Galaxy Rand

Galaxy Hand

Galaxy Rand

M. R. Tighe

Galaxy Rand

Published by Wheatmark®
1760 East River Road, Suite 145
Tucson, Arizona 85718 U.S.A.
www.wheatmark.com

ISBN: 978-1-62787-030-6 (paperback)
ISBN: 978-1-62787-031-3 (ebook)
LCCN: 2013949389

Contents

I raised my glass in a polite salute to my snitch, then leaned across the table toward her and muttered, "J'neen, some bastard's trying his damnedest to kill me!"

Her delicate, dark eyebrows made sharp arches. "*Again?*"

I scowled at the unwelcome reminder. "This time it's different!"

"Really? How 'different'?"

"This's nothing to do with any two-bit beef. Whoever the *fleggin* bastard is, he really has it out for me—two tries within a planet-hour! What's worse, I've got no idea in the Cosmos who the hell's behind these damn attacks."

"That does present you with a bit of a problem, Galaxy."

I got impatient and prodded, "Dammit, J'neen! Have you heard anything?"

She gave one quick shake of her dark head. "Not so much as a whisper. Sorry I can't help you, Galaxy."

"That's bad news, real bad news. Means whoever the hell's after me can afford to make damned-sure mouths stay shut. So that lets out the usual riff-raff I deal with!"

J'neen's bright eyes widened. "How in hell did you manage to make an enemy *that* powerful? And who in blazes could it be?"

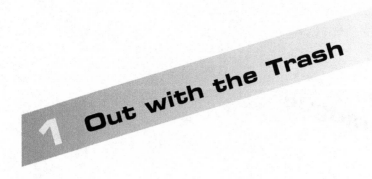

1 Out with the Trash

I know damned good and well I walked into the Star Dancer Saloon on my own two feet, but how I got outta there, Hell only knows!

The cheap swill the Star Dancer tries to pass off as high-grade *hahk-teem* sure wasn't to blame. Some of my "friends" swear I'm the one and only fem in this sector of the galaxy who could down disintegration accelerant without batting a single eyelash.

Naw, I was pretty damned sure it wasn't the *hahk-teem* that'd downed me. As I began to fuzzily recall, a fist half the size of Jupiter'd caught me square on the jaw. My lights'd instantly gone out. For once in my life, I hadn't ducked fast enough.

Huh! Maybe the lousy *hahk-teem* was to blame after all.

Anyhow, God only knows how long later, I came to. Found myself stretched out on my back on a lumpy surface. My jaw ached as if a ten-ton meteor'd hit me full-on. My back felt broken in at least five different places. At first, I couldn't see a whole helluva lot. Too bloody dark, wherever I was.

I sat up slowly, let out a groan, and had to hold my *fleggin* head between both hands 'til it stopped spinning. Soon as my head slowed down and my eyes focused, it hit me: I was inside some kinda moving vehicle!

The whole damn place stank worse'n a well-used *kareeb*'s burrow, if that's even possible. Putting two and two together, I figured out some lowlife bastard in the Star Dancer'd been rude enough to dump me down the bar's trash chute.

Then, I'd been "collected" by one of the mobile trash collectors routinely servicing Kaswali City.

A knife-thin slice of light cut through the stinking gloom. The intake hatch overhead hadn't closed all the way—faulty mechanism maybe. Anyway, there was enough light for me to make out the disgusting pile of trash I was perched on. That collector was one helluva place to wake up in! Wouldn't do wonders for any fem's disposition, and mine isn't exactly what you'd call "amiable" in the first place.

I stretched carefully, making sure all my limbs were still attached and in good working order, then got to my feet. That wasn't quite as easy as it sounds, not standing on the pile of quaking, shaking rubble I had to deal with. The collector jounced along its route, unaware it had an unwilling passenger.

As I quickly discovered, not even a six-footer like me could reach the intake—not even when I stood on tiptoe and stretched upward for all I was worth. I tried jumping. No go: I just sank farther into the crap. Tried heaping up trash to stand on, but the perch wasn't steady enough to do me one damned bit of good. I gave up in disgust and began to circle the collector's walls, searching for another way outta there.

I prayed there was an emergency exit, just in case of bloody stupid accidents like this, but if there *were* an escape hatch, I sure as hell couldn't find it. For the fraction of a microsecond, I thought about drawing the blaster from the holster at my right hip and blasting my way through the thick metal wall. Luckily, I was smart enough to figure out, with at least half a ton of flammable trash packed into the collector, a dumb-ass move like that'd be a great way to commit suicide!

As I circled the collector, I tripped over something sticking up outta the trash heap. I went down, sprawled flat on my face in the disgusting mess. Madder'n hell, I let out a few cusswords, picked myself up, and went back to see what the *flegg* had tripped me.

My own damn curiosity gets me into more trouble than I care to think about!

I groped around in the stinking darkness 'til my hand touched a hard, smooth, cold object that felt like an arm—not a flesh-and-blood *human* arm, of course; not a sim arm either. This arm was made outta metal. Somebody'd trashed the arm of a bot.

My brain cells—what little's left of 'em!—instantly fired on all cylinders. Just might be able to use that arm to reach the intake. Maybe I could pry it farther open and at least holler for help. But hard as I yanked and pulled on that bot arm, the damn thing wouldn't budge.

Swearing a mile-long blue streak, I began digging madly through the trash, bound and determined to find out what the hell the arm was stuck on. At its end, I discovered the knob of a shoulder, then a jointed neck, and, perched atop the neck, a smooth metal skull. With my bare hands, I dug furiously, tossing junk to all sides.

At last, the truth dawned on me: what I had here was a whole bloody bot!

The damn thing was lying on its right side with both arms straight down at its sides, stiff as a day-old corpse. At first, I didn't think finding a bot buried in the pile of rubbish was all that odd. Hell, the way the *fleggin* things break down, a bot must get tossed out every day of the week. Costs too damned much nowadays to bother repairing 'em. Besides, they're outmoded so bloody fast it's a far sight easier just to order an up-to-date model.

But something about this bot struck me as more than a little strange, so I took my time looking him over. Far as I could tell in this lousy light, the bot was all black, 'cept for the silver joints that allowed bots to move pretty much like a human. His housing was real heavy-duty. If you'd asked my opinion, I would've said he was one damned fancy model, sure as hell not your ordinary household bot. And he seemed brand-new. In fact, I didn't see a damn thing wrong with him, at least nothing a little metal polish couldn't cure.

Crouched hip-deep in stinking-to-high-heaven trash, I scowled as I stared him up and down. Couldn't help thinking of the bot as "him." He was one of those humaniform jobs, obviously male, bulges in all the right places. And let me tell you, whoever'd sculpted and cast that metal body of his had done one helluva job. The bot looked bloody magnificent!

I whistled my admiration for his awesome build. "Damn me if

you aren't a *fleggin* work of art, pal! Too bad you broke down and got tossed out like yesterday's garbage."

But that was the end of my interest in the bot. Far as I was concerned, he was just one more piece of useless trash in a whole stinking pile of useless trash.

Disgusted with the amount of time and energy I'd wasted on the damn bot, I got to my feet. Wading through the mountain of trash I'd created in unburying him, I headed back to the collector's outer wall, determined to make one last, desperate search for a way outta there.

An idea hit me like a brick of spectromium, square between the eyes. I went back and gave the bot a second look.

If I could get him to stand upright, he'd be at least six-feet tall, maybe a little over. And if I could get him to function, he might help me get outta this godawful place, before another load of trash was dumped on top of me. Or—worse thought!—before the collector completed its programmed route, and I came to one helluva bad end at the local incinerator!

Kneeling on one knee beside the bot, I pushed with all my might 'til I managed to roll him over onto his flat metal belly. He had to weigh as much as half a ton of spectromium! That metal shell of his sure as hell was more'n mere decoration; the bloody bot was as well-armored as a *fleggin* planet-tamer.

"Okay, pal! Now let's see what the hell's your problem."

Lifting the flap of the tool-pack on my belt, I pulled out a medium-sized simager: a multi-purpose tool I just happen to be damned good with; comes in handy in my line of work. I clicked on the tiny light at the simager's business end and pried open the small, square access panel centered between the bot's shiny, black shoulder blades.

Practically had to shove my nose into his innards, trying to ID his problem. Then I rocked back on my heels, flabbergasted by what I'd found.

"*Huh!* Disconnected! Now who in bloody-blue-blazes would deliberately disconnect your circuits, then toss a damn-fancy model like you out with the trash? Did you misbehave, pal? Maybe get a little too frisky with your owner's missus, or what?"

I knew damned good and well this bot wasn't some outdated

model. He was state-of-the-art: one *fleggin* expensive piece of machinery! Knew that without looking him up in any vid-catalog.

Using my simager, I reconnected his circuits. Hell, I'm no bot engineer—far from it!—but by the time I got through tinkering with him, the damn bot should've functioned. I heaved and rolled him over onto his back again. He just lay there, still as a life-size statue. Not one of his silver-jointed metal fingers so much as twitched.

I got to my feet and, in sheer disgust, shoved my simager back into the toolkit on my belt. Hands on my hips, I snarled down at the bot, "Why the bloody hell did I bother wasting what precious little time I've got left *on you*?"

The bot's black-and-silver surface gleamed, reflecting what little light was coming through the intake, 'cept of course, where it was smeared with kitchen grease and bits of rotten veggies. The two, shining crystal lenses he had for eyes gave me a blank stare.

Could've sworn the damn bot was silently mocking me. In frustration, I gave him a parting kick in the side and—boot or no boot—nearly broke my damn toe!

"Stay here where you belong then, you *fleggin* hunk of worthless junk! I'm getting myself the hell outta here. Somehow."

I turned and stalked away with as much dignity as I could muster.

Behind me, a male voice said, "You might at least remain civil, madam."

From sheer instinct, I whipped my blaster outta its holster and whirled to face—what? I searched for a target; my eyes darted to all four corners of the collector, but for the life of me, I couldn't spot any sign of danger. I squinted harder and scanned the stinking darkness once again.

"All right, you *fleggin* smart-ass, you wanna talk? At least have guts enough to come out where I can *see* you."

The damn bot sat straight up. Scared holy crap outta me!

I let out a loud curse and jumped backward, nearly tripping for a second time. The bot's black-metal dome instantly swiveled in my direction. His twin crystal lenses, set where human eyes were, fastened on me.

Every inch of skin on my entire body crawled!

"I repeat, madam: despite the unfortunate predicament in which we presently find ourselves, you might at least act in a civilized manner!"

I blinked stupidly at him. "*K'yoti* Hell! You scared the living—! Hey, I fixed you!"

The bot drawled, "To be perfectly blunt, madam, that procedure did not require a great deal of skill on your part."

I kept the muzzle of my blaster trained dead-center on his metal chest and dared to approach him. "If I were you, pal, I'd watch my damn tongue, or whatever the hell you bots talk with."

He—it?—stared at me without blinking and complained, "Historically-speaking, human beings have been extremely reluctant to acknowledge the existence of any intelligence other than their own."

I got the impression he was talking to himself, not to me. But all the same, that uppity tone of his made my hackles rise. I took the high-faluting statement as an insult aimed at me and snarled, "Is that so?"

"It is indeed the truth."

"Now you just look here, Blackie! *I* wasn't the one tossed out with the trash. *You* were!"

"Although my motor functions were disengaged from my main power source, I was aware that I had received company in this bin of disgusting refuse. If truth be told, madam, it would appear that we both were summarily discarded."

The bot didn't seem to be armed or hostile, and I wasn't all that eager to barbecue myself, so I holstered my blaster. I took one angry step toward him, eager to settle the matter and take back at least a shred of my wounded pride.

"Look here, you human-aping hunk of tin! I *wasn't* tossed out with the trash! Just somehow got dumped on top of it, you got that?"

"Ah, yes, indeed! The subtlety of that fine point obviously eluded me," the bot drawled, in the most irritating tone I could possibly imagine. With one silver-jointed finger, he flicked a piece of crushed fruit peel off his left bicep, as if he were the picky-neatest human on Milo's Planet!

Then the bot gave me a loud sniff—sounded all too human for my liking. "You positively *reek* of garbage and low-grade *hahk-teem*. Abominable! Have you no class whatsoever, madam?"

That latest insult was the last damn straw. My blood started to boil like the bubbling tar pits of Hell. "Watch those snarky remarks, pal! I got class coming outta my—! *Hey! Stop calling me madam!* I absolutely hate that! Nobody calls me 'madam' and gets the *flegg* away with it, y'hear me?"

In a snippy tone, the bot replied, "Indeed! When you employ that voice level, how could I help but hear you? However, since I remain ignorant of your proper appellation—"

Swearing, I deliberately turned my back on him and gave the first damn thing I came across a vicious kick. A badly-rusted accelerator bucket flew across the collector and, with a loud crash, bounced off its far wall.

I groaned. "Can't believe this crap is actually happening! How in the name of Unholy Hell did I manage to wind up ankle-deep in stinking trash, arguing with a *fleggin* piece of broken-down machinery like you?"

Blackie totally ignored my insult. He seemed to be listening to something I couldn't hear. "I beg your pardon, madam—"

At the top of my lungs, I roared, "*Quit calling me madam, damn you!*"

"Whoever you may be, then, I thought it might interest you that this mobile collector is rapidly approaching the end of its route."

Felt as if every damn drop of blood drained from my face. "*K'yoti* Hell! *The incinerator!*"

I was about to be dumped and burned, along with the rest of Kaswali City's trash.

"*Dammit all!* Unless you wanna get incinerated along with me, pal, you'd better stand the hell up—now!" I ordered, hoping the bot'd obey me.

Luckily, Blackie obeyed, without giving me any guff. At first, he stood a good bit over me, but his considerable weight made him sink deeper into the trash heap than I did. I made a rough estimate of the height needed to reach the intake chute. Maybe, just maybe—!

"C'mon over here, pal!" I urged, beckoning to him.

The bot followed, 'til we both stood directly beneath the chute. I asked him, "Can you do this?" and bent over, lacing my fingers together at my own knee-level.

Obedient as hell, the bot imitated me.

"Good! Now hold it right there, pal. Let me get a leg up. Don't you dare move!"

I put one booted foot into the step he'd made with his hands and grabbed onto his broad metal shoulders for support. Without waiting for further orders, the bot straightened and boosted me upward 'til my feet were level with his waist.

To steady myself, I clutched his smooth metal skull, wishing he had ears for me to hang onto. Somehow or other, I managed to get my right knee up onto his left shoulder. Carefully, I drew up my other leg. I was soon standing on his metal shoulders, wobbling like a day-old *kareeb* kitten just learning how to walk.

If I slipped now, it was all over but the burning!

I stiffened and let out a little gasp as the bot's metal fingers suddenly clamped around my ankles and steadied me. I stood up straighter, arms spread wide. Keeping my balance wasn't exactly easy; the damn collector was jouncing around worse'n a pleasure-house bed!

"Are you able to reach the intake?" the bot asked, his voice as calm as if he were asking me about the state of the weather outside.

Have to admit, I was more'n a little surprised by his actions. How in the name of Bloody Hell had the bot figured out what I was trying to do? Putting that question outta mind, I stretched upward for all I was worth. "I can almost reach it! Need just a tad more height. *Dammit all!* We're sinking into the crap!"

The bot's grip on my ankles tightened. I let out a louder gasp as he raised my feet above his shoulders. Now, my head was inside the chute. I stretched out both arms and caught hold of the rough outer edge of the intake. My fingers latched onto it.

"Got it! Let go, pal!" I hung on for dear life.

Bracing my legs against opposite sides of the chute, I pulled and kicked and inched my way upward. I got one arm and one leg through the narrow opening. I squeezed the rest of my body through, scraping my back in the process, then lay face down on top of the collector, panting for breath.

The outside air was a helluva lot fresher than the air inside the collector. Didn't stink nearly so bad, either. But the instant I raised my head to check out the situation, I froze in horror.

Dead-ahead, the incinerator's red maw gaped, belching flames and clouds of thick, black smoke, like the gate to Hell Itself!

As it closed in on the incinerator, the collector slowed down and tipped forward. Nothing under Milo's Sun was gonna stop its routine. My first thought was to get my ass outta danger as fast as humanly possible. I started to scramble over the side, then thought better of it.

Far as I could tell, the bot down there was in damned good shape. To let such a valuable piece of machinery be incinerated like yesterday's garbage would be a bloody shame, as well as a sheer waste of credits. According to the salvage rights recognized on Milo's Planet, if I hauled the damn bot outta the collector, he'd be my legal property.

With no overhead costs to be recouped, if I could sell him, I'd make one helluva nice profit—provided I could get him outta the collector before he got dumped into the incinerator and burned to cinders, or whatever.

Laying down on my back, I used both booted feet to kick the intake open wider.

I yelled down to the bot, "Find a length of wire, pal, something strong enough to hold your weight, and throw it up to me! Make it damned snappy or else!"

Faster than I could've, the bot found a coil of sturdy electrical wire and tossed it up to me. I caught it on the first try; in a helluva hurry, I wrapped a free end around one of the intake chute's hinges. After making sure the wire was secure, I dropped the rest of the coil back down to the bot.

"*Climb!*" I ordered, holding fast to the tied off end so it couldn't slip and send him crashing back down into the trash.

I braced myself. As the collector inclined, the angle of its top got steeper and steeper. In a matter of microseconds, I'd find myself sliding off, right into the *fleggin* inferno!

The bot's black-metal skull poked through the intake. One long, black-and-silver arm, then the other, reached out to grip the taut wire. Slowly, the bot drew himself through the intake. Hauling up a carcass as damned heavy as his sure as hell wasn't easy.

The collector ground to a halt and bumped into the incinerator—hard!—threatening to send both me and the bot tumbling into the roaring flames.

He made a grab for my arm, but I yelled, "*Bail out, pal!* Over the side!" Letting go of the wire, I scrambled to the edge and slithered over it, feet first. I landed on the filthy floor of the narrow alleyway that led to the incinerator.

A thud shook the ground under my feet, as the bot landed right beside me. The metal inner-works of the collector let out one long, ear-splitting squeal as the whole bin upended. The bot and I quickly stepped back. From a safer distance, we watched as the collector's stinking cargo slid into the incinerator's smoking maw. Flames shot twenty feet into the air.

I blew out a breath of sheer relief and couldn't help shuddering. With what was left of my long, once-white shirtsleeve, I wiped black streaks of smoke and sweat from my forehead and muttered to myself, "*K'yoti* Hell! Damned glad that's not *me* going up in flames."

The bot said, "My sentiments exactly, madam." For some unknown reason he thought I'd been speaking to him. As if! And there he stood—right at my elbow!—for all the Cosmos as if he considered himself my equal.

I shot him an annoyed glare. "Stop calling me madam, damn you, or I swear I'll take you apart with my bare hands and toss the pieces into the *fleggin* incinerator!"

Had to pause to clear my smoke-clogged throat. "And if you *must* know, the name's Rand—Galaxy Rand—as if that's any of your damn business."

The bot gave me a stiff, formal bow from the waist, which took me by complete surprise. "It is indeed a pleasure to make your acquaintance, Ms. Rand."

He sure as bloody hell didn't sound one bit pleased, but at least he had manners, I had to give him that. None of the *fleggin* space-scum I deal with in my line of work have manners.

But I screwed up my face in another scowl. "Can the Ms. part, too, pal. I'm just Rand. That's what everyone calls me."

"Since we would appear to be in the process of making introductions—"

The bot cut short his own sentence. His metal head swiveled

sharply on his silver neck-joints. Something farther down the alley'd drawn his attention, but I couldn't see any sign of danger. And all I could hear was the incinerator's ungodly roar.

In a low voice, the bot warned, "I beg your pardon, Rand, but two humans are approaching, in an uncommonly stealthy manner."

I frowned as I gave the alley an even closer look. Still didn't see a damn thing the least bit suspicious. Stacks of large plastic and metal drums lined both walls of the alley; they probably held toxics waiting to be incinerated. I wondered what in bloody hell the bot was talking about. Maybe the jouncy collector ride'd scrambled his brain circuits—or maybe I'd just discovered the reason he'd been junked in the first place.

Puzzled, I demanded, "What in bloody-blue-blazes makes you think someone's coming, pal?"

"I am equipped with state-of-the-art sensor systems, mad—that is, Rand." To my dismay, the bot sounded pretty damned sure of himself.

I hissed under my breath, "*K'yoti* Hell! Now what?"

Drawing my blaster, I scanned the alley in search of another way outta there, but it was a dead-end. The sheer walls were too damned high to be scaled without fancy climbing equipment and too damned thick to blast my way through.

The incinerator was the only other exit; that was not a route I cared to take!

Again keeping his voice surprisingly low, the bot said, "Might I suggest that, under the present circumstances, Rand, the best strategy would be to divide and conquer?"

I shot him a dark look, just to let him know how annoyed I was with him. "What in the name of Bloody Hell are you babbling on about? Oh—yeah! Okay, now I get the picture, pal."

At that very microsecond, a human head and the muzzle-tip of a blaster popped up from behind a stack of drums. As if the bot and I were on the same wavelength, Blackie jumped right, just as I dove left. A blaster-bolt exploded in the spot where we'd been standing. Shards of scrap metal and thick clouds of dust went flying in all directions.

I hit the dirt, slid forward on my left side, and raised my blaster.

My first shot burned down the *fleggin* bastard who'd had the gall to try to smoke me. Nailed him right through the metal drum he was using to steady his gun hand. Some kinda foul-smelling, greenish stuff spurted outta the hole burned through the drum and made green pools on the alley floor.

On the opposite side of the alleyway, Blackie charged into a tall stack of drums, as if he'd gone berserk. He bent down, lifted a full drum over his head, as easily as if the damn thing'd been empty! He tossed it down the alley. I heard one yelp, which was cut short, then nothing but silence, except for the incinerator's roar.

The bot turned in place and stood staring at me, for all the Cosmos as if he were waiting for my instructions.

Ignoring him, I scrambled to my feet and went to check out the damage. As usual, my aim had been perfect: The guy I'd smoked was good and dead. He lay face-down in a pool of the sticky green stuff, long past IDing. Farther down the alley, I found a limp, blood-covered hand sticking up between two drums full of toxins.

"Dead?" I asked, casting a glance over my shoulder at the bot.

"Most regrettably; he was crushed to death." He made an odd sound, way too damned close to a human sigh.

Shrugged off both deaths and holstered my blaster. "Out here on Milo's Planet, pal, it's either kill first or get killed," I told the bot. Something else struck me as mighty odd. "But I thought all bots were programmed *not* to kill humans. Isn't there some kinda law about it? Didn't some guy named Ass-something-or-other invent it one helluva long time ago?"

The bot gave me a blank stare. I couldn't begin to read those crystal lenses of his. "I am certain *Doctor Asimov* would indeed be gratified that you remembered the fact; however, I assure you, Rand, I had no intention whatsoever of killing this scoundrel. He was about to open fire upon you, thus forcing me to act in order to prevent you from being killed or injured."

I bristled. "Listen up, pal! I'm perfectly capable of taking care of myself. I sure as hell don't need you, or anybody else, to protect me. Understood?" He didn't answer.

Tried my damnedest to roll away one of the heavy drums pinning the second dead guy. Finally, I was forced to give up and order the bot to do it. I took a good look at the guy's mangled face—let me tell you, it was a bloody mess!—but there wasn't one damn thing familiar about him.

"By any chance were these two ruffians friends of yours?" the bot asked.

I shook my head. "Hell, no! Whoever they were, these guys were no friends of mine. In the first place, I don't have many to speak of. And far as I can tell, I never laid eyes on either one of these bastards before. *Huh!* Maybe they weren't gunning for me; maybe they were after you, pal."

The bot took a sudden step backward, as if I'd whacked him across the face with a laser-handle or something.

"*That* is hardly likely!" he snapped in a real uppity tone. He pivoted on one metal heel and stalked away from me, obviously insulted.

I straightened my spine, took a real deep breath, and wiped both hands on the seat of my pants. By that point, it wasn't exactly clean either.

"Well, as they say, pal, that's that! I'm all for getting my sweet ass the hell outta here before the local law or—God-forbid!—the *fleggin* ISF shows up! Don't wanna get stuck answering a slew of nosey questions."

I skirted the toppled drums and the toxic green puddles. Leaving behind the remains of the two dead guys, I made for the mouth of the alley, more than happy to forget the whole nasty incident.

But heavy footsteps dogged mine. I halted in mid-stride and turned to face the bot. "You following me, pal?"

"Not at all, Rand. I am merely pursuing an identical course."

"Well, *don't* follow me!" I warned him in my sternest tone of voice. "I've decided you're a helluva lot more trouble than you're worth, credit-wise. Rather not get caught with you in tow and have to do some fancy explaining to the authorities. I'm sick to death of answering their questions!"

The bot protested, "Rand, I assure you that I had not the slightest intention of following you."

"Good!"

At the mouth of the alleyway, I hit fresher air and brighter light. Instantly knew where I was; it was one of Kaswali City's main drags. I avoided the move-walk, which was crowded with folks who were too damned lazy to walk even a block or two. Took a quick sighting on Milo's Sun, made a sharp left, and headed for the city's main space-port, where I'd parked *Jammer* the night before.

Even after my change of course, heavy footsteps thudded behind me. Now riled as hell, I whirled to face the damn bot again.

"Thought you said you weren't following me, pal?"

"That statement was true—originally."

I planted my fists on my hipbones and glared at the bot. "And what the bloody hell is *that* supposed to mean?"

"The thought has since occurred to me that I currently lack an owner; therefore, I am, as humans would put it, 'at loose ends.' I find such an abominable state of affairs intolerable."

Somehow or other the bot managed to look downcast.

I rolled my eyes. "Oh, for the luva—! Go latch onto some other poor sucker! *Shoo!* I'm in one helluva hurry here, pal. For damn sure, I don't need you tagging along. I do better on my own."

"Indeed, Rand?" The bot swiveled his head and cast a long, meaningful look back in the direction of the incinerator. "Perhaps, under the present circumstances—?"

I got his drift pretty damned fast. "*No!* Forget it, pal! Leave me the hell alone, and blast off!"

The bot cocked his shiny black dome to one side. "Rand, I do not possess the apparatus necessary to achieve lift," he said, perfectly deadpan.

My mouth fell open. I stared at him. Got the feeling the damn bot wasn't putting me on. "*K'yoti* Hell! You're denser'n a ton of spec-tromium!"

"No, not at all, Rand. My specific density is—"

I gave a loud groan. "Can it, will ya, Tin Man? No pun intended there!"

The bot made another real odd sound; this one came too damned close to a human sniff. "My proper appellation is RBS02—*not* Tin Man!"

"Y'don't say? And who in bloody flaming hell gives a fast-flying damn what you're called? You're a *fleggin* bot, not a person. I'll call you whatever I damn please! Be seeing you around, pal. I hope not!"

I made a fast about-face and headed for the Port at a relaxing jog, so I could get back to *Jammer* as soon as humanly possible.

I was dead-determined to lose the damn bot along the way, but Blackie lengthened his stride to keep pace with me. I ignored him and kept jogging, hoping to hell he'd give up and go away.

"Rand, as you will no doubt observe, I am *not* following you, per your specific instructions," the bot pointed out in a smug tone.

At that, I lost my last shred of patience and snapped, "*Oh, for God's-green-snake!* I'm not your bloody owner! Do as you damn please! Just leave me the hell alone!"

"Rand, do you habitually contradict yourself?"

Disgusted, I growled back, "Do you ever shut up?"

Blackie refused to answer. I hoped he'd finally got my less than subtle hints. Sure as hell didn't want him hanging around. But the damn bot stayed alongside me, like some mangy, stray mutt I couldn't get rid of no matter how hard I tried.

I slowed down to a walk, just to give myself time to catch my breath and think before I reached the Port and *Jammer*.

I'd salvaged the bot; legally speaking, he was mine. Had to admit he was real intelligent and in damned good shape. Right at the moment, I happened to be a mite short of credits, and I figured the bot should fetch a fair price. With even a shred of luck, I might be able to pawn him off on some poor, unsuspecting sucker before I left Milo's Planet.

Then the damn bot'd have a willing owner, someone besides me he could follow around, and I'd gain some much-needed credits as well as a welcome return to peace and quiet.

So, much against my better judgment, I gave in and heaved a sigh. "What the hell! All right, pal, you can tag along with me for now, but don't you go getting attached, y'hear me? This arrangement's only temporary. Understood?"

The bot repeated, "Understood, Rand." He sounded perfectly happy with the deal I'd offered him.

I made it to the main entrance of Kaswali City's Spaceport without any more incidents. Picked up my pace, eager to get back aboard my ship; I never like leaving *Jammer* for long.

I wound my way through the maze of terminals, dodging surface-transports loaded with passengers. I gave the overcrowded commercial pads a wide berth and headed for the fast-ship pads and Beta 0221.

Blackie stayed glued to me, babbling a steady stream and asking questions about damned near everything we came across. But to be honest, I wasn't paying him a whole helluva lot of attention 'til outta the blue he asked, "If I may be so bold, Rand, exactly what profession do you practice?"

His question caught me off guard. I had no idea a bot could be so damned nosey. "I, uh, well, guess you could say I'm a—a bodyguard of sorts."

"Indeed?" The bot gave me a long, sideways look, which told me plain as day he didn't believe my lie for a microsecond. I wondered if those state-of-the-art sensors of his included a lie detector.

But I sure as hell had no plans to spill my whole life story—sorry as it is!—to any damn bot. I always say the less anybody knows about you, the better off you are.

I decided to take a breather, stepped up onto one of the move-walks that ferry pilots and passengers out to the fast-ships, which are parked all along the outer fringes of the Port. That's a good hike from the main entrance. The bot stepped up onto the move-walk, right beside me.

The closer we came to the pad where I'd parked *Jammer*, the more deserted the pads became. Pretty damned odd; then and there, I should've smelled a *kareeb*'s den.

At that time of day, the outer sections of the Port usually hum with off-worlders coming and going, transport jockeys trying to drum up business or tending to their ships. Hell, some days, the fast-ship pads get so damned crowded you can't spit sideways without hitting somebody in the eye.

Today, out here on the fringes, there wasn't a single, star-blasted soul anywhere in sight.

Blackie's nonstop babble distracted me. Lack of food and sleep, on top of a night of hard-drinking, had dulled my own normally-reliable senses. I didn't pick up on the danger signs 'til it was far too late.

That little mistake damn near proved fatal!

When we reached Beta 0221, I stepped off the move-walk and took my first good, long look around. My "uh-oh" sense finally kicked in.

No sign of the guard I'd hired to keep an eye on *Jammer* 'til I got back; he was a squinty-eyed, little half-breed B'treeni named Gamial Sang. I'd expected to find the lazy slacker sleeping on the job, as usual, but today Sang was nowhere in sight.

And what's worse, *Jammer*'s boarding ramp was *down*! I remembered damned good and well leaving it *up* the night before. All the landing pads surrounding Beta 0221 were quiet, as deserted as a bloody graveyard at midnight. The skin covering every inch of my body began to prickle a warning.

I muttered under my breath, "Damn you, Sang! If you had the *fleggin* gall to set so much as one toe aboard my ship—!"

Blackie was right at my elbow. "Trouble, Rand?" His shiny black skull made a one-eighty as he scanned the area.

I heaved a heavy sigh. "It'd be safe to bet your bolts on that, pal!"

"Rand, I detect several life-forms hidden behind neighboring ships."

"Great! Now the trick is to see if I can make it into *Jammer* without getting myself smoked." I nodded toward the old forties fast-ship that sat dead ahead.

The bot eyed my ship with less respect than she deserved. "*Humph!* That disreputable-looking vehicle belongs to you?"

For that insult to my beloved *Jammer*, he earned another glare. "You got a better way off this miserable excuse for a planet?"

"No, Rand; most unfortunately, I do not."

"So shut the bloody hell up and follow me—or don't!"

I took one real deep breath to steady my nerves and drew my blaster. Crouching low, I made a dash for *Jammer*'s ramp, zigging and zagging all the way. Figured it's a helluva lot harder to hit a moving target. Didn't give a fast-flying damn whether or not the bot chose to follow me. Right now, my main concern was keeping my own sweet hide in one piece long enough to get my ass off this *fleggin* planet.

The bot was expendable.

A blaster-bolt zinged past my shoulder blades, close enough so I could feel its heat right through the back of my shirt. "*Flegg* it!" I hissed.

From behind me, I heard the bot warn, "To your left, Rand!"

Without stopping to think, I ducked even lower and wheeled to my left. Before the bloody bastard who'd fired on me could get off a second shot, I burned him down. Sure enough, the cowardly son-of-a-bitch'd been hiding behind one of the fast-ships next door.

I dodged one more blaster-bolt that came too damned close for comfort and raced up *Jammer*'s ramp, hoping to hell I'd find safety inside my ship.

A couple microseconds behind me, Blackie trudged up the ramp. The bot was nowhere near as fast on his feet as I was, but then, nobody was gunning for *him*!

As soon as he'd come aboard, I punched in the lift order on the ramp's manual controls, which were located just inside *Jammer*'s hatchway. All my senses still on high-alert, I flattened my back against the inner bulkhead. The microsecond the ramp clicked into place, I secured the hatch.

I slid to my left with my back still against the bulkhead and poked my head around the corner to scope out *Jammer*'s main corridor. The corridor, which led to my control cabin, forward, was deserted; the cabin's hatch was shut, just as I'd left it. But something plain didn't feel right to me.

In a whisper, I said, "So help me, if I find Sang in my cabin, putting his damn feet up and taking a bloody fiesta—!"

The bot pitched his voice so low I could barely hear him, even though he was standing right next to me. "Siesta, Rand, *siesta*. My sensors detect a single heat source in the forward compartment. Judging by its mass and temperature, I venture to say one better than average-sized human being presently occupies your cabin."

I let out a little sigh of dismay. "It's not Sang, then! Read any other life-forms aboard *Jammer*?"

"Negative, Rand. There is only the one."

Under my breath, I swore fluently. "This's exactly what I was afraid of. That bloody bastard is between me and *Jammer*'s controls! Unless I can get into my cabin, *Jammer* can't take off. And while I'm wasting precious time trying to break in there, his pals outside will have plenty of time to call for reinforcements."

I did some real hard and fast thinking, something I'm used to doing in my true profession. "Listen up, pal! You stay here and guard the ramp in case they try to override my controls. I'll take care of the *fleggin* creep who's had the gall to hole up in my cabin. Then, we'll get the hell off this planet. Understood?"

"Understood, Rand."

Taking one cautious step at a time, with my blaster at the ready and my eyes glued on the cabin's hatch, I crept forward. The hatch stayed shut, but there was no way that piece of space-scum in my cabin'd missed the whine of blasters. And as sure as Hellfire's hot, he was ready to smoke me the microsecond I set foot inside my cabin.

Halfway down the corridor, I spotted the emergency ladder; it ran up the starboard bulkhead and across to the access panel in the center of the overhead. In zero G, the ladder wasn't necessary, but whenever *Jammer* was on-planet, that ladder came in damned handy. A brilliant idea suddenly hit me: a tactic that was a helluva lot safer and saner than busting through my cabin's hatch and possibly getting myself smoked in the process.

I slipped my blaster back into the holster at my right hip, then grabbed the rungs of the narrow ladder and began to climb. Where the ladder met the overhead, I crawled across, upside down, 'til I reached the access hatch. There, I clung to the ladder with both arms and both legs, like a web-crawler waiting for a fly to get trapped in its sticky net.

Time dragged by, but when I didn't open the cabin's hatch on cue, the bastard inside got nosey. He cracked the hatch to see what the hell was going on. Seeing nothing in the corridor, he dared to step out. His blaster clutched in one hand, ready to take me out, he started toward *Jammer*'s ramp.

I held my breath and prayed he'd be too much of a dumb-ass to think to look up. Sure enough, he walked right underneath me. Like a freighter load of spectromium, I dropped on the bastard and flattened him.

Scrambling to my feet, I whipped out my own blaster and trained it on him, then waited to see how he'd choose to play this. The jackass made one helluva mistake: he fumbled for his blaster and dared to swing it on me. Not a smart move!

One well-aimed kick to the jaw took him outta action. But it also left him in no shape to answer any of the hundred-and-one questions I had for him.

I growled, "That'll teach you to mess with *my* ship, chum!" I pulled both of his arms up over his head and dragged him the length of the corridor. At the outer hatch's control panel, I punched in the order to lower *Jammer*'s ramp. The bot watched me, but he was smart enough to keep his damn mouth shut.

I couldn't help chuckling, "His pals out there'll be expecting to see him, but not in this condition!"

I dragged the unconscious creep to the top of the ramp and gave him a kick. Arms and legs flapping like a rag doll's, he rolled down *Jammer*'s ramp, all the way to the bottom and a good distance out onto the landing-pad to boot.

"Good riddance, you bloody bastard!" I yelled after him. "And tell your *fleggin* friends to keep their distance, or they're gonna get fried to a crisp!"

Quickly, I punched in the lift order. Leaving the bot to secure the hatch this time, I dashed forward. Inside my cabin, I dropped into the pilot's seat, located on the port side of the control console, and strapped myself in. I started checking *Jammer*'s systems, one by one, getting her ready for immediate lift-off.

Lucky for me, my uninvited visitor hadn't damaged my ship. Maybe my attackers figured, once I was dead, they could sell *Jammer* and make themselves a hefty profit.

Anyway, it felt damned good to be back in control of my own ship. I took a deep breath and relaxed. Then, I realized Blackie was standing in the open hatchway.

Too damned busy taking readings and executing standard lift-off procedures to pay much attention to him, I shot over my left shoulder, "Well? What in bloody hell are you waiting for, pal? An engraved invitation? If you're coming with me, you'd better sit down and strap in. *Jammer*'s no luxury class. She's zero G, in case you hadn't guessed!"

As Blackie made his way to the starboard side of the console, where the co-pilot's station was located, he drawled, "I might have expected as much, or should I say, as little?"

Gritting my teeth, I shot him a nasty glare, just to let him know I didn't see the humor in his snarky remark.

The bot lowered himself into the co-pilot's seat as if he were expecting to be electrocuted. Couldn't help sneering while he tried his damnedest to figure out how to strap himself in.

"Rand, before we take leave of this planet, should we not report these unprovoked attacks to the Interstellar Space Force?"

That dumb-ass idea earned him another glare and a loud snort. "The ISF? Are you kidding me, pal? I'd probably end up locked in stasis for the next three or four hundred years. Naw! I don't deal with the ISF—not if I can bloody-well help it!"

"I see," the bot said. "But, Rand, is it not illegal—"

"Now you look here, pal! Either shut the hell up and hang on, or you'll be the next one I roll down *Jammer*'s ramp!"

The microsecond I completed the hasty pre-flight sequence, I engaged lift-thrusters. With what sounded like a roar of sheer joy, *Jammer* rose eagerly into the sky: a vertical launch, as usual. She was damned sick and tired of sitting a launch-pad. Sweet piece of machinery, my *Jammer*.

As she rose through the atmosphere, just to be on the safe side,

I kept my eyes glued on her aft monitor. Below, first the space-port, then the whole of Kaswali City, rapidly shrank. Milo's Planet itself was soon nothing but a mottled, red-brown-and-gray dust ball, streaked with a few puffy, white clouds.

As gravity released its grip on me, I relaxed my guard and glanced over at the bot, a broad grin on my face. "Ever pilot a two-man fast-ship, Tin Man?" I asked casually.

"Never, Rand."

His serious tone made me chuckle again. "Guess that makes us even, then. Never had a co-pilot before, human or otherwise. Never needed one."

"Is that not another violation of interplanetary regulations?" the bot demanded.

"Regs are for other people, not for Galaxy Rand."

The bot seemed to be running that info through the nano-computer he had for a brain. "Then, technically speaking, I suppose I would be categorized as 'non-essential personnel'?"

I shrugged. "Or cargo. All depends on how you look at it, I guess, pal."

"Cargo! *Humph!*"

Blackie's metal dome swiveled on his silver-jointed neck to face forward. He sat without speaking—an improvement as far as I was concerned!—and stared straight ahead, as if I'd called him a filthy bastard or some other nasty name.

After a bit, though, what was left of my conscience started pricking me, so I made an awkward attempt to apologize to him. "Uh, look, pal, I'm sorry if I offended you—or whatever. It's not that I don't appreciate what you did for me back there on Milo's. You probably saved my damn neck once or twice. But I don't exactly know what to make of you. Never had to deal with a bot before; you sure as hell aren't *human*."

"Now there is an astute observation if ever I heard one!" the bot said in a real snarky way.

I lost the last shred of what little patience I had left and snapped, "*Flegg* it! If you don't watch those smartass remarks of yours, I am gonna classify you as *excess* cargo and jettison you in mid-space!"

In an icy tone, the bot replied, "I begin to suspect I might prefer to suffer such a fate, rather than be forced to endure your company very much longer."

Angry as hell, I swung the pilot's chair sideways to confront Blackie face to face. "For God's-green-snake! Listen up, you insufferable, tin-plated son-of-a-bitch—!"

The bot eyed me with obvious disgust and demanded, "Rand, is your conversation habitually laced with profanity as well as vulgarities?"

"Don't you *dare* lecture me, you useless pile of tin!" I snarled.

Outta the blue, the bot's attention shifted. "Rand, I realize interruptions are considered extremely rude, but you ought to be monitoring your rear."

"My *what?*" For a fraction of a microsecond, I couldn't figure out what in bloody hell the bot meant by that. I gave him a blank stare, then my gaze flashed to *Jammer*'s aft monitor. Sure enough, two fast-ships were hot on my tail, closing fast.

I let out a loud groan. "*K'yoti* Hell! Whoever these *fleggin* bastards are, they don't discourage easily!"

I jacked *Jammer*'s energy converters up to maximum. Her aft scanners suddenly screamed a warning. I swung *Jammer* hard aport to dodge the laser-cannon blast aimed at her stern. Lucky for me, the shot didn't connect.

Jammer pulled away, quickly putting more cold space between her and her pursuers. In her wake, both fast-ships fired salvo after salvo, even after they were too damned far outta range for a lucky hit.

I growled, "I'd love nothing better than to turn around and blast those s.o.b.s to bloody hell. There's only one slight problem."

"And that would be—?"

I made a face at the bot. "Afraid *Jammer*'s down to her very last laser-cannon charge. Tried to wangle a recharge back at the Port, but didn't have enough credits left to pay for it. And for some strange reason, they wouldn't let me put it on my tab."

"Then, for all intents and purposes, *Jammer* is unarmed."

"Told you she was no luxury class!"

The bot shook his head. "So you did, Rand; so you did."

As I continued to eye *Jammer*'s aft monitor, a smug grin spread across my face. The images of our two attackers were shrink-ing. Soon, they became only pinpoints of light, then disappeared entirely.

"Those bloody bastards never had a prayer of catching up with *Jammer!*" I chortled. "That's the main reason I don't bother refur-bishing this old gal's exterior, pal. Rather have my many enemies underestimate the speed she can make. Comes in damned handy at times like this, wouldn't you say?"

All too grimly, the bot reminded me, "Someone certainly appears to have made your death their top priority, Rand."

That remark sobered me up pretty damned fast. "No doubt about it, Tin Man. Only question is: who wants me dead that badly?"

"I take it, then, you have more than one mortal enemy!" the bot exclaimed, making his dismay obvious.

His reaction amused me. I let out a snort. "Does a mine-rat have more'n one flea? A couple dozen beings in this sector'd love to see me dead and broiling my brains out in Hell. Trouble is, not a damn one of 'em has both the freedom and the credits to see the job through. Lucky for me, most of my worst enemies are doing time on one penal planet or another."

Blackie's gaze was still fixed on *Jammer's* aft monitor. Without turning his head to look me straight in the face, he said matter-of-factly, "Rand, I find it extremely unlikely that a lowly 'bodyguard', such as you claim to be, would attract such determined enemies, especially in such large numbers."

I played with *Jammer's* navcomp settings a helluva lot longer than I needed to, stalling for time to think. "Yeah? Well, about that—"

"You lied."

I shrugged off the blunt accusation. "Another nasty habit of mine, I'm afraid. I learned the hard way to protect myself at all times. Take my advice, pal: never give anybody any info they might use against you."

"*Humph!* A prime example of paranoia, if ever I heard one," the bot noted dryly. "Are you willing, as yet, to disclose your true occupation, or shall I attempt to deduce it?"

I gave the damned cocky bot a scornful snort and decided, just for the hell of it, to challenge him. "Since you think you're so bloody clever, go ahead. Try and guess what I do!"

I sat back with my arms folded across my chest and waited to be entertained at his expense.

At first, Blackie didn't say a damn thing, then he started ticking off clues faster than a *fleggin* computer could kick out a stream of data!

"You work alone. You are accustomed to finding yourself in dangerous situations. You own this fast-ship and, therefore, must have—or have had at one time—a fair amount of credits at your disposal. You are highly skilled in the use of weapons, as well as in hand-to-hand combat. You often find yourself at odds with the ISF. You have an extraordinary number of enemies of low class and low morals, including many of the criminal element."

Without pausing so much as a fraction of a microsecond, he kept rattling off facts: "You travel frequently and at a moment's notice, and are—at least on occasion—pursued. And as I have observed, your ship is equipped with a tractor-arm, which is definitely *not* standard equipment. Therefore, I venture to say that you, Rand, are in all likelihood a recoup agent."

My lower jaw dropped so damned fast it almost bounced off *Jammer*'s deck. Soon as I could get a word out, I demanded, "How in bloody hell did you guess?"

"My astute deduction, rather, was a simple process of logical reasoning, based upon our recent experiences and conversations. This information, combined with the deplorable appearance of your vessel as compared with its remarkable speed and accouterments, as well as with all available data regarding human occupations in this sector of the galaxy, led me to one inescapable conclusion."

Instead of admitting I now had a grudging respect for the bot's reasoning abilities, I stubbornly shook my head. "*Huh!* Just a lucky guess, I'd say."

"Not at all, madam. In fact, I do not believe in the existence of luck."

I bristled. "Thought I told you to ditch that *madam* crap!"

"Very well; if that form of address offends you—although I hardly see why—"

I leaned in close to the bot. To get my point across, I poked my right index finger into his metal chest—hard! Note to self: don't pull *that* dumb-ass stunt again; it hurt like hell!

"Listen up, Tin Man! This is *my* ship, and aboard my ship *I* give the orders, and *you* obey me, or else! You got that?"

In a real huffy tone, the bot said, "My auditory receptors are functioning perfectly well."

But he finally shut up, thank God!

I sat there, fuming in silence and drumming my fingers on *Jammer's* command console. For the first time—but not for the last!—I came to a conclusion: I'd made one helluva mistake by salvaging the damn bot. And I'd made an even bigger one by actually bringing the *fleggin-* obnoxious hunk of tin aboard my ship!

3 Close Quarters

I switched *Jammer* to autopilot, while I visited the head. Inside the cramped cubicle, which was located just aft of my cabin, I stripped off my filthy gear and clothes and discovered, from head to foot, I was just as filthy. Since we were in zero G, I took a quick sonic shower, then changed into some fresh duds. My usual outfit: a pair of black pants and a long-sleeved white shirt.

I cleaned my belt and fastened it around my waist again. Cleaned and checked my blaster, its holster, and my tool-pack. Luckily, after what I'd been through, none of 'em were any the worse for wear. Polished my boots and slipped into them. Lastly, I tucked my laser-handle into the top of my right boot where it belonged.

Once I'd cleaned up, I felt a whole helluva lot better. Had to admit the bot'd been right: I'd smelled pretty damned ripe.

On my way back to *Jammer*'s cabin, I stopped in the open hatchway. Hanging onto a restraining strap with one hand, I let myself float in midair while I spied on the bot. On the co-pilot's screen, the son of a bitch was running through my data files! He was so intent on whatever he was scanning he hadn't noticed I'd returned.

"Snooping, Tin Man?" My angry words cut across the cabin like a laser-bolt.

But calm as calm could be, the bot swung his chair to face me. "Your ship's data banks lack any trace of *accurate* information in regard to you, Rand. In fact, I suspect most of your documentation is fabricated."

"So what?"

"Current interplanetary regulations require every spacecraft to log the correct identity of its legal owner, as well as the ship's planet of registration, do they not?"

I glared at the bot. "Not *my* ship, pal!"

"And why, may I ask, not?"

I gave him a casual shrug, trying to pass off my all too shady actions. "Not my style. Like I told you before, I never give out any info that could be used against me."

For a few microseconds, the bot stared at me. Then he said slowly, "Rand, by any chance, are you in difficulty with the law?"

Planting the sole of my right boot against the frame of the hatchway, I launched myself across the cabin. Snagged the back of the pilot's chair with one hand, and shook a clenched fist in the bot's metal face.

"Quit snooping and just mind your own damn business!" I warned him in no uncertain terms.

His voice still calm, Blackie replied, "I have decided to make *you* my business, Rand, and I am of the opinion that you are, at least at present, in dire need of both my help and my protection."

When I heard those words coming outta him, I couldn't help letting out a harsh laugh. "Protection? From a bot? *Ha!* I don't need one damn thing from you, pal, let alone protection. You're nothing but a worthless hunk of junk!"

"I beg to differ, Rand. I am very much afraid you do need my protection," the bot insisted. He sounded dead-serious.

Swearing and grumbling under my breath, I pulled myself down into the pilot's seat, grabbed the floating ends of my restraining straps, and yanked them tight about me. "Look here, pal, there are a few things—okay, maybe a helluva lot more than a few!—I'd just as soon forget about and have the rest of the Cosmos forget about. Get my drift?"

The bot mulled that over for several microseconds, then said, "I gather you are implying your past is rather unsavory."

Obviously, he got my drift and got it way too damned well.

"Uh, that might be part of it. Just don't snoop, y'hear me? You might learn a helluva lot more'n you'd really care to know."

Thinking the matter settled, I heaved a sigh of relief. While I was in the head, I'd tucked a polishing rag into my belt. Now I pulled out the large square of cloth and offered it to the bot.

"Here! I, uh, thought you might like to clean up, too. After my shower, I feel a whole helluva lot better."

Blackie hesitated before taking the cloth from my fingers.

"Go ahead. Give yourself a good rub-down," I urged him. "That rag's got metal polish on it. I use it to clean *Jammer's* console."

The bot tried to wipe off the kitchen grease and bits of garbage stuck to his metal hide, but only managed to smear the gunk around.

His clumsy attempt to clean himself irked me no end. I snatched the polishing rag right outta his metal hand. "For God's green snake! Haven't you polished your own chassis before?" I stretched my right arm toward him. "Better let me have a go at it, pal."

He drew back and started to protest, "Rand—!"

"Shut up and let me get to work. You don't exactly smell so sweet yourself, pal. If you're gonna share close quarters like *Jammer's* cabin with me, you need—to get—washed up!"

I scrubbed his black dome until it gleamed like a *Garzantine* mirror, dug some caked-in grease outta his silver neck-joints, then polished his broad metal shoulders and chest. Rubbed so damned hard I could see the reflection of my face in his black pecs.

"Rand! Enough, if you please!" the bot begged.

My hand fell to those black-and-silver washboard abs of his; suddenly, I stopped polishing. Tried my damnedest, but couldn't curb the heat rising to my cheeks. I drew back my arm and flung the cloth in the bot's direction. He let the rag pass him; it went floating across *Jammer's* cabin.

I snapped, "Get the general idea, pal? Finish polishing your chassis later, while I'm sleeping or something. You'll have a helluva lot more privacy."

Blackie cocked his head and flashed me an odd look. "Am I mistaken, Rand, or are you embarrassed?"

I gave him a loud snort. "Me? Embarrassed? *Hell, no!* Just

damned tired! Not gonna waste any more energy on you!" I focused on plotting a new course projection on *Jammer*'s navcomp.

After that disaster, the damn bot kept his mouth shut for one helluva long time. Should've known he was only thinking up more nosey questions, still looking to pry into my private affairs.

"Rand, have you considered that your past might very well provide the motive behind the recent attempts upon your life?"

"I don't follow you, Tin Man. You saying some bastard wants me dead because my past isn't exactly flawless?" I had to shake my head. The whole idea was *fleggin* crazy! "Naw, I can't buy that load of bilge."

"Do not dismiss my theory quite so hastily, Rand. Let us hypothesize that someone from your past does indeed intend to kill you or to have you killed. The motive would most likely be one of two: either fear or hatred, or perhaps a combination of the two."

I got a real chuckle outta that one. "Lots of people in this solar system hate my bloody guts, Tin Man! But fear? Hell, nobody's afraid of me—'cept the jackers and smugglers operating in this sector. I do my job. I recoup, period! Otherwise, I make it a firm policy never to stick my nose into other people's business, whether it's legal or illegal. Too damned dangerous!"

"But as a recoup agent, you are paid to recover hijacked goods, are you not?" Blackie demanded, as if he thought I needed reminding about my own profession.

"Yeah, and I'm damned good at it, pal."

"Have you recovered any stolen property of late?"

My pride was stung; felt my face go flame-red, so I turned away from the bot's nosey stare. "Uh, well, I have to admit the job's been a helluva lot tougher than usual lately. Besides, I never claimed I recouped one hundred percent," I grumbled.

I pictured the microchips or nano-circuits, or whatever the hell the bot had for brains, clicking and whirring like crazy inside that black metal skull of his.

"As rumors would have it, Rand, the ISF suspects that a criminal mastermind is responsible for the most recent hijackings plaguing this sector of the galaxy. You would not be at all familiar with the subject of these rumors, now would you?"

I growled, "Wouldn't give you two damn credits for any unsubstantiated rumors, pal."

The bot pounced. "*A six-syllable word!* Absolutely astounding! That must be a new verbal record for you, Rand!"

I glared daggers at him, not appreciating the snarky remark one damn bit. "Look here, you smart-ass—!" I started to snarl, then checked myself. "Why in the name of Unholy Hell am I sitting here arguing with a *fleggin* piece of machinery? Especially one that thinks it's God's greatest gift to the whole damn Universe?"

Switched off the autopilot so I could take over the controls and swung *Jammer* hard aport, just for the hell of it. A real dumb-ass move on my part, if ever I'd made one, but by that point I was boiling mad.

I was too damned stubborn to speak to the bot again. But if I'd been speaking to him, there was no way in hell I'd let him know what was going through my mind. He'd dredged up a nagging fear from some far-back corner of my brain. That old fear was so damned scary I didn't have guts enough to take it out, dust it off, and stare it straight in its ugly face.

My *fleggin* past deserved to stay where it was: dead and buried on the planet Esperance!

Just then, the incoming transmission signal on *Jammer*'s comm system squawked. I jumped, leaned forward to punch in my private code—along with an order to unscramble the message—and hit receive. A fuzzy visual came up on the comm's vidscreen.

As the image gradually un-fuzzed, I recognized the face of Krol Kramer, head honcho of Surety Galactic Insurance: my boss. I almost let out a groan, but managed to stifle it in the nick of time. Kramer looked cool and composed, as always, and nattily dressed. Never a single hair outta place, that's Krol Kramer.

"Greetings, Rand," he said in his usual brisk tone, without cracking so much as the hint of a smile.

I gave the image on the screen one curt nod of my wildly-tousled head; zero G doesn't exactly do wonders for any fem's hairdo. "Kramer. What's up?"

Never one to beat around any bush, large or small, Kramer got right down to business. "Remoxa has filed another large claim for losses incurred."

I let out a low, shrill whistle. "*K'yoti* Hell! Another jacking? So damned soon?"

Krol Kramer's thin, prissy lips got even thinner; the creases in his forehead got deeper. "Correct, Rand. That makes the *third* such loss Remoxa has suffered in the last planet-month. No wonder Roman Aguilar wants his cargo recovered ASAP, as does Surety."

Kramer went on, "If you *flegg* up this time, Rand, Surety stands to lose a substantial amount. Putting it simply, so you can understand, we can't afford to keep paying out on such huge losses and remain in business much longer. And we certainly can't afford to offend the great and powerful Roman Aguilar by canceling our contract with him, now can we? That would be tantamount to Surety committing financial suicide!"

I took Kramer's snarky remarks personally and gave him a dark scowl of my own. "I'm already doing my damnedest to crack this case! The bastards behind these latest jackings are real pros, not your run-of-the-mill, easy to catch amateurs. Solving this one's gonna take me some time and some serious credits. Right at the moment, *Jammer*'s basically unarmed, and I'm strapped for credits, if you know what I mean?"

Kramer didn't look even a nano-bit concerned. "Surety isn't about to invest further in your so far futile efforts, Rand. You're on your own, I'm afraid. And this time, Roman Aguilar not only wants his cargo recouped, he wants the culprits apprehended as well. In point of fact, he's out for their blood. He's meeting with all interested parties at Remoxa Headquarters, tomorrow, promptly at ten hundred hours. Have you got that, Rand? I advise you to be there—*or else!*"

I scratched my head. "Uh, Kramer, going back to Milo's Planet right now might present a wee bit of a problem for me."

Kramer gave one of his overly dramatic sighs, making it pretty damned obvious how put out he was with me. "What the devil's your problem this time, Rand?"

"Well, first, a couple bastards tried to smoke me; then, just before I left Kaswali City, a little send off party was waiting for me at the Port, if you get my drift."

Kramer wagged his head in disgust, careful not to muss up his expensive, classy hairdo. "That's your problem, Rand, not mine.

You're the one who gets herself into these ridiculous predicaments, time and time again. Surety most certainly does not. And as Mr. Aguilar made eminently clear to me, he wants every last soul involved in this endeavor to attend his meeting. He'll accept no excuses whatsoever. Have I succeeded in making myself clear?"

"Yeah, I get your point, Kramer. I'll be there—one way or another."

"Please don't fail us, Rand. You'll sincerely regret it if you do, that I can promise you. I'll see you at Remoxa Headquarters, then. Tomorrow, ten hundred hours. Kramer out."

The vidscreen faded to gray, then went blank. I let out a long groan and leaned back in my seat to mull over this latest glitch in my sorry life. The tail end of Kramer's little speech'd sounded to me mighty like a threat. Surety must be getting pretty damned desperate.

"*Dammit!* Another jacking, just when I need some downtime to iron out my own bloody headaches!" I grumbled out loud, speaking to myself.

For some reason, the damn bot thought I was talking to him. He turned and eyed me with those off-putting crystal lenses of his. "Recouping is your chosen profession, is it not, Rand?"

"The timing's damned lousy, Tin Man. How in hell am I gonna nab those *fleggin* jackers and watch out for my own ass? Get distracted at the wrong microsecond and I could get smoked!"

To make myself feel better, I swore a helluva lot more. Finally, I decided to play it safe: I'd head back to Milo's all right, but by a roundabout route. I'd come in on the far side of the planet, park *Jammer* up at one of the space stations, and avoid the surface ports like the bloody plague. With any kinda luck, the bastards out for my blood wouldn't expect me back on Milo's Planet so damn soon.

As I plotted the course correction on *Jammer*'s navcomp, I muttered, "Bloody Hell! If word gets around I'm on-planet—!" I shivered and couldn't finish that grim thought.

"Your mortal enemies, whomever they might be, will most certainly come in search of you," the bot finished for me, as if he were tuned in to my frequency.

"Sure as hell, pal, sure as hell! You can bet your metal ass on that."

For a long spell, the bot didn't say another damn word. He was probably thinking again, maybe worrying about going back to Milo's. But of course, that was ridiculous. Bots didn't worry, couldn't worry— not about anything in the whole bloody universe.

But before long, I got bored. Just to make conversation, and scratch the itch of my own curiosity, I asked the bot, "How long've you been operational, Tin Man?"

To my surprise, he practically jumped down my throat. "That information is none of your business, Rand!"

"Why in hell are you getting so damned huffy?" I asked him. "I just asked a civil question, and you act all offended!"

Blackie gave me a long, sideways look. That look told me plain as day he didn't trust me—shocked the hell outta me. Making his suspicion even more obvious, he demanded, "*Why* do you require that information?"

I gave him a shrug and leaned forward to give the course projection a totally unnecessary tweak.

"Just curious, I guess. That's a human trait, y'know? *K'yoti* Hell! Will you stop looking at me as if I were starting a new Spanish Exposition? So don't answer me! Just ignore me! Pretend I'm not even here, and I'll do the same for you, pal! I swear, the microsecond it's safe to land *Jammer* on the surface of Milo's, I'm selling you to the highest bidder. Can't come any too damn soon for me, you tin-plated, *fleggin* bastard!"

Furious, I swung the pilot's chair back to him, so I wouldn't have to look at him. I crossed my arms on my chest and ran through a catalog of every cussword I knew, in every language I knew, which made for one helluva long list. Then I invented a few of my own. I felt a little better.

Blackie finally broke the awkward silence. "Rand, I have no wish to offend you; however, I am entitled to some privacy, am I not?"

Coming from him, that word was mighty damned odd. I forgot my anger and swung my chair to face him again. "A *bot* entitled to privacy? *Huh!* That's a good one, pal! Didn't know bots knew the meaning of the word."

"As you previously pointed out to me in no uncertain terms, Rand, you have several, ah, unfortunate incidents in your own past, incidents which you prefer not to discuss."

"Yeah, well, that's different. I'm human. You're not. Humans make mistakes. We do a helluva lot of things we're sorry for later on. Bots are supposed to be perfect, aren't they?"

"Although robots are a vast improvement upon the human race, at least in some respects, we most certainly are not perfect."

After getting such a humbling confession outta the bot, I had myself a good chuckle. "You don't say! Well, doesn't that crush your ego to smithereens, Tin Man?"

Blackie muttered something under his so-called breath; I thought I caught the words "...machine bigot!"

Once again, hearing such a damned odd remark come outta the bot's mechanical mouth set me back on my heels.

"*K'yoti* Hell! There you go again, getting all huffy on me! Look, for all I know, pal, you murdered the entire family you used to serve! I don't give a fast-flying damn what you did in the past. You don't wanna talk about it? We won't talk about it. Deal? Forget I even asked the bloody-question!"

Gritting my teeth, I turned my attention to the navcomp and concentrated on keeping *Jammer* dead-on course. Sternly reminded myself I'd be rid of the damn bot soon enough, which made me feel one helluva lot better. The bloody smart-ass was an unbearable bastard, best left to his own devices. I wanted him outta my hair—for good!

Still, somewhere deep down in my gut, I had an uneasy feeling; there was something fishy about the *fleggin* bot, something I couldn't quite put my finger on. But I knew damned good and well that something about him sure as hell wasn't right.

One of my frequent hunches whispered into my ear, *The sooner you get rid of that damn bot, the better!*

4 Five Million Credits

For my own health and safety, I docked *Jammer* on the mid-level of one of the space stations parked in low orbit above Milo's Planet. Station security tended to be a helluva lot tighter than security down at the surface ports.

I left the bot aboard *Jammer*, with orders to guard my ship at all costs, and hopped a shuttle for a flight down to the center of Kaswali City. Figured the farther away from the main port I stayed, the better. I was pretty damned sure I'd find a welcoming party there waiting to greet me.

From the shuttle terminal, I planned to hop a surface tram headed in the general direction of Remoxa HQ. Having to take a crowded, downtown tram might be a royal pain in the ass, but right at the moment, I figured it was a helluva lot safer than landing *Jammer* at any of the surface ports.

As soon as the shuttle landed at one of the city's midtown terminals, I shouldered my way onto a packed surface tram. Spent the entire trip standing with my back plastered against its rear wall. I kept my eyes on my fellow passengers, watching for signs of hostility or the slightest hint of interest in me.

My nerves twitched like crazy the whole way, but the ride was so damned dull I was bored half to death.

The microsecond the tram reached my stop, I pushed my way to the exit and jumped off. I stood staring up at Remoxa Tower like some overawed rookie-tourist. But I had to admit that tower was one helluva feat of hover engineering!

Remoxa Tower'd been built almost entirely outta the huge crystals native to Milo's Planet. The tower was suspended in midair, as weightless as a pillar of cloud. Its crystal skin reflected Milo's Sun like one gigantic *Garzantine* mirror. A globe made outta gold wires sat atop the blazing tower. Inside the golden globe, blue-white bolts of energy snapped and arced. Reminded me of desert lightning trapped in a cage. Let me tell you, the awesome sight gave me one helluva case of goose bumps!

I took a deep breath and headed toward the fiery tower. But before Remoxa's army of heavily-armed security guards would let me, or anyone else, near the tower, we had to pass through a series of checkpoints. At the first scanner, the guard forced me to hand over my weapons: my blaster, the laser-handle tucked in the top of my right boot, even the tool pack on my belt.

Hate being unprotected! Feels as though I'm walking around in public stark-naked.

The next guard used a small, hand-held wand to scan my ident chip. Years ago, when they'd first hired me, Surety insisted on implanting one in my chest wall, just inside my ribcage. The better to ID my remains, I suppose, if and when I turned up dead. The guard read the ID that came up on the wand. His upper lip curled in a sneer. I practically heard the dumb-ass thinking, *A damn recoup agent—hah!*

He swept the wand over the rest of me in one final check to see if I'd come into recent contact with any dangerous stuff—biological or chemical—or had any weapons implanted in my body. Once that guy cleared me, I returned his nasty sneer before walking away.

I strode straight beneath the hovering tower, headed for the lift-compartments located in the central area. The state-of-the-art lift-complex was shiny, spotless, and damned expensive-looking. I stepped inside the nearest one-man lift and stated my reason for being there.

The lift door closed instantly. I felt a brief, familiar sensation in the pit of my stomach, as if I were aboard *Jammer* just as she was going into zero G. Anti-gravs raised the lift upward and into the tower floating high overhead.

Microseconds later, when the lift door slid open, I stepped out and found myself on the sixty-fifth floor. A fem's voice directed me to Conference Room 65 Zeta, at the far end of the fifth corridor on my right. I followed directions. Sure as hell didn't know my way around; I'd never actually been inside Remoxa HQ before.

But I knew damned good and well if I tried to get in, no way in hell would I make it past the first security checkpoint—not unless I'd been invited by the great Roman Aguilar himself. Galaxy-famous, bigwig philanthropists and multi-billionaires like *him* wouldn't be caught dead anywhere near a lowly recoup agent like *me*.

Hell, Roman Aguilar wouldn't stoop to wipe his damned expensive boots on me!

At the door to Conference Room 65 Zeta, a force-field barred the way. Before I could get through it, I had to pass yet another security check. And this time I was forced to suffer an actual pat-down!

After that humiliating experience, I was allowed to set foot inside the room. Seemed Roman Aguilar wasn't at all the trusting type. All those layers of security made me wonder what in bloody hell he had to be afraid of.

I strolled into the conference room, trying my damnedest to act as if I came here every day of the week. But when I got a load of all the unfamiliar faces around the room, my stomach did one helluva flip. Roman Aguilar's other "guests" were way too damned respectable for me to know a single one of 'em.

A huge oval table took up most of the conference room. Its shiny black surface was as polished as a *Garzantine* mirror. For a fraction of a microsecond, that table reminded me of the damn bot. I wondered how he and *Jammer* were getting along. Wished to hell I were back aboard my ship, back in my own comfort zone.

I slid into the nearest empty seat and leaned back in the well-padded chair. Crossed one ankle over my knee and tried to look casual, as though I really belonged there. Then I did my damnedest to blend in with the furniture.

As luck would have it, a few microseconds later, Krol Kramer himself breezed into the conference room, neat as a bloody pin and fashionably late, so everyone there'd be sure to notice him. On his way in, he stopped to greet several people, then took up the seat on my right. He gave me the barest nod, not to risk disturbing his expensive hairstyle. Either that or he was hoping to hell no one there'd think he actually knew me.

"Rand."

I gave him a slight nod of my own head. "Kramer." Nothing more'n that; hell, it's not like we're friends or anything close to it. He just happens to be my boss, that's all.

After that, Kramer and I ignored each other. Bored outta my *fleggin* skull, I passed the time by playing a sorta game. Tried to guess why all the long faces seated around the big black table'd been invited. It was easy enough for me to pick out the insurance 'gents, the ISF bozos, the local law, and so on down the line. I suspected several guys dressed to the nines were Remoxa bigwigs.

Far as I could tell, though, I was the one and only recoup agent who'd been invited to this little shindig of Aguilar's. Damned strange! How in bloody hell I'd earned that honor I had no idea.

I hate waiting for anything; that's just one of my many flaws. Waiting gives me a damn headache. Never been known for my patience. It might be a virtue and all that crap, but never once in my whole sorry life has anyone ever accused me of being virtuous. I drummed my fingers on the boot crossed over my right knee; sighed, and shifted in my chair, letting everyone in the room know how bloody bored I was. Wished to hell I could stand up and stalk outta there, but I couldn't do that, not without getting myself fired.

I wanted nothing more in the whole *fleggin* universe than to get back to *Jammer* where I belonged. But Krol Kramer and the rest of the stuffed shirts in charge of Surety Galactic Insurance wouldn't be one damn bit pleased if I walked out on the great Roman Aguilar. They were annoyed enough with me as it was, so I sat there and suffered and glared at the jackasses around the room—especially at a couple letches seated across the table from me who kept giving me more'n a once-over with their eyes!

I was teetering on the brink of losing my mind when a stuffy-looking little dumb-ass—one of the guys I'd pegged as Remoxa bigwigs—got to his feet. At long last, the damn show was about to get on the bloody road! He cleared his throat loud enough to make everyone in the room stop talking and look at him.

"Gentlemen and gentlefems—let me introduce myself: I am Laird Bokner, CFO of Remoxa, Incorporated. As you all know, Mr. Roman Aguilar, the galaxy-renowned CEO of Remoxa, has invited you here. He wishes to speak to you regarding the reprehensible spate of hijackings currently plaguing our company. Now, if you will kindly attend to his presentation, Mr. Aguilar will address you in person."

Mr. Laird Stuffy-Pants resumed his seat. With a grand gesture, he passed his hand over an almost invisible control panel set into the table before him. Instantly, lightproof panels dropped down from above, covering the crystal windowpanes that ran from floor to ceiling. The conference room went dark.

A huge hologram appeared, hovering over the middle of the oval table, mirrored in it's polished surface. It was the image of a man's head, and that head belonged to Roman Aguilar. From the vidcasts I'd seen of him, I recognized the great man right off the bat, but of course, I'd never met him in person.

My guess was this was about as "personal" as Roman Aguilar ever got.

I sat back in my padded chair, arms folded across my chest, and watched the holographic image slowly revolve. When it faced my direction, I saw a hawk-nosed face topped by a thick mat of blue-black hair: a transplant job if ever I saw one! Aguilar's smile showed perfectly-even, whiter-than-white teeth: damned expensive implants, no doubt. There wasn't so much as a single line or crease anywhere on his face, no hint of his age. Roman Aguilar was tanned, well-groomed, damned good-looking—and as phony as hell!

These days, if you have the credits, you can buy just about anything, I mused, *including a total rejuv-job whenever you feel the need.*

"I am, as of course you must already know, Roman Aguilar, the President and CEO of Remoxa, Incorporated. I would like to take this opportunity to welcome you all to Remoxa's Universal Head-quarters."

My lips twitched. Did my damnedest to stifle a sarcastic grin, but I couldn't help thinking, *And here we all took you for God Almighty. You sure as hell seem to think you're Him!*

Smooth as smooth could be, Aguilar went on with his little speech. "As you are no doubt aware, we at Remoxa are facing a rather serious problem, albeit a relatively minor one. These repeated hijackings of our shipments are rapidly becoming a thorn in my proverbial side. I wish that thorn removed. I want the problem resolved—immediately, *if not sooner!*

"Therefore, I am prepared to spare no expense to see that these nefarious thefts are halted and the culprits, brought to swift and final justice. To that end, I am offering a substantial reward: five-million credits to the agency or individual responsible for bringing a halt to these despicable crimes—one way or another!"

Aguilar's tone was ice-cold, deliberate, pointed.

The microsecond I heard those words, my chin rose, as if the great man'd challenged me personally. He hadn't left the slightest doubt what he'd meant by "one way or another." I'd heard Roman Aguilar was a man you'd never want to cross—not if you had half an ounce of brain cells left in your skull. Power, wealth, fame, thousands of loyal employees, Roman Aguilar had it in spades, and Roman Aguilar meant to *keep* it all, no matter what he had to do.

To a super-bigwig like him, five-million credits was splurge money, but to me, five-mil meant a helluva lot more: something a lowly recoup agent like me could only dream about, nothing but sheer fantasy!

Quickly shelved those thoughts and forced myself to focus as Aguilar went on, "Before you leave, each of you will receive detailed information on the most recent hijackings: date, time, location, cargo manifest—every last bit of relevant data Remoxa has accumulated. Whoever possesses the requisite brainpower to solve the puzzle, and has guts enough to apprehend the perpetrators, will find himself five-million credits richer."

A wave of greed, matched by nothing I'd ever witnessed, rippled around that conference room.

"Before I leave you to the task at hand, I must inquire whether there are any questions," Aguilar said curtly.

Not a damn soul spoke up. No one in the room so much as twitched. I risked offending the great man by raising my hand.

The giant holo-face swung in my direction. Great dark lines scrawled across Roman Aguilar's brow. "Yes, Ms.—?"

"Rand, sir, Galaxy Rand. I'm a recoup agent with Surety—"

Aguilar cut me off. "I am well aware of your credentials, Ms. Rand. Your question?"

That shocked the hell outta me! *How in the name of Unholy Hell did Roman Aguilar know who I was?*

I stuttered, "Wh-what if the guys responsible for these jackings turn out to be yours? I mean, maybe someone in your employ's leaking info to the jackers."

The great brow smoothed out. "Of course, I have taken that possibility into consideration, Ms. Rand, incredibly faint though it might be! But to date, I have found no evidence whatsoever to support such a theory. Without exception, my employees are noted for their unswerving loyalty and devotion, both to Remoxa and to myself, personally.

"You see, in my organization I tolerate nothing less than total loyalty, total honesty, and total dedication. I expect this from *all* my employees. And you, Ms. Rand, as an agent of Surety Galactic Insurance, are in my employ, are you not?"

I had no chance to mask my shock. My eyebrows shot skyward. "Uh, guess I really never thought of it quite that way, Mr. Aguilar. But whoever the hell I work for, I always do my damnedest."

A faint smile twitched the corners of the holographic lips, as if my bold remark amused the great man. "An excellent philosophy indeed, I must say, Ms. Rand."

Then Roman Aguilar lost all interest in me. "If there are no other issues to be addressed at this time, gentlemen and gentlefems, I expect your full cooperation in this matter. I also expect nothing less than complete success. You are dismissed."

In the blink of an eye, the holo-image vanished; the panels covering the crystal windows rose. Light from Milo's Sun flooded the room, making it so damned bright I couldn't make out a bloody thing.

I heard a faint click and a whir right in front of me and looked down. A paper-thin plastidisc shot outta a slot in the table. I took the disc, stood up, and slipped it into my pocket. Around the room, others were doing the same, murmuring among themselves in low, excited voices. Most of 'em were awed at seeing Roman Aguilar "in person" and by the once in a lifetime chance to earn five-million credits.

I headed for the door, eager to leave, but Krol Kramer dogged my heels and demanded, "Well, Rand, what did you think?"

"Roman Aguilar's in one helluva solar flare over these jackings," I noted wryly, keeping my voice low, so no one else in the room could hear.

"Solar flare? *Humph!* Much too mild a description for his reaction, believe me," Kramer said, giving me a prissy little sniff. "This entire, unfortunate business is making him look bad: weak, impotent, so to speak. Here's the most powerful conglomerate in the galaxy, being victimized repeatedly, and at will, by a band of petty hijackers. *Tsk-tsk!* An intolerable situation! Aguilar simply can't afford to allow that blight upon his sterling reputation to continue. Especially not now!" Kramer gave me a wink. "Not when he's about to announce his candidacy for the presidency of the Galactic Consortium!"

Once again, my damn eyebrows shot skyward. "The Consortium! *K'yoti* Hell! Where the *flegg*'d you hear this, Kramer?"

His thin chest puffed out; he reminded me of a male peacock strutting in full plumage. "I'll have you know, Rand, I heard the news directly from the lips of the great man himself, not an hour ago. By tonight, the news will be on every vid-network on every planet in the Consortium. That's the real reason Roman Aguilar's so dissatisfied with our efforts to recoup his stolen property and with our customary reimbursements for the full value of those losses— as he pointed out to me, in, ah, no uncertain terms!"

I took those last remarks as an insult aimed at me and gave Kramer one of my darkest scowls. "Now you look here, Krol Kramer, I don't give a fast-flying damn about Aguilar's bloody image problems! I do my job the best I can, same as always. *Surety* pays me. I work for you—*not* Roman Aguilar!"

A cold glint lit up in Krol Kramer's eyes, an evil glint I didn't care for in the least.

"What the devil's the matter with you, Rand? By any chance are you getting a wee bit nervous, perhaps due to your dismal failure to stop these latest hijackings?"

"*Hell, no!* Just don't like Roman Aguilar telling me I work for him! He may be Surety's number one client, Kramer, but he sure as hell doesn't own *me*! Nobody owns me!"

"Oh, that I am very well aware of," Kramer drawled in a sarcastic tone, eyeing me from head to toe. "But if you wish to continue your employment with Surety Galactic, Rand, you'll do your job particularly well in this case. And I'm quite certain you don't want Roman Aguilar—personally—annoyed with you, now do you?"

I bristled and snarled, "For all I care, Kramer, Roman Aguilar can go take a little dip in the tar pits of Hell!"

"Temper, temper, Rand! I wouldn't be at all surprised if the illustrious Mr. Aguilar has this entire premises, ah—closely monitored, shall we say?" Kramer pointedly eyed the conference room's crystal walls and overhead, then gave me a snarky grin.

"I don't give a *fleggin* damn what Aguilar overhears! He's not my business!"

Kramer's thin face sobered. "Then may I suggest you stop wasting precious time and get down to business, Rand? If you'd care to let me know exactly where you intend to go next—?"

I gave him a firm shake of my head. No real reason not to trust Krol Kramer; it was just force of habit. "Naw! I'm better off keeping my damn mouth shut and my plans to myself."

I had more'n enough reason to keep my cards close to my vest. I was playing a bloody dangerous game here; my damn life was at stake.

Kramer's prissy mouth got even tighter. "Play it anyway you see fit, then, Rand, but remember this: your career as a recoup agent depends on your success. Surety is on an extremely short umbilical. As I warned you before, you'd better not fail us!"

"I *won't* fail, damn you!" I snapped. "Count on it!"

I'd had more'n my fill of Krol Kramer. I pivoted on the heel of my boot and stalked outta the conference room. All the way back to the lifts, my temper simmered. Under my breath, I griped colorfully, telling Krol Kramer and Roman Aguilar what they could do to each other.

Then, from outta the clear blue, a thought hit me; maybe Surety'd decided it was past time to put me out to pasture—permanently!—and without having to pay me retirement benefits. After all, I knew a whole helluva lot more'n was good for me. Was *that* what Krol Kramer'd been trying to warn me about? Was Surety itself behind the recent attempts on my life?

I was sunk so damned deep in those grim thoughts that I let my guard down for a fraction of a microsecond. As I stepped into the one-man lift, someone else slid in right behind me. The door closed.

I whirled to face my unexpected and unwelcome company. From force of habit, my right hand reached for my blaster. My holster was empty. I let out a colorful cussword, flattened my back against the lift's far wall, and got ready to kick the bloody bastard's lights out. But a one-man lift's damned close quarters for hand to hand combat!

My whole body tense, I waited for my new "friend" to make the first move. The guy just stood there, grinning like an idiot. "Hello, Rand. Heard a lot about you. Now we finally get to meet, face to face."

"Who the bloody hell are you?" I demanded, giving him my worst glare, still on guard and prepared to fight for my life if need be.

He raised both hands to show me they were empty. Moving with care, so I wouldn't misinterpret his actions, his right hand went to the breast pocket of his shirt. He gave it a sharp tap with his index finger. Where the pocket'd been, a holo-badge appeared.

I groaned in disgust. "ISF! Are you *fleggin* kidding me?"

Should've known! Who but a dumb-ass ISF 'gent would be stupid enough to follow somebody like me into a one-man lift? Nobody, unless they were bloody crazy.

"Smart move, chum, real smart!" I growled at the guy in front of me. "If I hadn't waited for you to make the first move, you'd be a dead man right about now."

As if he didn't hear one damn word, he said in an even tone, "Jeffries." A voiceprint crawled across the top of the badge, matching the permanent one printed below. A small, revolving holo-image of his head appeared; a line beneath it read: *Jeffries, Armando: Inspector Second Class.*

The two of us were standing way too close. Got a real good view of his badge and of him. I had to admit the guy wasn't half bad to look at. He had a pair of deep-blue eyes you could get lost in, a shock of slightly-thinning blond hair, and a body he obviously kept in damned good shape.

Allowing myself to relax a bit, I leaned back against the lift wall and crossed my arms on my chest. "Okay, chum, let's get this over with as fast as humanly possible. What in bloody hell does the ISF want with me now?"

"Not the ISF; this's my own idea, Rand. Two heads could get to the bottom of these jackings a hell of a lot faster than one," Jeffries said, eyeing me up and down, without showing any particular interest in my head.

If the bloody jackass expected me to jump at his offer and pant at the golden opportunity to work with him, he must've been real disappointed.

"As in you and me?" Without giving that crazy idea so much as a microsecond's thought, I let him have a scornful laugh. "I work alone, chum. Didn't your ISF data banks tell you that? And it's plain as day nobody bothered to warn you I can be damned dangerous, even when I'm unarmed."

Jeffries looked a tad uncomfortable. His feet shifted, and his jaw tensed. "So I checked you out, Rand. I'm not a *fleggin* moron! I thought half of five-million creds would be a hell of a lot better than nothing at all. Now that Roman Aguilar's offered such a huge reward, everybody and his baby brother will be scurrying all over this sector, frantically trying to solve the damn case."

I scowled. "So why in bloody-blue-blazes did you pick *me* outta the mob of possible candidates? Why not choose some other poor sucker for that honor? For instance, you could share the wealth with one of your ISF buddies."

Jeffries leaned in closer and lowered his voice, which told me he was afraid our private conversation was either being overheard or recorded. "There're some rumors floating around that your old buddy Torrance is back in business and operating in this sector again."

A light-orb roughly the size of Jupiter lit up inside my skull. Outwardly, I gave Jeffries a slight shrug. "Might've heard something like that, but to be honest, chum, I never put much stock in rumors. Does the ISF really believe Torrance's the one behind this latest rash of jackings?"

Jeffries' nod was solemn. "Right now, he's our prime suspect. If the bastard is up to his old tricks, would you have any idea where he might be holed up?"

"Even if I knew for a damn fact exactly where Torrance was, I sure as hell wouldn't tell you, or feel the slightest obligation to report his whereabouts to the ISF," I said, being perfectly blunt, perfectly honest. "I gave the bloody ISF enough help the last time. Paid one helluva price for it."

Jeffries' eyes shot angry blue sparks into mine. "You must realize Torrance has good reason to be out for revenge. If I were you, Rand, I wouldn't play games on this one. You could lose and lose bad!"

I gave the arrogant jackass another offhand shrug. "Hell, Torrance'll just have to take a number and wait his *fleggin* turn." I raised my voice and ordered the lift control: "Ground level and make it damned snappy!"

All the way down to the ground, Jeffries fumed in sullen silence.

The lift drifted to a stop beneath the crystal tower hovering overhead. The microsecond the door opened, I shoved my way past Jeffries before he could stop me. But the bastard came after me and grabbed my upper arm.

"Don't be so damned sure of yourself, sister!" he hissed. "You're gonna get yourself into serious trouble somewhere in this sector, then scream your pretty little head off for the ISF to save your sweet ass! Trust me on this!"

Angry as hell, I pulled my arm outta his grip, then turned to look Jeffries straight in the baby-blues and drawled, "Hope to bloody hell I never get *that* desperate!"

Jeffries turned red in the face, like a neo who'd guzzled his first glassful of cheap *hahk-teem*. "All right! Play this your own way, then, Rand. Since you insist on being so *fleggin* stupid, you can go it alone. See how damn far that gets you. I offered you your best chance of success, and you refused it. Do me a favor? Remember *that* when your ass lands in the frying pan!"

With one hand, Jeffries smoothed his shirt pocket. The holo-badge instantly vanished. Hackles still up, he took off.

For a couple microseconds, I stared after him, before striding over to the first security gate to reclaim my property. I shoved my blaster back into its holster, tucked my laser-handle into the top of my boot, and fastened the tool-pack to my belt. It felt damned good to be armed again. Without my weapons, I'd felt as naked and as helpless as a newborn babe.

A sudden thought made my skin crawl; if I'd had my blaster on me in the one-man lift, I might've smoked that *fleggin* bastard Jeffries—and found myself swimming up to my damn eyebrows in one cosmic-sized vat of pickles!

5 The Black Hole

With a surge of relief, I caught the next surface tram headed for the transport station. Soon enough, I was aboard a shuttle and on my way back up to the space station where I'd parked *Jammer*. My thoughts were on the five-million credits Roman Aguilar'd dangled right under my nose, as if he'd offered poisoned bait to a starving mine-rat.

Five-mil was one helluva lot of credits! Made quite an incentive, more'n enough for someone like me to retire on, before I got myself killed, or worse! With five-mil I could buy a private little bungalow somewhere out in the boondocks on one of the barely-populated outer colonies: some nice, peaceful place beyond the hustle and bustle of the mainstream.

Against my will, a half-forgotten memory bubbled to the surface. I shoved it back down where it belonged, hard and fast! But that was all it took to shake me outta my pleasant daydreams of wealth and ease.

I'm smart enough to realize that kinda life sure as hell isn't meant for me. Daydreams are only empty dreams. Reality has thorns, great big, sharp, pointy thorns—and thorns draw blood. At a tender age, I'd learned *that* the real hard way, twenty-two long years ago—back on Esperance. And right now I had no intention of letting the faint hope of earning five-million credits blind me to life's harsh realities.

As for retirement—aw, hell! I know damned good and well that's one thing someone in my line of work never has to worry about!

When I got my butt safely back aboard *Jammer* and found every-thing quiet there, another wave of relief washed over me. Naturally, the damn bot peppered me with a slew of nosey questions about the meeting at Remoxa: blah, blah, blah! I kept my answers short, curt, and not terribly useful. Meanwhile, I set about making plans and deciding exactly what I had to do next.

In the back of my mind, I knew bloody well it wasn't safe for me to stay in one spot for long, not even up on a space station. But much as I hated to face the fact, my best source of informa-tion was on Milo's Planet. I decided my best strategy was to beat a temporary retreat and wait for darkness to cover the planet's western hemisphere. Then, I figured, it'd be safe enough to land *Jammer* in the backwater port closest to Habeeb's Outpost. Right at the moment, that plan was the sanest one I could come up with.

Once I'd decided to leave the station, I requested departure clear-ance from station control, released *Jammer* from her berth, and set course out into deep-space. With my ship a good, safe distance from the surface of Milo's, well outta the way of its heavy traffic, I could keep an eye out in all directions and avoid a possible sneak attack.

But by that point, I was running on fumes and needed to get some sleep. So, leaving the bot to keep watch, along with *Jammer*'s automated warning system, I released my restraining straps and launched myself forward. In the ship's bow, two sleeper-cocoons were attached to the overhead. I wrapped myself up in one and soon dropped off to sleep.

When I woke up from my nap, I checked the monitor on the console below me. Darkness was creeping over the near side of the planet. Letting out a groan, I struggled to unwind myself from the cocoon.

The bot heard me and called my attention to *Jammer*'s vidscreen. "Rand, I was about to wake you, since this upcoming vidcast may prove of interest." Evidently, he'd come across some breaking news.

"Why?" I grumbled, my tone surly as hell. To quiet my stomach's growling, I took a bite outta a power bar I'd stuffed into my pocket, then propelled myself toward the control console.

"Your friend Roman Aguilar is about to make a major announce-ment," the bot told me.

"Y'don't say? Heard he was gonna run for the presidency of the bloody Consortium, but he's sure as hell no friend of mine, Tin Man!"

My mouth stuffed full of power bar, I pulled myself down into the pilot's seat and strapped in. The bot turned up the volume on the vidcast. Aguilar's face came on-screen: the same face I'd seen up close and "personal" via the giant hologram at Remoxa HQ.

"Gentlefems and gentlemen, allow me to introduce myself: I am Roman Aguilar, President and CEO of Remoxa, Incorporated. Tonight, after due deliberation and much soul-searching, I announce my candidacy for president of the Interstellar Consortium. Temporarily putting aside my own considerable business interests, I intend to bring the welfare of this entire galaxy to the forefront. And, if elected, I shall boldly lead the Consortium into a peaceful and prosperous twenty-fourth century!"

The *fleggin* hypocrisy of Aguilar's speech made me wanna puke. I knew damned good and well Roman Aguilar never did anything that didn't benefit Roman Aguilar. But as the great man posed for the vidcams, looking presidential, loud cheers rose from the crowd of loyal supporters surrounding him.

I fumed. Didn't the bloody bastard already have more than enough of everything in the Cosmos? So why in hell was he grabbing for *even more?*

"Turn that damn thing off, Tin Man!" I ordered grumpily. "I've had as much of Roman Aguilar's bilge as I can stomach for one day!"

"You believe the gentleman in question has ulterior motives, I take it?" the bot observed.

"You can say that again, pal! And that bastard had the *fleggin* gall to tell me *I* work for *him!* *Hah!* That'll be the day!"

"Indeed? From what little you have told me about your meeting, Rand, I gather Roman Aguilar is well-accustomed to buying people—and their loyalty."

"Not mine, pal. Nobody buys me!" After making the necessary course corrections on *Jammer*'s navcomp, I sat back with a little sigh. "But I sure as hell could use the five-million credits Aguilar's offering for the capture of the jackers. And I wanna keep my damn job—at least for now."

"So where, then, are we heading?"

I shot a hard, nasty look at the bot. "*We?*" I repeated, raising one eyebrow.

"I may, perhaps, prove to be of some assistance to you, Rand, although you appear skeptical of that."

I heaved a resigned sigh before answering, "This won't mean one damn thing to you, pal, but if you must know, we're headed for a spaceport just outside Habeeb's Outpost. There's a sleazy little dive there that's known as The Black Hole."

The Black Hole, on the outskirts of a backwater settlement commonly called Habeeb's Outpost, has a real bad rep; it's one of the roughest joints in this sector of the galaxy. Sooner or later, most of the scum of the universe washes up in the sketchy bar, like so much space-debris caught in a vortex.

Going in, I stood just within the energy barrier that kept out the dust and heat of the street. To be on the safe side, I gave my eyes plenty of time to adjust to the low lighting before making my way farther inside.

Rowdy voices and bursts of drunken laughter couldn't quite drown out the off-key tune coming outta the music-pod in the far corner. Too damned bad about that! I was sorely tempted to draw my blaster and silence the *fleggin* thing.

I caught the high-pitched laughter of my snitch, so I drifted in her direction. Had to shoulder my way none too gently through the noisy, milling crowd.

I found J'neen lounging at the bar with both elbows planted on it's sticky surface. The grubby-looking, stub-legged asteroid miners on either side of the laughing, dark-haired fem took one good look at me, choked on their booze, and lost all interest in J'neen. The pair of 'em melted into the crowd like the shadows of ghosts.

As they say, guess my rep preceded me.

J'neen turned her head from one side to the other, obviously wondering where the hell her two admirers had suddenly gone to. But the microsecond she saw me, her small, sharply-pointed white teeth flashed in a real smile.

"Galaxy!" she cried.

"How're ya doing, J'neen?"

She gave me a little shrug of thin, sun-browned shoulders that were barely holding up a shimmery, red evening gown. Even I realized how outta place her fancy getup was in that classless joint.

J'neen replied, "Same as always, my sister. And you?"

"I'm okay."

She looked damned tired to me. This rotten way of life must finally be getting to her.

"Uh, J'neen, I really need to talk to you—in private."

She swept a nervous glance around the crowded dive, licked her lips, then nodded toward the darkest corner.

"Let's take a table, then—over there, where we won't be so *fleggin* conspicuous. And for God's sake, Galaxy, lighten up, will ya? You're attracting way too much attention."

Doing my best to oblige, I followed her to a small table shoved into the corner opposite the one where the damnable music-pod sat. We took seats.

With her index finger, J'neen tapped out an order on the servo-disc set into the center of the dingy table. A couple microseconds later, the disc rose. Under it sat a glassful of *hahk-teem* and a solar-*rudj'di*. I reached over, dropped a couple cred chips into the payment slot, then grabbed hold of the *hahk-teem*. Fem or not, cocktails'd never been my style.

I took a sip, not expecting a whole helluva lot, and got a big surprise. The stuff in my glass was high-grade *hahk-teem*, mighty fancy for a low class dive like the Black Hole, The bar's owner hadn't come by it legally, that was for damned sure. Most likely, the *hahk-teem*'d been part of some smuggler's wares old Brody, or one of his many sons, had lucked into. But right this minute, that crime didn't concern me. Remoxa didn't deal in shipments of booze.

I raised my glass in a polite salute to my snitch, then leaned across the table toward her and muttered, "J'neen, some bastard's trying their damnedest to kill me!"

Her delicate, dark eyebrows arched sharply. "*Again?*"

I scowled at the unwelcome reminder. "This time it's different!"

"Really? How 'different'?"

"This has nothing to do with any two-bit beef! Whoever the *fleggin* bastard is, he's really got it out for me—two tries within a planet hour! What's worse, I have no idea in the Cosmos who the hell's behind these damn attacks."

"That does present you with a bit of a problem, Galaxy," J'neen reluctantly agreed. She stared into her solar-*rudj'di*, watching the green and gold liquors swirling and mingling in the glass. The motion seemed to fascinate her, almost as if she were hypnotized.

After several microseconds of getting nothing but silence from her, I got impatient. "Dammit, J'neen! Have you heard anything?"

She gave me one sharp shake of her dark head. When they caught the light from the bar, the long, dangly *star-shi* earrings she was never without danced and sparkled.

"Not so much as a whisper. Sorry I can't help you, Galaxy."

Sorely disappointed, I took another bracing gulp of my *hahk-teem*. "That's bad news, real bad news. Means whoever the hell's out for my blood, he can afford to make damned sure mouths stay shut. So that lets out the usual riff-raff I deal with."

J'neen's bright eyes got wider. Her mouth dropped open. "How in hell did you manage to make an enemy that damned powerful? And who in blazes could it be?"

I could only shake my head. "Beats the hell outta me, J'neen! Can't for the life of me figure out who's to blame, or why they're after me. Haven't pulled anything shady since, ah—"

I paused to take another swig of my *hahk-teem* and quickly changed the subject. "Happen to catch any rumors floating around about these latest jackings?"

J'neen swirled the dregs of liquor in her glass and avoided my eyes. "Yeah, well, about that—word's out that Torrance's back in this sector." She winced when she said his name. "I heard a while ago he'd been paroled, for good behavior, or some such crap."

The sun-browned hand holding her glass started to tremble.

I took in one sharp, deep breath. *"Torrance!"* Not the news I'd wanted to hear! Jeffries had it right. "So the *fleggin* bastard's really back, is he? And up to his old tricks, I'm willing to bet. When he was sentenced to that bloody penal planet, I was praying he'd die out there!"

"Galaxy, you don't suppose *Torrance* put the price on your head? He wouldn't dare go after you himself, but he sure as hell would pay to see you dead!"

The look in J'neen's dark eyes told me she was worried, scared even. She knew Torrance every bit as well as I did. And she knew he had damned good reason to hate my guts. He hated me enough to want me taken out.

Did my damnedest to shove down my own fear, so I could think straight. "Torrance's no friend of mine—not yours either," I reminded J'neen, "but there's no way in hell he could've got his hands on enough credits to pay all the creeps who've tried to smoke me. At least not this soon. And much as I hate to disagree with you, J'neen, if I know Torrance, his business with me is too damned personal to be settled with hired guns. Bad as he wants revenge, I just don't see him hiring somebody to smoke me; that'd spoil all his fun!"

J'neen gave the barroom another quick scan, as if she were looking for someone. She was acting real nervous; something'd spooked her, maybe just the mention of Torrance.

"Afraid that's all I can tell you, Galaxy. I-I gotta get back to work. You take damn good care of yourself." She stood up to leave the table. As she passed me, she bent over and whispered in my ear, "Don't trust anyone, you hear me? *Not one damn soul!*"

I flashed J'neen one of my cocky, lopsided grins—a grin I wasn't quite feeling at the moment—and slid my last twenty-cred chip toward her. "Never do, J'neen. You oughta know me well enough by now to realize that's the damn truth. Just watch your own back, huh?"

Without being obvious, she palmed the cred chip and sashayed back to the bar to spend it. God, I felt sorry for J'neen! Damned sorry. She'd had a life as rough as mine. Out here on the raw frontier of space, a lot of kids were orphaned young, just like me and her.

But unlike me, J'neen had never fought back. Or maybe she had—for a while.

But her problems were her problems. Right now, I had way too damn many myself. Saving my own sweet skin had to be my main concern. Finding Torrance, capturing the bastard, and claiming Aguilar's five-mil reward came a close second.

I'd left the bot outside the bar to stand guard. He was hiding in the shadows of the narrow alley running between The Black Hole and the equally-sleazy joint next door. I whistled low, once, as a signal, and the bot came to join me. Gas orbs hovering over the deserted street offered a few splotches of dim light. The bot's black-armored body gleamed like polished glass.

"Did you acquire any pertinent information, Rand?" he asked.

"Not a whole helluva lot," I had to admit. "Confirmed some current rumors, though. Seems an old friend of mine's back in this sector, and I'll give you hundred to one odds *he's* the one behind the latest Remoxa jackings."

"Could the individual in question be responsible for the recent attempts upon your life as well?"

I shook my head. "Don't see how the bloody hell that's possible, Tin Man. Torrance can't have enough credits to hire that many hit men. If he jacks one or two more shipments like the last one, he'll have more'n enough to take me out, no doubt about that. But it's beginning to look as if somebody's beat him to the punch."

"Then where does that leave us?"

"*Us?* Again with the us!" For some unknown reason, that two-letter word raised my hackles to full-staff.

"Now you look here, pal! There is no us! You have absolutely nothing at stake. Got that? Not a *fleggin* soul in the whole bloody Cosmos gives a fast-flying damn what happens to you. Hell, you're nothing but a bot: just a walking, talking, human-aping collection of nuts and bolts, servos and nano-circuits—nothing more!"

In his most annoying, most uppity tone, Blackie snapped, "Thank you for reminding me of the cold, hard facts, madam. I had almost succeeded in forgetting my present state of being."

"Oh, for the luva—! Will you stop being such a *fleggin* smartass?"

I hissed at him. "Tonight I'm in no mood for your snarky remarks, pal!"

"That would appear to be quite true. You are in an extremely vile mood, even for you, Rand."

"Hell, you'd be in a vile mood, too," I grumbled, "if you had a price on your head, some bastard had painted a target on your back, and you didn't have one single damn clue who to blame. Five-million creds at stake, and I gotta worry about staying alive! Couldn't expect a bot to appreciate the fix I'm in, now could I?"

For once, Blackie held his tongue, or whatever, but the way he stared at me made me downright uncomfortable.

"Quit looking at me like that, damn you!"

I started down the street, headed back to the port where *Jammer* was parked, praying the damn bot was insulted enough to take off on his own and leave me the hell alone.

But in a few strides, he'd managed to catch up with me. I groaned out loud and kept on going. Side by side, in an uneasy silence, we walked down the dusty, deserted main drag of Habeeb's Outpost. The whole way, I kept my right hand on the grip of my blaster, just in case trouble showed up.

Lights shone out from the doorways of the few bars still open. As we passed, haunting music and hollow laughter drifted into the street. I fought a feeling I'd disowned a helluva long time ago, just one feeling outta many.

Suddenly, the bot started babbling. "Rand, I realize that by your discriminating standards I may not qualify as a living being; however, much like you, I fear one thing above all else."

Once again, my damn curiosity got the better of me. "Oh? And what the hell's that, Tin Man? Rust?" I chuckled at my own lousy joke.

"No, Rand—brain-death."

Those two words stopped me dead in my tracks. I turned and stared into Blackie's metal face, as if he'd gone haywire.

"For God's sake! You're a bot! You don't have a brain, not a living brain anyway. Hell, you're practically immortal, aren't you?"

The bot made that weird sound, way too damned close to a human sigh for my liking! "Should this metal shell cease to function, it can, most likely, be repaired or replaced. But *my mind* is another matter entirely, Rand. Should those nano-circuits be severely damaged, destroyed, or erased, I would cease to exist as an individual entity— and I fear that as much as humans fear death."

I started to scoff, to boast I wasn't afraid of one damn thing, but quickly changed my mind and kept my mouth shut. I got the creepy feeling that, for once anyway, the bot'd been completely honest with me, more honest than most flesh and blood beings'd ever been. Didn't exactly know what to make of that, but I sure as hell didn't like the feeling it left me with.

Being reminded of my own mortality—especially by a bloody bot!—wasn't a comforting thought. For damned sure, it wasn't welcome. Given the danger I was facing, that reminder scared the hell outta me.

In my surliest tone I growled, "You aren't as smart as I thought you were, Tin Man. Hanging around me could get you killed. You'd be a helluva lot safer on your own or attached to somebody who leads a much duller life than I do."

"Your statement may very well be true, Rand, but who, then, would prevent you from getting killed? Who else would bother attempting to correct your innumerable shortcomings or to expand your woefully-limited vocabulary?"

I gritted my teeth, muttered some of my most colorful cusswords under my breath, then snarled at the bot, "You're *not* my teacher, and you sure as hell aren't my *fleggin* nursemaid! Why don't you smarten up and get lost, pal?"

Blackie drew himself up to his full height. Like an iron giant, he towered over me. "Because, madam, I know precisely where I am and what I am, which is considerably more than you can truthfully say! That is assuming you are capable of recognizing truth in the first place."

By that point, I was trembling with fury. I went chest to chest with the damn bot, my blood boiling, ready for a fight.

"*K'yoti* Hell! If you aren't the most damned stubborn, high-handed, insulting son-of-a-bitch I've ever had the bloody bad-luck to run into—!"

"And you, Rand, appear to have entirely forgotten where we are.

At any microsecond, we may find ourselves in extreme danger. Might I suggest we table this, ah, discussion for the time being, at least until we reach the safer environs of your ship?"

With a bit of a shock, I came to my senses. The damn bot was dead-right. For a few microseconds of blind, insane rage, I'd forgotten all about the price on my head. Suddenly, I knew how one of the targets in a shooting gallery felt!

Stifling a last twinge of wounded pride, I had to admit, "Damned good suggestion, Tin Man! Let's get the hell outta here, while the pair of us can still walk!"

The bot and I made it safely back to the spaceport on the outskirts of Habeeb's Outpost and climbed aboard *Jammer*. I had to visit the head before resuming her controls. Drinking even a small amount of *hahk-teem* will do that to you.

In the cabin, the bot'd already made himself comfortable at the co-pilot's station, focused on *Jammer*'s vidscreen. As I dropped into the pilot's seat, the flickering image on the screen drew my attention.

There again was Roman Aguilar; he sure wasn't wasting any time! Baring his whiter-than-white teeth in a broad, phony-as-hell smile, he waved to an audience made up of rough-and-ready jedite miners. He was sealed, all safe and secure, in a blaster-proof transparent bubble, which floated above the heads of his wildly cheering fans.

Off-screen, a vidcaster was reading a typical spiel: a poor boy who was born the son of lowly asteroid miners, a determined youth who'd worked his way up to become the head of a struggling mining company, Aguilar'd now become a multi-billionaire, but still remembered his humble roots, blah, blah, blah! The usual *fleggin* political crap.

Son of asteroid jumpers, now *that* I'd be tempted to believe!

The microsecond the great man himself started to speak, the crowd quieted down and raised their dirt-streaked faces to him, as if they thought Roman Aguilar were some kinda god.

"My friends and fellow miners," Aguilar was saying, "you all know me. You are well aware that I once lived under the same wretched conditions in which you now find yourselves. I was forced to claw my way up through the grime and the gloom of the asteroid mines, until, at long last, I attained my present position of great wealth and great power. Constructing a vast empire from nothing was not easy, but I finally accomplished the ambitious goals I set for myself as a young man. One last, major goal remains to be fulfilled, my lifelong dream: to improve *your* lot as well!"

Right on cue, the miners cheered. When the cheering died down, Aguilar went on with his sickening speech. "My friends, I truly desire to help you, but first, you must help me. As you may know, I recently announced my candidacy for the presidency of the Galactic Consortium. Once I am elected to that exalted position, you may be assured that I will never, ever, forget from whence I came, nor will I forget the invaluable assistance I received from my own kind."

The crowd went wild, cheering and shouting and jumping into the air, as if they'd all gone bloody crazy. Aguilar raised one hand in a grand, dramatic farewell. The bubble encasing him floated higher and drifted toward a transport hovering in the background.

I reached out and punched the vidscreen's controls with my clenched fist. The screen went blank.

"Damn that *fleggin* son-of-a-bitch to Bloody Hell!" I snarled, my temper on overload. "He won't 'remember' one damn thing 'cept how to crush the people who voted for him!"

"You seem to be extremely cynical, Rand," the bot noted.

"*Huh!* There's a lot in this old universe to be cynical about, Tin Man—*one helluva lot!*"

I could only curse silently and pray Roman Aguilar'd never realize his grand dream. Couldn't imagine what'd happen if he grabbed even more power and more wealth than he already had.

Still, I wasn't above taking his five-million credits; that is, if I lived long enough to earn 'em!

6 Esperance

Jammer lifted off, eager to leave Habeeb's Outpost in its own dust and squalor. She left Milo's Planet far behind and headed out into the dark currents of open space, where she belonged.

But my thoughts were a helluva lot darker, weighing me down.

The microsecond J'neen'd mentioned Torrance, deep down in my gut I felt sick. I had a pretty damned good idea where the bloody bastard would hole up if things got too hot for him. But tracking him down meant I'd be forced to go back to Esperance! That wasn't gonna be easy on me.

Hadn't set foot on Esperance for over twenty-two years, 'cept in my worst nightmares. I tried my damnedest not to let myself think about the place or remember the godawful things that'd happened there.

I glanced over at the bot. He pinned me with a disapproving stare.

"Now what in bloody-blue-blazes is the matter?" I demanded.

"I am simply attempting to comprehend why a reasonably-intelligent, healthy young woman like yourself would pollute her internal systems, both physical and mental, with that abominable excuse for spirits you persist in imbibing. The devastating aftereffects alone ought to—"

"And what in the name of Bloody Hell would a bot know about

a hangover?" I growled, shifting in my seat so I could look him right in the, uh, eyes.

A tad too quickly for my liking, Blackie replied, "I am not, of course, speaking from *personal* experience, Rand."

My suspicions raised, I asked, "Then from *whose* experience are you speaking, Tin Man?"

He hesitated a couple microseconds before replying, "Why, my former master's, naturally."

Still suspicious, I cocked an eyebrow at the bot. "He a drinking man?"

For once, the bot seemed at a loss for words. Finally, he replied, "My master overindulged somewhat, shall we say, on one notable occasion. He found that experience so intensely repugnant he never imbibed another drop of liquor."

"So he became a teetotaler, eh?" Couldn't help chuckling at the picture my brain conjured up: a skinny, timid, nervous little professor-type with his prissy nose pressed against a comp screen or a 'tron-scope.

"This former master of yours, he a real persnickety type?"

Somehow Blackie managed to look offended. "My former master was a highly-intelligent, responsible, fastidious individual. If you choose to call those admirable traits 'persnickety', then I suppose that is your prerogative, madam," he said, giving me a put-out little sniff.

I let out a loud groan. "Are we gonna go back to that *madam* crap? Look, Tin Man, sorry if you're offended, but—hell, it's just that—that you're *a bot*, for God's-sake! But you don't act like any bot I ever heard of!"

"Indeed?" he said, giving me another sniff.

One of my frequent hunches crinkled it's way up my backbone. I followed its lead. "Uh, tell me something, Tin Man: was this guy we're talking about an educated man?"

"Well-educated indeed! He held several degrees from a variety of prestigious institutions of higher learning located back on Terra One."

"He a wealthy man?"

"No, he was not particularly wealthy—comfortable rather, I would say—reasonably well off."

My hunch burst into full-bloom. Over the years, I've learned to trust my hunches. More often than not, they're pretty damned reliable.

"This guy wouldn't happen to be a scientist?"

"Yes."

"An engineer to boot?"

The bot answered with greater care, "One might say so."

A flash of intuition hit me like a bolt of lightning right between the eyes. "Not a *robotics engineer* by any chance?"

Blackie outright refused to answer, so I pounced with glee, pointing a finger at him.. "Your so-called 'master' built you, didn't he? He was your creator!"

Now the bot refused to so much as look in my direction. He sat motionless and stared straight ahead. When it came to snooping, the tables had been turned, and he didn't like the change one damn bit.

"So tell me, pal, what happened to this guy? How in bloody hell did you end up in that mobile trash collector? Nobody in his right mind—especially if he weren't a rich man!—would junk a valuable piece of machinery like you without a damned good reason. You say your master wasn't a drinking man, but he had to be either stinking-drunk or outta his *fleggin* skull to toss you out like yesterday's garbage!"

For one helluva long time, the bot kept silent. I was sure he wasn't gonna answer me, but he said quietly, "If it will serve to satisfy your insatiable curiosity once and for all, Rand, my master did not discard me. In fact, he could not have done so—he had been murdered."

"*Murdered!*" I gasped, so shocked I almost sent *Jammer* tumbling end over end. I fought to regain attitude control. "Why the *flegg* didn't you tell me this sooner, Tin Man?"

"I thought it prudent to keep my own counsel until I knew you better."

The bot's mistrust was totally logical. I nodded my approval. "That's the smartest move you've made yet, Tin Man. It's not safe to trust people. I don't completely trust one single soul in the whole damn galaxy."

I mulled over what Blackie'd just told me, 'til my "insatiable" curiosity got the better of me again, and I wondered out loud, "So how, exactly, did this super-intelligent science-geek go about getting himself murdered?"

The bot's voice fell so low I could barely hear it. I leaned toward him to catch his reply. "If you do not mind, Rand, at present, I prefer not to discuss the subject further. The entire experience was traumatic, to say the least."

The whole bloody-raw truth hit me with the force of a punch to the gut. I drew back with a gasp. "*K'yoti* Hell! Don't tell me you *witnessed* his murder!"

All the stuffiness drained outta the bot, like air escaping from a kid's balloon. He sat still, as if he'd been deactivated again. At last, in a flat tone he admitted, "I was indeed present when the crime was committed. My master's murder was brutal, inhumanly brutal. He did not deserve to die in such an horrendous manner!"

That startled the hell outta me. I was more shocked than when I'd learned about the murder.

"You *cared* about your master? But I-I thought bots didn't—couldn't—give a damn about humans! Bots have no feelings; they do what they've been programmed to do, nothing more!"

"*I* cared!" the bot said. His tone was solemn, sounded as if he were testifying under oath before a jury in a Galactic Court.

I shook my head in sympathy for him. "I'm sorry as hell to hear that, Tin Man. Caring causes too damned many problems. I quit caring long, long ago. Could've saved yourself a helluva lot of grief if you hadn't cared."

The bot didn't answer. He kept his metal jaws shut tight longer than I thought possible. I concentrated on piloting *Jammer* and let him have a moment or two.

Grief—now that's one feeling I'm too damned familiar with.

Some time later, the bot said, "Rand, may I ask where we are presently headed?"

Now, *I* had a damned tough time answering *his* question. "Esperance!" I snapped. Getting out that one word in anywhere near a normal tone of voice cost me a helluva lot.

"Esperance?" Blackie repeated, obviously not impressed. "If my recollection is correct, Esperance is an uninhabited backwater planet located in Milo's Solar System. Now why in the Cosmos are we headed there, of all places?"

To be honest, I didn't wanna talk about Esperance any more'n the bot wanted to talk about his master's murder. But by this time, I knew Blackie well enough to realize he'd never let the subject lie. He'd keep chipping away at me 'til I gave in.

I took one deep breath before answering, "Because *that's* where Torrance's most likely to hole up—the one place he'd hide if things are too hot for him."

"And exactly how did you come by this remarkable piece of information, Rand? Did your snitch tell you this?"

"Naw! Just another one of my hunches, and I believe in playing my hunches."

The sound Blackie made came damned close to a human snort. "A hunch? What remarkable detective work! Hunch indeed!"

With a helluva lot of effort, I managed to ignore him, but I couldn't ignore the funny feeling gnawing at my gut. "How much d'you know about Esperance, Tin Man?" I asked, as casually as I could, testing him.

The bot cocked his shiny black dome to one side, for all the Cosmos like a human trying to recall some half-forgotten info. "Again, if memory serves, Rand, Esperance is a small, barren planet orbiting Milo's Sun. Once rich in metal ores, the planet was heavily-mined in the past—and of course, it was the site of the infamous Esperance Massacre."

That all too familiar term struck a raw nerve. My jaw clenched; so did both of my fists. Had to take a couple real deep breaths, trying my damnedest to relax. "That's why Esperance's also known as the Death Planet," I muttered. Even to my own ears, my voice sounded grim as death.

"And *that* is where we are presently headed?"

"You got it, Tin Man."

"Marvelous indeed! I cannot imagine there is much demand for conducted tours of Esperance."

"Not on your life, pal. Right at the moment, some two-bit outfit called Omega Mining Enterprises owns the ore rights, or at least it did last time I bothered checking records at the Mines Bureau. The mining rights've changed hands so damned many times over the years I kinda lost track."

I took another deep breath and added, "Rumors say most of the valuable ore's played out, so Omega probably had no luck selling the rights. Hell, I'd bet my ass they couldn't even *give* 'em away! But I know one spot on Esperance that'd make the perfect hide out for a gang of jackers. Not a single damn soul in his right mind, 'cept for Torrance, would have the *fleggin* guts to even try!"

Shoving the whole grim subject outta my mind, I switched *Jammer* to autopilot, unstrapped, and pushed off in the direction of my sleep-cocoon.

"Need to grab some more shutdown time, Tin Man," I told the bot. "You can keep half an eye on our course, if you want to."

Damned and determined to get some sleep, I wound myself in the snug folds of the mesh cocoon attached to *Jammer*'s overhead. But I couldn't resist opening one eye a slit to check on the bot.

"Uh, don't bots ever relax—or something? How d'you conserve energy?"

"I do not require sleep as humans do, Rand, if that is to what you are referring," the bot said. He didn't bother turning his head to look in my direction. "If there is need, be assured I will awaken you promptly."

"Don't worry about it, pal," I told him curtly. "*Jammer*'s programmed to wake me up in case anything outta the ordinary happens."

"Then, I take it, my full attention is not absolutely necessary?"

"Damned right! So you can power-down or whatever the hell bots do to conserve energy."

"Very well, Rand, if you insist upon it."

With my own arms and legs all nicely tucked into place, my body tethered to the overhead so it wouldn't drift off, I settled down to sleep. But for some reason, I had an urge to take one last look down at the bot.

As I watched, Blackie swung the co-pilot's chair to one side. He raised one black metal leg at a time, letting them float in midair, and casually crossed his metal ankles.

He folded both metal arms across his broad metal chest and tucked his metal fingers under his silver-jointed armpits—to keep his arms from drifting upward, I guessed. Then he leaned his gleaming, black metal skull back against the headrest.

My skin crawled. It was like watching a human being making himself comfortable. I bristled and thought, *That damn bot has one helluva nerve!*

Catching him at that was something like watching your freezer-unit break into a *ji'jen* dance and start twirling madly! Had to remind myself the bot was nothing but a machine; a machine did whatever it was programmed to do and not a blasted thing more. Blackie was a machine, and at least for the moment, I was his master.

I drifted off to sleep, but not before wondering what else in Bloody Hell the damned obnoxious bot'd been programmed to do.

Uncle Clive was in one of his drunken fits, yelling at me at the top of his lungs, knocking my stuff off shelves, upending my bedroom furniture. He stopped ranting long enough to shake a bony fist under my runny nose. His watery, blue eyes bulged like a madman's. Terrified, I cringed and cowered in a corner.

Uncle Clive shouted, "Yer a good fer nuffin' whiny little troublemaker! Yer a bloody disgrace t'the family name! Nuffin' but one helluvan unwanted burden upon us, that's what yer are!"

With one sweep of a long, scrawny arm, he cleared my desk. My school things scattered in all directions. I rushed to protect my precious belongings.

Hot tears stung my eyes, blinding me. Quivering from head to toe with anger, I stood and faced my uncle, small fists clenched by my sides.

"Leave me the hell alone, you crazy old coot!" I screamed at him. "I never asked t'be sent here in the first place! Hate it here! Hate you! Wish *you* were dead 'steada them!"

Tears spilled down my blazing-hot cheeks. I started picking up my things from the floor; one by one, I hurled them at my uncle.

But everything flew right through him!

I woke up, thrashing against *Jammer*'s overhead, my clenched fists full of mesh-cocoon. *Just another damn nightmare!* I told myself. *Not so bad this time!*

I tried to relax, but my heart kept pounding like some wild thing trapped within my ribcage and desperate to escape. Hate left its bitter, metallic taste in my mouth.

After all this time, and after all the horrors I'd managed to survive, Uncle Clive still held the power to reduce me to *this!* Damn the drunken sot to bloody-*fleggin*-hell!

And after all these long years and all the solemn vows I'd made to myself, over and over again, damned if I wasn't doing the one thing I always swore I'd never do: go back to Esperance!

When I took over *Jammer*'s controls, the bot said, "You spent a rather restless night, Rand."

I scowled at him and snarled, "My nights are none of your damn business!"

He didn't seem the least bit put off by my surly tone. "While you were sleeping, I took the liberty of scanning your ship's data files, looking for information on Esperance. I must say, the data is rather extensive—unusually so, considering that the planet is so unprepossessing."

Had no idea what that word meant, but I took it as an insult. I stiffened and snapped, "Thought I told you *not to snoop!* You're trying my patience, pal, and I'm not known for having a whole helluva lot to begin with. Keep this up, and you're begging to take a mighty-long, mighty-cold spacewalk!"

As if the bloody bot hadn't heard one damn word I said, he kept talking. "Over thirty years ago, a quasi-religious cult, which originated on Terra One, journeyed here to Milo's Solar System on a quest for a new home. The cult members claimed Esperance, an uninhabited but habitable planet, and made a valiant attempt to colonize it. For a time, they eked out an existence and enjoyed a modicum of success in terraforming the planet—until an asteroid mining company happened to scan Esperance.

"They discovered extensive, extremely rich ore deposits beneath the very land the colonists had settled upon. Consequently, the company made repeated and increasingly-lucrative offers for the mining rights to the entire planet, but the colonists stood their ground. To a man, they refused every offer.

"Not long thereafter, every last colonist on Esperance was brutally murdered, and their settlements, torched—burned to the ground in an apparent attempt to conceal the horrific crime. But the massacre was eventually discovered and made galactic news."

Through clenched teeth, I hissed, "Let it lie, damn you! That Massacre's ancient history!"

"Ah, but so much more of the tale remains to be told, Rand! Subsequently, the ISF's prime suspects, a notorious gang of mercenaries, were killed when their ship mysteriously exploded in midspace. Thus, the suspected murderers became victims themselves.

"At the time, the ISF theorized that the rebuffed mining company—Alpha Mines, Incorporated—hired the mercenaries to massacre the colonists. Apparently, the company's owners silenced the culprits in order to shield themselves from possible prosecution, as well as to avoid the threat of future blackmail. However, due to an appalling lack of hard evidence, the case could never be proven. No one has ever been brought to justice."

"So what in bloody hell has this bilge got to do with *me*?" I demanded. I tried to keep my voice sounding normal, but it came out a helluva lot gruffer than usual.

"According to your files, a single individual survived the massacre: a female child. Several weeks later, the two ISF agents who discovered the crime found her wandering amid the carnage and scavenging for food like a wild animal. I suspect *you* are that sole survivor, Rand."

My face burning like the fires of my long dead past, I roared, "*The hell I am!*"

"At this point, denying the fact makes no sense whatsoever, Rand, since *I* pose absolutely no threat to you."

I faced Blackie and gave him a stern warning: "You're straining to the breaking point what little's left of my sanity, chum!"

But as usual, the damn bot ignored me. "Your reaction to visiting Esperance was what first aroused my suspicions. Since you do not appear to be at all the superstitious type, Rand, why should the mere mention of the planet's name effect you so deeply?

"And according to my estimation, you *are* of the correct age to be that lone survivor. Although your name matches none of those listed as colonists, a name can easily be changed. And with a bit of effort, one's background can be covered up—or invented."

"Got nothing *to* cover up, pal," I insisted stubbornly, grinding my teeth in anger.

"Contradicting yourself once again, are you not, Rand?"

"Shut the bloody hell up!"

"If your limited patience will allow, bear with me a moment longer, Rand. Let us suppose that at least one of the individuals who masterminded the Esperance Massacre is still alive and desperate never to be connected with the horrendous crime. That alone would provide you with more than enough motive to cover your tracks and hide your identity. Indeed, had you *not* done so, and done so extremely well, most likely you would no longer be alive."

I fussed with *Jammer*'s navcomp and lied with a straight face. "That *fleggin* massacre hasn't got one damn thing to do with me! Like I said, pal, it's ancient history. Your brilliant deductions are dead-wrong. Those nano-circuits you've got for a brain must be on the fritz."

"My 'brain' is functioning quite normally, thank you, and my deductions *are* most certainly correct," the damn-stubborn bot insisted.

"Just my dumb-ass luck!" I muttered. "I had to stumble across a bot who thinks he's *fleggin* Shylock Holmes!"

"I believe you meant *Sherlock* Holmes, Rand. And, yes, I do rather fancy myself something of a sleuth. My master's talents ran in that particular direction, and, of course, he was the one who programmed me."

I groaned and cursed under my breath, then held my aching head between my hands. "If that bastard weren't already dead, I'd sure as hell like to thank him—*with my fists!*

Jammer approached the godforsaken ball of dust and rock the colonists had dubbed "Esperance." Suddenly, her forward sensors screamed a collision warning. The bot drew my attention to our monitor, to the image of an object headed straight for us!

I was mighty damned shocked to find traffic in this sector, but my nerves instantly switched to high-alert. I sent *Jammer* into a steep nosedive in time to avoid a head-on collision. The huge object sailed overhead harmlessly.

"*K'yoti* Hell! Is that thing a space station or a *ship*?" I demanded.

"According to the scan report, it is most definitely a ship."

"Who'd be way the hell out here? Smugglers maybe?"

The bot's crystal lenses were glued on the scan readouts. "I do not believe so, Rand. That ship is devoid of life. It appears to be a disabled ore freighter, abandoned long ago and locked in orbit: a derelict."

"*Huh!* And the *fleggin* mine company just left her up here—'til her orbit decays and she falls into the planet's gravitational pull and burns up. Mighty thoughtful of them! To be on the safe side, Tin Man, I'm giving her a wide berth, in case she's been booby-trapped."

The doomed derelict drifted past us and continued on its lonely orbit of Esperance.

The gray-brown, dusty-looking planet was rapidly filling our forward viewscreen. As *Jammer* drew closer, I began to make out the spots where our humble settlements'd once stood. Nothing was left but scars scattered across the plain. No ships parked below, no signs of life.

The wide plain spread between two rugged mountain ranges, one to the north and one to the south. Only the areas surrounding the settlements'd once been fertile. Now, the whole plain looked like the tortured surface of an asteroid: pockmarked with mine shafts, strewn with piles of tailings and other trash the miners'd left behind. The hovels they'd built to house themselves were either crumbling to ruins or had already collapsed. In a few places, deep, ugly pit-mines scarred the plain.

All in all, the scene below was pretty damned bleak.

But here and there, in the shade of the low foothills, a few pockets of scraggly trees'd somehow managed to survive. I was surprised, and a bit cheered, to see the trees planted so long ago by colonists brimful of hope.

"*Dammit!* This area used to be *green!*" I muttered, then caught myself and quickly added, "Or so I heard tell."

I was shocked to my core; damned little was left of the place I'd once called home. I took one deep, ragged breath and tried to relax, but the microsecond I'd set eyes on the ruins, my jaws'd clenched together tighter'n a vise.

As *Jammer*'s automatic sensors continued to scan the planet, Blackie pored over the images and data scrolling across the readout screens.

"Rand, if I am interpreting this data correctly, every last gram of ore was stripped from the planet's surface. Shafts were sunk deep into the bedrock, allowing the removal of what ore remained. Once the ore was played out, it appears mining operations ceased, and the planet was abandoned."

I gritted my teeth, but couldn't keep from grumbling under my breath, "The greedy bastards *raped* the place! They left *fleggin* little behind that I even recognize! Damn them all to Bloody Hell and back again!"

The cagey bot—damn him, too!—pounced on my latest slip up. "Aha! Then you now *admit* you have been on Esperance before!"

"Uh, yeah, only once—one helluva long time ago, Tin Man. You might say I, er, took a guided tour."

"Indeed?" Blackie stared at me. I swear I could feel those lenses of his boring right through me like twin diamond drills. Knew damned good and well he didn't believe my lie for a microsecond.

The bot tapped one silver-jointed index finger against the scan-screen, now indicating the altitudes of surface features. "This mountain appears to be the most prominent feature in the hemisphere; therefore, it is a likely reconnoitering point, would you agree, Rand?"

"*Mount Hope?*" My laughter sounded damned scornful. "Now that's what I'd call one helluva bad idea, Tin Man! See this?" I stretched to point out a dark spot in the image.

The bot studied it. "I would venture to say a rather large cave or cavern exists within the mountain—naturally occurring, I presume?"

I flashed him a sarcastic grin. "*Huh!* Suppose you could say that. Probably started out as a natural feature, but it's mainly the work of an asteroid eater. One damned nasty beast, let me tell you—nothing but a traveling gut! It can digest anything that gets in its path, and I do mean *anything!* By this time, the *fleggin* eater's probably turned that whole damn mountain into one gigantic honeycomb!"

For several extra-long microseconds, the bot mulled over what I'd told him. "If, as you say, Rand, such a creature were capable of digesting solid rock—?"

"Hell, like I told you, Tin Man, an eater can digest damn-near anything, including metal, which happens to be the stuff *you're* made outta."

The bot sat back, as if I'd given him one helluva shock, and murmured, "What an absolutely abhorrent thought!"

"Now I guess you have a pretty damned good idea why the wise avoid Mount Hope like the bloody-plague." I took gleeful pleasure in draining the bot of some of his damn-cocky attitude. "Any dumb-ass miner who dared set foot inside that cavern sure as hell never came out!"

Blackie's polished dome swiveled to face me. "Then *why* am I left with the distinct impression that this Mount Hope is our destination?"

Couldn't help snickering. "Because, Tin Man, that cavern is the *perfect* hideout for Torrance and his gang of space-scum."

"And why, pray tell, is that?"

I gave the readout screen a sharp tap. A cross-section of Mount Hope appeared on it, but the image was too damn fuzzy to read.

"Think, Tin Man: layers and layers of solid rock laced with metal ore. It interferes with deep-scans from passing ships. Not to mention the fear factor; keeps nosey visitors far-and-the-hell away. That's the crowning touch!"

The bot's crystal lenses focused on me; he seemed to be scanning my brain to see if I'd gone space-happy. "Rand, no intelligent being in his or her right mind would deliberately venture into such eminently dangerous surroundings, let alone take up residence therein!"

"'Cept for smugglers and jackers," I disagreed. "I know how the bastards think, Tin Man. Used to be one of 'em myself."

Damned good thing the bot was strapped into his seat and *Jammer* was in zero G, or he would've fallen outta the co-pilot's chair onto the deck.

"You, Rand—*a hijacker?*"

I gave him the slightest shrug of one shoulder. "Not too smart of me, eh? That what you're thinking, Tin Man? Hell, back in those days I was a mixed up kid, barely sixteen when I fell in with Torrance and his lot, just to keep myself alive. And once you're into that way of life—well, let's just say it's a damn-sight easier to get *in* than it is to get *out*—alive and in one piece, anyway."

"But you did, as you say, 'get out'?"

I nodded, not exactly happy about having to recall my past mistakes. "I managed to get out in the one and only way I could think of: I ratted out Torrance to the ISF. Turning him in put my own damn neck into the noose. Had to swear to go straight for the rest of my life or suffer the consequences. Got off on probation."

For once, the bot didn't have a snarky come back, but I took his dead-silence as disapproval. "Look, pal, I had to turn in the bastard before I got myself killed, or caught and sentenced to a *fleggin* penal planet! It all boiled down to self-preservation—nothing heroic. I don't do heroic."

But whatever the hell was inside Blackie's metal skull, his mind seemed light-years away. He murmured absently, "You did the right thing, Rand, whatever your motives."

I wasn't expecting the bot's approval. Made me squirm in my chair and cough. "Yeah, well, doing 'the right thing' cost me big time. Made me socially unacceptable on *both* sides of the law, marked as a damn squealer! How's *that* for justice?"

I knew damned good and well I sounded bitter, but, dammit! I *was* bitter.

"Is that the true reason you turned to recouping as an occupation?" Blackie asked.

"Unlike you, Tin Man, a fem's gotta eat. Knew the jacking and smuggling business inside and out. I simply turned my experience, along with my many other talents, to my own advantage."

For one helluva long time, the bot sat staring at the image of Mount Hope on *Jammer's* scan-screen. Then he said slowly, "Rand, perhaps this is not a wise course of action. I wish you would reconsider."

"No way in Bloody Hell! I *can't* leave Esperance 'til I check out that cavern to make damned sure Torrance isn't in there."

"Have you considered what might happen should we encounter the asteroid eater while searching for Torrance?" the bot demanded.

I shrugged off that thorny question, putting all thought of the terrible risk outta mind. "Hell, maybe the eater's dead. Maybe the jackers drove it out. For all I know, Torrance tamed the bloody beast and made it his *fleggin* pet!"

All too obviously, the bot was annoyed with me. He clamped his metal jaws shut and stayed silent. But I noticed him intently studying the images on the scanner, as if he were damned and determined to memorize every last feature of the planet below.

I swung *Jammer* to starboard and got ready to make an approach. Brought her in low on the opposite side of Mount Hope from the mouth of the cavern. If Torrance were hiding there, I figured it worked both ways: if I couldn't see him, he sure as hell couldn't see me.

Jammer skimmed the barren plain while I searched for a landing area: level and fairly close to the foothills. I engaged thrusters and brought my ship to hover above the most likely spot I could find, then gradually powered down the thrusters.

Jammer came in for a soft landing; she settled neat as you please onto the rough plain. All my senses on high alert, I watched and waited, prepared to take off in one helluva hurry. Not a damn thing moved anywhere on the plain around us or in the foothills to our left.

No greeting party appeared.

The bot still seemed pretty damned unhappy with my plans. "Rand, has it occurred to you that this venture is foolhardy and *dangerous* in the extreme? You could very well be killed!"

I sighed. "Hell, like I told you, we can't scan that cavern! There's only *one sure way* to find out whether or not Torrance's in there, and that's to go in myself. *You* don't have to go, Tin Man. *I* do."

The bot made an attempt to mumble something under his breath, obviously hoping I wouldn't hear him. But I caught his words clear enough: "I begin to have serious doubts that your pretty head actually contains *a brain*!"

Said head instantly snapped in his direction. "What'd you just say?" I demanded.

"The remark does not bear repeating, Rand," Blackie said, giving me an annoyed sniff.

"You said something about me being *pretty*! Now what in bloody-flaming-hell would a bot know about human looks?"

"My programming was quite thorough, Rand. My master was a man who appreciated beauty in all its many forms; thus, comparison of one object, or one human being, with another is entirely within my capabilities."

"Keep your damn opinions to yourself, then, you prissy piece of hardware!" I snarled at the bot. Had no idea in hell *why* I was so upset with him.

I let a fair amount of time pass. As soon as I was pretty damned sure our landing hadn't attracted attention, I shut down *Jammer*'s engines, released my straps, and got my legs under me. Getting used to gravity again took a little doing.

I double-checked my blaster, making sure it had a full charge, then patted the laser-handle I kept tucked into the top of my right boot. I figured if Torrance and his gang *were* holed up inside Mount Hope, a concealed weapon might come in handy. Knew damned good and well I'd be in for one helluva fight.

I had high hopes of taking Torrance alive, so he could answer a ten-mile long list of questions. But whether I took him dead or alive, I was bound and determined to collect the five-million creds Roman Aguilar'd put on the bastard's head.

Once I was ready, I set out for *Jammer*'s ramp. The bot followed.

"Rand, if by any chance you are entertaining the moronic notion that, just because I am a robot, I will automatically come to your rescue should you find yourself in grave difficulty—"

"I'm *not* gonna let them catch me!" I assured the bot. "And if I do get caught, I sure as hell don't expect *you* to rescue me!"

He stopped dead in his tracks and demanded, "Why ever not?"

I pivoted and glared into that man-made face of his. "You may be damned obnoxious, Tin Man, but you aren't *fleggin* crazy, are you?"

"Indeed not!"

"So you get my point?"

Soon as I reached the hatch, I punched in the code to lower *Jammer*'s ramp. Blackie waited to see me off, but when I started down the ramp, heavy footsteps trudged behind me.

I whirled and demanded, "Just where in bloody hell d'you think you're going? I got the impression this mission was a little too risky for your, ah, blood or whatever."

The bot hesitated a fraction of a microsecond before answering. "Rand, should anything unfortunate befall you, I would find myself stranded on this desolate, godforsaken excuse for a planet, quite possibly forever."

"Stranded? What the bloody hell d'you mean by 'stranded'? You'd have *Jammer* all to yourself!"

"Have you entirely forgotten space-faring regulations, Rand, or did you neglect to learn them in the first place? Robots are strictly prohibited from piloting any space vessel, unless all humans aboard have been disabled."

"Disabled? Dammit, Tin Man! If the *fleggin* jackers get their hands on me, I'll be *dead*!"

"But not, technically, disabled."

In total disgust, I gave up and threw both hands into the air. "You and your blasted laws! Do as you damn please, then. Just don't get in my way. If you do, I won't hesitate to smoke you myself! Got that, pal?"

At the bottom of *Jammer*'s ramp, I paused long enough to stifle a shudder before stepping off onto the dust-dry soil of Esperance. Long ago, I'd made myself a solemn vow never to set foot on this cursed planet as long as I lived. Couldn't help grumbling under my breath about this unexpected turn of events.

As if he were my faithful watchdog, Blackie chugged along at my heels, doing his damnedest to keep up with me in spite of the rough terrain. I groaned inwardly and came to a silent conclusion: the bot'd been sent as punishment for my countless sins. More'n likely, the stubborn piece of machinery was gonna get me killed!

For the ten-thousandth time I wished to Unholy Hell I'd never stumbled across the damn bot, never so much as laid eyes on him. I wished I'd made the smart choice back in Kaswali City and left him to burn in the *fleggin* incinerator!

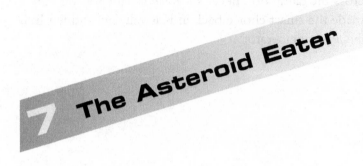

We scrambled through the rugged foothills surrounding Mount Hope; it sure wasn't an easy job. When I was a kid, I was used to hiking the rough terrain, but I had to admit the mountain'd seemed a helluva lot *taller* then.

If the climb was tough on me, it was even tougher on the bot. He wasn't built for struggling up mountainsides, slowed me down a helluva lot. But by the time we reached the flanks of Mount Hope, I was tired and panting for breath; the bot wasn't.

"A long time ago—I discovered this shortcut," I told the bot between breaths, pointing up the rocky slope. Far above our heads, an ancient planet quake'd split the solid rock like an overripe melon. The deep crack led right into the heart of the mountain.

Blackie studied the opening. "No doubt you discovered this fissure during your—ahem!—'tour' of Esperance. Is there indeed no easier access, Rand?"

"Hell, the only other way in is through the mouth of the cavern. I'm pretty damned sure we'd find it well-guarded, that is, if Torrance's really in there. Didn't see his ship parked on the plain below, so who the hell knows *where* he is right now?"

I was beginning to have second thoughts of my own. I sized up the narrow opening. Wasn't looking forward to squeezing my six-foot frame down into Mount Hope. Sure as hell wasn't gonna be easy. As for the bot, he was even taller than I was and a helluva lot bulkier and less flexible.

I made a face at him. "To be honest, I don't think you're gonna fit, Tin Man."

But the bot insisted, "I am going wherever you are going, Rand."

"The *hell* you are! You'll be nothing but a damn nuisance to me, as usual. Stay here, and that's an order!"

"I *am* going with you," he repeated stubbornly.

When he refused to obey my orders, I got mad as hell. "For God's-green-snake!" I snarled at him. "Bots are supposed to be programmed to obey humans! What the *fleggin* hell's *wrong* with you, Tin Man?"

Blackie refused to answer. Now I might not be a genius, but I'm smart enough to know when I'm licked. Didn't waste any more breath arguing with the big metal bastard. I scrambled up the side of the mountain. The bot struggled to follow me.

I reached the crack and told him, "I'll go in first, Tin Man. If I get stuck, you can pull me loose." I took a deep breath and stepped inside Mount Hope.

For the first hundred yards or so, the going wasn't too bad. The passageway was a bit more cramped than I remembered, but it was passable and fairly level. Then, the crack narrowed and began to slope downward. To fit through, I was forced to turn sideways. Flattening my back against the rough wall, I inched my way forward.

The growing darkness was the worst problem. I'd been too damned stupid to bring a tube-torch with me, too concerned about my weapons to think about other possible problems. I swore under my breath.

Damned poor planning on my part! But why in bloody hell didn't the bot think of bringing a torch with us? He knew we were going into Mount Hope.

I decided Blackie wasn't quite as *fleggin* smart as he thought he was!

With my left hand, I groped through the darkness and discovered that, up ahead, the crack got even narrower. I started to feel more than a little cataclysmic—or catastrophic—or whatever the hell that big word was!

"*K'yoti* Hell! This's gonna be a damned tight squeeze, Tin Man. Think you can make it?"

"Scraping metal against solid rock does little damage to either, Rand, but human flesh *bleeds*, or had you forgotten that relevant fact?"

In the darkness, the bot couldn't see my face, so I stuck out my tongue at him. "Just mind your own metal hide, pal, and I'll mind, uh—mine! Ouch! *Dammit!*"

"Are you injured, Rand?"

"Naw! Took a little skin off my elbow, that's all! Watch your chest here, Tin Man. It's not as flexible as mine."

I heard the bot mumble, "Nor as shapely."

"*What?*" I turned my head so damned fast I bumped it on the opposite wall. "*Owww!* Shut the bloody hell up, will you? I hit my damn head trying to listen to your nonsense!"

I wriggled onward, able to make only an inch or so at a time. I heard metal grating against rock; the sound gave me goose-bumps, and I shivered. Still, the damned-stubborn bot refused to give up and go back.

"*K'yoti* Hell! If this *fleggin* crack gets any narrower—! Stay back, Tin Man. Let me see how much farther we can go."

"*No, Rand!*" the bot warned. I caught the unmistakable note of panic in his voice. "We have made a terrible mistake! As the larger of us, *I* should have gone into the aperture *first*. Should you become trapped, it may well prove impossible for me to reach you. You could *die* in here!"

"Now's one helluva time to decide we made a mistake, pal!" I growled. "We can't exactly change places!"

A couple feet farther on, I came to a real tight spot and explored it with both hands. If my guess were right, we weren't far from where the crack broke through into one of the asteroid eater's tunnels. Like I'd told the bot, the bloody beast'd tunneled all through this mountain, leaving it like one huge hunk of Swish cheese. I scrunched down, trying to make myself as small as humanly possible, but still couldn't quite squeeze by.

"Dammit! This stretch's way too narrow to get through!" As a scrawny kid, I'd been able to wriggle past this spot, but that'd been over twenty years ago, and I'd grown a bit since then.

"Back out toward me, Rand—*carefully!*" I heard the worry in the bot's voice; it hit me hard: the bot was worried—*about me!* "Would it be possible to employ your blaster to widen the aperture?" he asked.

Sounded like a helluva good plan to me, at least worth a try. "Good idea, Tin Man—if I don't cook us both in the process!"

I wriggled backwards until I bumped into hard, cold metal. "Uh, sorry about that, Tin Man," I muttered, then wondered why in bloody hell I was bothering to apologize to a bot.

Blackie and I backed up the way we'd come. After a good distance, the bot came to a halt. "According to my best estimate, Rand, you should be able to safely fire your weapon from here."

I drew my blaster, extended my shooting arm full length, and took aim. In the total darkness, I couldn't see one damn thing. I expected my first shot'd be a bit off-target.

"Aim approximately five degrees to your left, Rand," the bot instructed. He sounded pretty damned confident; without question, I did as he said.

"This shot's gonna make one helluva racket, Tin Man. Better block your ears."

"You forget, Rand: I have no ears *to* block."

"Here goes, then!"

I pressed the firing button and ducked. A bolt of pure energy shot into the gloom ahead. It burst against the spot where the rock walls nearly came together. The explosion almost deafened me. Violet light flared to blinding white. I shielded my face with both arms.

Chunks of rock pinged off Blackie's armored body. I got one damned good pelting myself. Soon as the hail stopped, I dared to take a peek. Where the blaster-bolt had hit the walls, they glowed dull-red. Gave off enough light for me to see the way ahead; it was wide enough now for even the bot to pass, with room to spare.

My ears were still ringing. "Let's hope to bloody hell Torrance didn't hear that blast," I whispered to the bot.

"Slight chance of *that*, Rand, unless he and his entire gang are stone-deaf!" the bot said in his usual snarky tone. "We can only hope they attribute the noise to a natural cave-in."

I gave the passage walls time to cool before inching forward again. But I was damned careful not to brush against the scorching-hot rock. We hadn't gone far when the passageway petered out again. This time, the bot and I were forced to drop to all fours and crawl on our hands and knees.

The bot was having an even harder time of crawling than I was. To encourage him, I panted, "It's not much farther, Tin Man! There's an opening right up ahead."

Just then, the passageway came to a sudden end. I bumped my head again. Swearing a blue streak, I groped for the hole I knew opened onto a familiar ledge. That ledge ran along the top of a tunnel the eater'd chewed through Mount Hope a long time ago.

Lying flat on my belly, I wriggled through the hole; had to use my elbows and knees to push myself forward. Once I made it onto the ledge, I went to my hands and knees again and felt around blindly, searching for the edge. Sure as hell didn't want to tumble head-first into the tunnel below!

That ledge'd seemed a helluva lot *wider* when I was six. But maybe the damn eater'd grown as much as I had. Maybe, over the years, it'd made the tunnel larger, shaving down the ledge in the process. I sat at the edge and let both legs dangle, while I gathered the courage to jump into the pitch-blackness below.

Heard the bot's metal butt scraping through the hole. After a bit of struggle, he made it onto the ledge and got to his feet.

"We have to jump from here, Tin Man," I told him.

"Good Lord, Rand! Wait!"

I laughed and said quietly, "Don't worry. It's not much of a drop—seven, maybe eight feet by now. I used to bring a torch in here with me, once upon a time, long, long ago."

Taking one deep breath, I slid over the edge on my backside. My feet hit the tunnel's slippery floor, slid on some loose pebbles, and went out from under me. With a tooth-rattling jolt, I landed flat on my ass.

Blackie landed beside me, feet-first, with an earth-shaking thud. Sounded as if half a ton of spectromium'd dropped off the ledge.

"Rand, do not tell me you were actually foolish enough—and brave enough!—to enter this unspeakable place as a small child!" the bot said in a whisper. The tunnel's gloom seemed to be getting to him, too.

I scrambled to my feet and dusted off my butt, even though no one was there to see it. "We have to be mighty damned quiet here, Tin

Man. Sound travels through these tunnels in a real odd way. Of course, as a kid, I never dared to go any farther than the ledge up there, so I have no idea what the *flegg*'s down here."

I put out one hand and touched the tunnel wall. It felt cold and smooth, not rough like the walls of the crack above. I knew damned well why the tunnel walls were slick as glass: the rock'd dissolved and hardened again.

I started forward, hoping to hell I was going in the right direction, toward the cavern, and grumbled under my breath, "Now I know how it feels to be completely blind."

A heavy, metal hand clamped onto my right shoulder. I jumped an Akadran mile. "*K'yoti* Hell! Don't *do* that, Tin Man!"

"I beg your pardon, Rand! I forgot you cannot see without a light-source, since I myself am equipped with infrared sensors. Please forgive me for neglecting to inform you of that."

"*Infrared?* You mean you can actually *see* in this *fleggin* gloom?" I hissed. "Damn you to Hell and back! Why in bloody-blue-blazes didn't you say so?"

"I just did, a bit belatedly perhaps. But under the circumstances, I believe I should take over the lead, Rand."

With a mocking sweep of one arm, I stepped aside and got the hell outta his way. "Only too damned glad to let you lead from here on out, pal!"

I followed on the bot's heels, moving as fast as I dared to go in the pitch-darkness. Sure as hell didn't want to be left behind or to get lost in this godawful tomb of a place. Still fuming, I glared daggers at the broad metal back in front of me—a back I couldn't see. Suddenly, I smashed face-first into a wall of solid metal!

"*Dammit!* Don't stop short like that! Give me some kinda warning first!" I complained. I felt my nose gingerly to see if it were broken or only squashed.

"Once again, I must sincerely beg your pardon, Rand," the bot apologized. "I truly forget you are unable to see in the dark, since I can. Here, put your hand on my shoulder and allow me to guide you."

Cold metal fingers clamped around one of my wrists. Without thinking, I pulled my hand away and shuddered.

"Uh, really rather not—thanks anyway!"

The bot snapped, "Rand, will you *cease* being so pig-headed, and do as I say for once?"

My jaw dropped. I'd never heard him use that tone of voice before. Something about it made me stop giving him grief and obey.

I shuffled along behind Blackie, one hand gripping his hard-as-a-rock shoulder. "There's something awfully fishy about you, Tin Man," I muttered.

"If you will recall, Rand, I informed you previously that I am *a prototype*," the bot replied, as if that simple fact alone explained all his oddness!

"What in the name of Unholy Hell was your creator trying to do? Build a bot so *fleggin* obnoxious nobody in the entire universe could stand to be around it?"

"*Humph!* Absolutely not! But my master did endow me with certain highly-advanced modifications. Shall we leave it at that? You most definitely are *not* scientifically inclined, Rand, and therefore, could never comprehend the innumerable state-of-the-art technological advances that went into my design and construction."

"So I don't have a bloody nano-computer for a brain, unlike you! What the hell did science ever do for anybody? Besides suckering a bunch of unsuspecting, defenseless colonists into coming way-the-hell out here—luring them to a godforsaken world on an impossible mission and leaving them there to die like *fleggin* mine-rats caught in a trap!

"Being a bit cynical, are we not, Rand?"

"Not cynical, realistic. I'm only being realistic, Tin Man. I'm always realistic."

I shuffled through the blackness for what seemed like miles, one hand clutching the bot's cold-as-ice metal shoulder. A damned eerie feeling crawled its way up my spine. Felt as if I'd died and been sentenced to Hell: a very cold, dark Hell! Couldn't help shivering. In one helluva hurry, I brushed off the awful thought and did my damnedest to concentrate on the job ahead.

Years ago, my parents'd warned me over and over again that an asteroid eater made its home inside Mount Hope. That's why I wasn't allowed to go there. God only knows how long the monster'd been making its way back and forth through the mountain.

And how long the eater'd been on Esperance, or how it got here, no one alive could say. There was no way to tell if the monster were still alive or not. I was pretty damned sure of only one thing: somewhere in that network of dark tunnels, my old pal Torrance was waiting for me.

But I wasn't anxious to run into the asteroid eater, either. Not one poor soul who met up with it ever got a chance to tell the tale. So, even though I hated like hell having to depend on anything mechanical to do my seeing for me, I kept close on Blackie's heels.

The bot warned softly, "Rand, my sensors detect light up ahead."

I leaned sideways to peer around him—a real dumb-ass move, since I couldn't make out so much as a hint of light. "I can't see a damn thing!"

"Nevertheless, a light-source lies ahead."

"Could be the *fleggin* eater."

"Should we continue to approach, or would retreat be wiser?"

I sighed. "Hell, more likely, it's the jackers, Tin Man, so damn right we approach!"

"Rand, may I remind you there are only *two* of us?"

"So what? You want an award for being able to count, pal?"

The bot made that odd sighing sound to let me know he was put out with me—again. "I was merely pointing out the obvious; we are bound to be outnumbered."

"I'm used to being outnumbered, Tin Man!"

"Well, *I* am not!" the bot protested, suddenly getting all huffy on me.

I hissed, "Then why the *flegg* don't you turn the hell around and get your metal butt back to *Jammer*?"

"And abandon you in this godforsaken place, leave you to face a gang of ruthless hijackers alone? I most certainly will *not* do so!"

My turn to let out an annoyed sigh. "Then stop your bellyaching and get a move on. Head for the light-source!"

The bot seemed reluctant as hell, but he obeyed. A couple meters farther on, he slowed.

Again, I urged him to keep going. The tunnel *was* getting a bit brighter. I saw reflections on its glassy walls. The hair on the back of my neck prickled and stood at attention. I reminded myself that probably nothing human'd been through this tunnel for one helluva long time, if ever—unless the eater were dead.

The bot stopped dead in his tracks, as if he were frozen in place. The silence in the tunnel suddenly felt thick and eerie. "Rand—," he whispered.

I hissed back, "Thought I told you to shut up and *go*?"

"Indeed you did, Rand; however, I now detect a faint sound coming from our back trail!"

"Huh! I don't hear a damn thing. The silence must be getting to you, Tin Man. You're starting to imagine things."

But instead of moving ahead, as ordered, the bot spun around and stared down the tunnel behind us. I couldn't see a damn thing but the darkness we'd already come through. Then I got a real creepy-crawly feeling between my shoulder blades.

In a hoarse whisper, I croaked, "Use your damn sensors!"

"I am attempting to use them, Rand! I sense a heat-source approaching rapidly. A rather large mass—essentially, a hollow tube."

I gasped, "*Oh, God*—the eater! Run for it, Tin Man! *Run!*"

Without waiting so much as a fraction of a microsecond to see if the bloody bot would obey me, I turned and ran for my own life. Behind me, I heard Blackie chugging along at his best possible speed, but he wasn't able to keep up with me.

Knew damned well and good I risked running smack into the jackers up ahead, but figured they'd be a helluva lot easier to deal with than the *fleggin* eater. And I doubted that jackers, being cowardly bastards, would stick around long anywhere near the godawful beast.

All the tales I'd ever heard said the eater could dissolve and digest even the hardest materials known to man, at least over time. Far as I was concerned, that'd be one damned hideous way to die!

The bot was lagging farther and farther behind me. I shouted over my shoulder, "*Move your metal ass, damn you!*"

His silver-jointed legs pumped hard and fast. "I *am* moving it as fast as I am able! I was *not* constructed for speed!"

I half-turned and took one quick look at our back-trail. Not far behind the bot, something huge glistened.

And no way in hell was Blackie gonna outrun it!

From between clenched teeth, I swore, "*Flegg* it!"

Before I realized what a dumb-ass stunt I was about to pull, my back was against the cold tunnel wall, and my blaster was drawn. I pulled the weapon in close to my chest and ordered the bot, "Go on by me! *Go by, dammit!*"

The microsecond Black passed me, I raised the blaster in both hands, stepped out into the middle of the tunnel, and fired. One bolt of energy hit the slimy mass that was bearing down on me dead-center.

The eater halted. Like a giant red-and-purple flower blossoming, its maw opened. I found myself staring straight down the monster's throbbing gullet. Hoping to cook the *fleggin* beast, or at least slow it down, giving Blackie a chance to get away, I loosed a blaster-bolt right into the gaping maw.

The energy-bolt burst inside whatever the beast had for guts. Its maw snapped shut. Violet light shone through its jelly-like flesh. The eater quivered violently. I didn't hang around to see what happened next. Ran like hell 'til I caught up with the bot.

He was smart enough to keep running. "Is the asteroid eater dead?" he wanted to know.

"Dunno—maybe!" I panted. "Maybe only stunned. We'd better try to lose it! Duck into the first side-tunnel we come to, Tin Man!"

Without checking our back-trail, Blackie answered his own question, "Rand, the beast *is* coming on!"

"Then I hope to bloody hell the *fleggin* thing's blind!"

A bit farther on, the bot said, "I detect an exit, approximately ten meters ahead on our left. Unfortunately, it appears to be the source of the light!"

I raised my blaster in both hands, spun, and gave the eater one more bolt to slow it down. "The damn thing sure as hell doesn't discourage easily!"

Just ahead, the bot made a sharp left and ducked into the side tunnel he'd detected with me right on his heels. This tunnel was a helluva lot brighter, so bright I had to shut my eyes. Without warning, the bloody bot stopped short. I skidded on the tunnel's slick-as-glass floor and crashed into his broad metal back.

I pulled away with an angry hiss. "Dammit! Told you *not* to do that!"

"Rand—," Blackie began in a damned odd voice. He didn't go on.

Wondering what in bloody-blue-blazes his problem was, I stepped out from behind the bot and got one of the biggest shocks of my whole damn life.

"*Torrance!*" I gasped.

The stocky, scruffy-looking man with the dark beard gave me a broad smile. But his smile sure as hell wasn't meant as a friendly greeting. I tightened my grip on the blaster clutched in my right hand, but, on either side of Torrance, stood his twin shadows. The muzzles of their blasters were trained on me.

I froze, not daring to move a *fleggin* muscle.

Torrance drawled, "We've been expecting you, Rand. You make one helluva lot of noise. If I were you, I wouldn't risk getting off a shot. You remember my cohorts here, Drake and Morgan? You know damned well they're your equals when it comes to target shooting. Better drop your weapon. Easy does it!"

I had no choice. I bent down and carefully placed my blaster on the tunnel floor. Raising both hands, I nudged the weapon in Torrance's direction with the toe of my boot.

He came over, picked up my blaster, then had the *fleggin* gall to turn it on me! "Now, hand over your tool-pack—and the laser-handle in your boot."

Torrance caught the look of surprise on my face. In a cold voice he said, "I remember your habits well, Rand—all your habits! Heard you were looking for me. Well, you've found me!" Spreading his arms wide, he gave me one of the nastiest laughs I'd ever heard.

I was itching to punch his lights out, but if I tried, I knew I'd end up with a smoking hole or two blasted in my chest. Using two fingers, I took the laser-handle outta my boot. With the other hand, I unsnapped the tool-pack from my belt. I passed both to Torrance.

Once I was unarmed, he turned a wary eye on the bot and demanded, "Who's your big metal friend here?"

I shrugged, trying to pass off Blackie as harmless. "Him? Just some stray bot I picked up in my travels. He's not worth bothering with."

Torrance obviously didn't trust me. He sized up the bot before giving him a sharp warning: "You so much as twitch the wrong way, my mechanical friend, and the lady here gets smoked—and I use the term 'lady' very, *very* loosely. Do you understand what I said?"

"Yes," Blackie replied in a toneless voice that sounded nothing like he usually did.

I couldn't keep from fuming. The bot's damn laws wouldn't let him put my life in danger, not even to save his own *fleggin* hide, or *mine*! "Aw, forget him, Torrance. He's only a dumb-ass service-bot. You and I need to sit down and have a real heart-to-heart talk."

"*Talk!*" Torrance's shaggy eyebrows shot skyward; he laughed, as if I'd told him one helluva good joke. "Talk? After you *betrayed* me? *S*old me out to the ISF to save your own ass, then had the *fleggin* gall to testify against me! Do you take me for a damn-fool, Rand?"

My life was at stake here, so I made a desperate attempt to sweet-talk the bloody bastard. "Torrance, old pal, I realize you think I'm some kinda Jude's-ass, but—"

In an all too loud whisper the bot said, "I believe you meant to say Judas, Rand." The s.o.b. couldn't resist correcting me! I shot him a dark scowl, hoping to shut him up.

"Look, Torrance, I came across a piece of info I thought you might be interested in, maybe interested enough to let bygones be bygones? Start our partnership fresh?"

But Torrance wasn't buying my act. He shook his scruffy head. "Nice try, Rand, but that trick's so damned old it has wrinkles! Won't work on me. I made one helluva mistake by trusting you once. Never again! Trusting you cost me five long years of *fleggin*-hard labor! After that rude lesson, I'm not about to forgive and forget. Oh, no!"

I refused to give up. Kept trying my damnedest to convince him I was sincere. "Hell, I'll be the first to admit I made a cosmic error in judgment back then—"

"*And you made another one by coming here!*" Torrance roared. White-hot fire flashed from his eyes, scaring the crap outta me! "I spent the last five years of my life planning—in graphic, gory detail—what I was gonna do to you when I finally got my hands around your pretty little neck!"

I swallowed hard and tried not to picture what Torrance had in store for me. "Dammit, Torrance! The *fleggin* ISF forced me to talk! You know their methods. I had no choice! Can't you see that?"

Torrance took two quick steps, closing the gap between us. He grabbed my upper arm. His fingers curled like talons and sank deep into my muscles. He yanked me toward him, so my face was right in his. It was seething with rage and raw hatred.

"Oh, I'm sure turning me in just about broke your tender little heart, Rand! But I intend to start collecting on the huge debt you owe me—right now!"

From behind Torrance, a fem's husky voice purred, "Tori?"

He shot a look over his shoulder. A curvy blonde stood in the cavern entrance, framed by its rocky walls. She wore a long, metallic-gold gown; it was so *fleggin* outta place here I almost snickered. She came and sidled up to Torrance. I got a real good look at her face and decided she must put on her makeup with a trowel. She gave me a glare full of hate.

Blondie wrinkled her nose at me, as if I smelled bad. "This someone *I* should know about, Tori?"

Torrance dropped my arm like a hot coal, but the look on his face let me know how much he hated letting go of me. Blondie kept glaring daggers at me.

"Allow me to introduce Galaxy Rand. She's the one you have to thank for my being outta circulation so damned long!

I wasn't paying the least bit of attention to either one of them. I was staring at the earrings dangling from the blonde's ears: the crystal earrings danced and sparkled in the light from the cavern.

They were *star-shi* earrings, and they belonged to J'neen!

I bit down on the tip of my tongue—hard!—to keep back an outburst I knew damned good and well would get me killed on the spot. But I couldn't stop trembling, as I battled the wave of cold fury rising from deep down in my gut.

Blondie gave me the evil eye. Not so much as a micro-speck of pity in that look! Her red mouth pouting, she latched onto Torrance's arm. "Five-years is one helluva long time, ain't it, Tori? I know how bad you want this fem dead, but *five-minutes* of her pain won't make up for all the years you suffered, now will it?"

"No, it sure as hell won't!" Torrance said, as if he hated to admit the truth. From the way he was scowling at me, I knew he was itching to tear me apart with his bare hands. "Not five-minutes, not five-hours—*not five-damn-days*!" He was getting angrier and angrier by the microsecond.

Blondie wriggled her generous hips against his side and purred, "Bet you a hundred creds your new pal Breego'd pay a damn-good price for her, wouldn't he, Tor?" She aimed a giggle in my direction.

I saw the greed dawning in Torrance's eyes. Obviously, Blondie's idea appealed to him. He let out an evil laugh. "Are you kidding, sweetheart? That fat pig'd pay half his *fleggin* fortune to get his hands on the likes of her!"

Blondie reached up and stroked Torrance's scruffy beard with one red-nailed hand. She pouted again. "That's the fate she really deserves, ain't it, Tori? Spending whatever's left of her miserable life as a slave—Breego's little plaything! That's what I'd call perfect revenge."

"Then that's exactly what I aim to have: p*erfect revenge!*" Torrance vowed, his mind evidently made up.

My fists unclenched; slowly, I relaxed. Whatever fate had in store for me now, at least I wasn't gonna die right on this very spot.

"Boss, what the hell are we gonna do with this bot?" Drake asked, jerking the muzzle-tip of his blaster in Blackie's direction.

Torrance circled the bot. Keeping himself at a safe distance, he eyed Blackie up and down. "This gizmo should fetch a fair price, too. Breego's *second* favorite thing is tinkering with all kinds of gadgets. The bloated bastard has delusions of grandeur. He sure as hell won't be able to resist getting his hands on a damned-fancy machine like this one."

Outta the corner of my eye, I shot a glance over at the bot. He stood still and stiff, looking for all the Cosmos as if he couldn't move a metal muscle 'cept on command.

Torrance stuck his ugly mug right in my face. "And d'you know what Breego's gonna love even *more* than tinkering with this bot, Rand? Getting his chubby mitts on you! All over you, in fact!" He chuckled evilly.

At that sickening thought, my self-control cracked. "You *fleggin* piece of space-scum! I'm *damned* glad I turned you in to the ISF! I'm only sorry you didn't get a helluva lot *longer* sentence, you bloody bastard!"

Torrance bared his teeth in a snarl of rage. He knotted his fist and drew back his arm. I flinched, shut my eyes tight, expecting a punch in the face. But the blow never landed; I heard Torrance grunt, then swear loudly. I opened one eye a slit to see what the bloody-blue-blazes was going on.

The bot had Torrance's fist locked in an iron grip. Torrance struggled and twisted, but couldn't break free. His face screwed up, as bright-red as a *kareeb*'s behind. Drake was the first one to use what little he had for brains. He aimed his blaster square at Blackie.

"Not at the bot, you *fleggin* idiot!" Torrance howled. "*Aim at her, damn you!*"

Drake swung his blaster on me. At the same microsecond, the bot let go of Torrance.

From the murderous gleam in that bastard's eyes, I could tell he was having second thoughts about revenge. But it was my lucky day; Torrance got himself back under control mighty damned fast. He drew a deep breath and ordered, "Don't damage either of them seriously, but if this *fleggin* bot gives you any more trouble, rough up the fem. Understood?"

"Yeah, Boss," Drake said dully. "Understood."

Plain to see he wasn't the swiftest ship in the space-fleet!

Torrance added, "If you're smart, Rand, you'll order this bot to leave me and my men the hell alone from here on out. If it misbehaves again, I swear *you'll* pay a very steep price!"

I said, "Tin Man, do as he says." Damn near choked on the words as they came outta my mouth. Rather've ordered Blackie to tear the lot of 'em to bloody shreds!

Giving me a nasty chuckle, Torrance told his gang of thugs, "They'll both be Breego's problem soon enough. I'll have my revenge for, say, the next twenty years or more—that is, *if* you manage to survive Breego's amorous attentions that long, my love!"

Torrance gave me a smirk and a wink, obviously taking a helluva lot of pleasure in the evil thought. But he made a real dumb-ass mistake by using the "L" word. I saw Blondie's hackles go up. She wasn't about to put up with any competition, whether it was real or imaginary.

"Tori, Breego's already on the way. Don't you think you should go contact his ship? If he's dying to inspect the goods and haggle over price, won't the deal go a helluva lot better?" Blondie purred, batting jet-black eyelashes at Torrance.

"Damn right! I'm sure as hell not gonna let you go cheap, Rand, if that's any consolation to you," he growled with sadistic glee. He turned toward Drake and Morgan, then beckoned to a third member of his gang who was standing behind the matched set of goons.

Torrance jerked one thumb down the tunnel, back the way the bot and I'd come. "Toss their asses into the pit until Breego gets here. That's the best place to keep 'em. Not a chance in bloody hell they'll escape!"

Leaving me and the bot in the clutches of his three well-armed henchmen, Torrance strolled back into the well-lit cavern. Blondie clung to his arm like a *fleggin* gold-skinned leech.

8 Old Rat Eyes

Like a trio of trained mine-rats, Torrance's blaster-armed goons hustled me down the side tunnel. They made a sharp left and shoved me into the eater's main tunnel. The farther we walked, the darker it got, 'til two goons brought out tube-torches to light our way.

Blackie followed along behind me, like a faithful dog sticking to his master's heels no matter what. He seemed to be all too aware that the muzzle of Morgan's blaster was jammed between my shoulder blades.

When the bastards finally brought me to a halt, I found myself standing on the rim of a round hole sunk into the middle of the tunnel floor.

I teetered on its raw edge, staring down into total darkness. No telling how damn deep the pit was or what might be waiting for me in it. Morgan planted a rough hand in my back and pushed. I was forced to jump into the black unknown.

I hit bottom on both feet, but lost my balance and pitched forward onto my hands and knees. Heard one of Torrance's goons order the bot to jump, so I flattened myself against the pit-wall to get outta his way. Judging by the sound, Blackie landed flat-footed and managed to keep his balance. The pit floor shook from the impact.

Drake leaned over and tossed down one of the lit tube-torches. I let it lie where it fell.

"Here!" the dumb-ass said, giving me a real snarky laugh.

"Y'might need this! The *fleggin* eater don't like light. Y'better *pray* the torch keeps it at bay—at least until the charge runs out!"

Their laughter and jeers echoed and re-echoed through the tunnel network before fading in the distance. When Torrance's goons were gone, I heaved a sigh, grateful to still be alive and in one piece.

"Rand—" the bot started to say.

"You keep your damn mouth shut!" I snapped. Bending down, I snatched the tube-torch and began to circle the pit with the light held high.

That was one of the damned-nastiest places I ever had the rotten luck to find myself in! Tiny bones—the remains of mine-rats that'd starved to death!—littered the floor. Their bones crunched under my boots; the sound gave me the shivers. Using the tips of my fingers as well as my eyes, I searched the pit-walls for a crevice, a bump, anything that'd help me climb the hell outta there.

But the sides of the pit went straight up, smooth and slippery as a *Garzantine* mirror. I figured the pit was the work of the asteroid eater. Most likely, it was some sorta den—or nest. That thought made me sick to my stomach; I shuddered and thought, *What if there's more'n one of the godawful beasts?*

Getting desperate, I ordered Blackie to boost me up to his shoulders. Then, he lifted me by the ankles, 'til I was above his head. We both stretched as high as we could stretch, just as we had back in the mobile trash collector in Kaswali City. But all our efforts were bloody-well-useless! No matter how hard we tried, we couldn't reach the rim; the pit was too damned deep.

The bot lowered me carefully to the floor. "I regret that our efforts proved unsuccessful, Rand."

"Not your fault," I said, giving him a sigh. "You did your best, Tin Man. Wish to bloody hell your master'd equipped you with wings or some kinda boosters!"

In an off-hand tone, the bot replied, "Wishes will never hold water."

I gave him a sharp look. In the light of the tube-torch, his armored body looked silvery, like some ancient knight. "*Huh!* That's one damned-odd saying, coming outta a bot. Old-fashioned as hell! There's something *awfully* fishy about you, Tin Man!"

"Indeed?" he replied, sounding innocent as all get-out. "For example?"

"Some of the spacey remarks you come out with and the uppity way you say things. Your accent's pretty damned odd, too. You sure as hell don't *sound* like any bot I ever heard before."

"Are you now proclaiming yourself an expert on robotics?" the bot asked in a huffy tone. "As I previously attempted to explain to you, Rand, robots respond according to their programming. Indeed, we cannot do otherwise."

Not totally convinced Blackie was telling me the God's-honest-truth, I shook my head. "My gut tells me there's a helluva lot more to you than meets the eye, Tin Man. Too damned bad I'm not gonna get time to figure you out. Nothing I like better'n doing a little detective work."

The bot didn't answer. He just stood there like a statue made outta bronze. In frustration, I began pacing the pit. Felt like an animal trapped in a *fleggin* cage! I circled helplessly, trying my damnedest to think my way outta the fix I was in.

"Sooner or later, Torrance's goons have to take us outta here. When they do, you might be able to escape, Tin Man. You can make your way back to *Jammer* and send a message to Krol Kramer or to the ISF—God forbid! There's one 'gent there named Jeffries who *might* be persuaded to help me out, though I hate like bloody hell having to ask for help from any of those jackasses!"

"Rand, may I remind you that Torrance's men are armed with energy-blasters and at present you are unarmed? In addition, you seem to be completely forgetting the asteroid eater, which is prowling about somewhere in these tunnels!"

"So?"

"Contrary to what you may presume, I am *not* invulnerable. If you do not mind, I prefer to remain in one solid piece. I have no wish to become the asteroid eater's next meal! But no matter what may happen, Rand, I intend to remain with you."

Sick to death of the bot's *fleggin* excuses for not taking action and angry as hell, I planted my fists on my hipbones. Glaring into his face, I snarled, "For God's-green-snake, pal, stop playing knight in shining armor! Damn your metal hide! If you get the chance to escape, *take it!* Don't worry about me. I'm used to getting myself outta tight spots like this."

"And of late you have done so exceedingly well at extricating yourself! There is a price on your head and a target on your back. You are currently trapped in an inescapable pit, not to mention that Torrance intends to sell you into lifelong servitude. Ah, yes! What a *marvelous* recommendation for the independent life!"

At that point, I crossed my arms on my chest, turned my back on the obnoxious hunk of junk, and fumed. "*K'yoti* Hell! I'll get myself outta this mess—somehow. Always do. I may not have your *fleggin* nano-computer for a brain, pal, but I've got stuff you don't have: horse sense, savvy, street smarts! I spot things other people miss. My hunches are pretty damned reliable, too."

The damn bot couldn't resist making a snarky comment. "And despite your many resources, Rand, you succeed magnificently in ensnaring yourself in an extraordinary amount of difficulty!"

"Like I said, pal, nothing I like better'n a challenge."

For a change, the bot kept his mouth shut; in fact, he was too damned quiet. But after a while, he said, "Rand, have you never once considered the benefits of settling down and enjoying an ordinary life?"

Coming outta a bot, that was one helluva strange question. I turned and cocked a suspicious eyebrow at him. "*Hell, no!* This's the life I chose to lead."

"Hah!"

Unable to hold my temper in check a microsecond longer, I let it boil over. "And exactly what the bloody hell is *that* supposed to mean?" I sputtered.

"I was simply expressing serious doubt that you had much choice in the matter, Rand. In fact, I have come to believe that, in a desperate effort to escape your sordid past, you fell into this way of life and are unable to extricate yourself. You have succeeded in convincing yourself *this* is the life you wish to lead."

Still fuming, I shrugged both shoulders. "Believe whatever the hell you please, pal! I'm not getting mixed up in another useless debate with you. It's like arguing with a *fleggin* computer! No human could ever hope to win *that* argument."

I kicked a spot on the pit floor clear of rat bones and dust, then sat down with my back pressed against the glassy wall. I drew both knees up under my chin and crossed my forearms on top of 'em. Reminded myself how vital it was for me to conserve my energy. No telling how long I'd be trapped down in this bloody pit without food or water: trifles the bot didn't need to worry about, damn his metal hide to Hell and back again!

But I get bored all too easily, and there wasn't one damn thing to do down in that pit 'cept sleep. The bot wasn't speaking to me, which made for a nice, quiet change. At least for a while.

Against my will, I started thinking about him, trying to figure him out. I remembered how he'd killed the guy gunning for me back in that alley in Kaswali City. And how he'd followed me like stray dog ever since. I recalled some of the spacey remarks he'd come out with.

Knew damned good and well I'd regret asking him a question, then thought, *Oh, what the hell!* and asked anyway. "This guy who designed and built you—what was his name?"

Blackie's shiny dome swiveled sharply in my direction. He stared at me for several microseconds. I thought he was gonna refuse to answer. In a strained voice, he finally said, "Robert Benton-Smythe." That name seemed to bring back some real bad memories.

"*Huh!* Figures! A snooty little professor-type would have a hoity-toity name like Robert Benton-Smythe!"

"'What's in a name?'" the bot said, so quietly I barely heard him.

I gave him a shrug of one shoulder. "I dunno. Damned good question, Tin Man. A name's only a name, I guess, and, like you said before, a name can be changed easy enough."

The bot let out a loud sniff and drawled, "I suppose William Shakespeare would agree with you on that."

"And who in bloody hell's he? Aw, never mind, Tin Man! I just think it's mighty damned odd a harmless guy like RBS made an enemy dangerous enough to get himself *killed*."

I halfway expected the bot to accuse me of prying, get all huffy, and give me the silent treatment again.

But instead, he answered my question. "As I previously told you, Rand, my master fancied himself an amateur sleuth. He enjoyed delving into mysteries and inconsistencies whenever he encountered them. Ultimately, that fondness for sleuthing led to his demise."

"You mean, he stumbled across some info that got him into real deep crap, huh?"

The bot stiffened, probably offended, as usual, by my poor choice of words; he let out a little sigh. "If you insist upon the entire truth of the matter, Rand, in order to satisfy your *insatiable* curiosity, my master uncovered data that implicated the ISF in the latest rash of hijackings."

That hot news item got my full attention mighty damned fast. "You're *fleggin* kidding me, Tin Man! *Not the ISF*—the holier-than-thou ISF? *K'yoti* Hell! They're supposed to be squeaky-clean! Never did trust the bastards myself, even though—!"

To shut myself up, I clamped my bottom lip between my teeth, but I'd already let slip way too much for my own damn good.

"Even though *what?*" the bot asked, picking up on my slip.

"Nothing! Forget it, pal!"

As if he hadn't heard me, Blackie went on, "Even though two ISF agents rescued you from amid the carnage and destruction left in the wake of the Esperance Massacre?"

I stared at my boots, scuffed the tiny, dust-dry rat bones at my feet into a small pile, and changed the subject. "So this Robert Benton-Smythe of yours stumbled across some info damaging to the ISF. What'd he do about it: sit around on his hands, timidly waiting to be bumped off?"

"No, not at all, Rand," the bot said. "My master realized full well that, sooner or later, his covert activities would be discovered and, ultimately, traced back to him. He knew that his life would undoubtedly be in extreme danger. He covered his tracks, so to speak, as best he could and began working around the clock to complete a personal project: he created *me*.

"A matter of hours after he completed my programming, two masked men broke into his private residence. They attacked him, bound him, and demanded he hand over the incriminating data. Of course, Robert Benton-Smythe was intelligent enough to realize that, regardless of whether he did so or not, his attackers had every intention of silencing him. Therefore, he stoutly refused to comply."

Any injustice was one too damned many for me! I sputtered, "But if *you* were there, Tin Man—if you witnessed all this!—why in the name of Unholy Hell didn't you *do* something? Why didn't you stop those bastards from killing RBS? What happened to your *fleggin* laws about protecting human life?"

The bot's metal head drooped; his tone of voice deepened. "Unfortunately, mere moments prior to the attack, my master decided the better course of action was to deactivate me. Hence, I was unable to lift so much as a single finger in order to prevent his murder. I could only bear silent witness to the tragedy.

"Rand, have you any idea what it is like to actually *witness* a murder, to be forced to stand by and *watch* as the horrendous crime is committed—and be absolutely helpless to prevent it?"

Didn't want to admit I knew damned well how that felt! I squirmed and avoided the bot's eyes. "Uh, not a pleasant thought, Tin Man," were the only words I managed to get out.

Blackie went on, "That horrific experience gave me a taste of human mortality, but as I soon came to realize, I was beyond death, trapped within a metal body that to all intents and purposes is immortal, unable to—" The bot stopped in mid-sentence, too upset to go on.

"Then, ah, forgive me for asking, Tin Man, but how in hell did you end up in that trash collector?"

"After murdering my master, the two fiends wrecked his private laboratory in an apparent attempt to make the crime seem to be a simple case of research theft. They forced me down the rubbish chute, along with my master's vidrecords and sundry other projects. Later that night, the bin was dumped into the mobile trash collector. You arrived shortly thereafter in a similar manner."

Another question hit me: "Tin Man, could you ID Robert Benton-Smythe's killers?"

"Possibly, although both wore masks to conceal their faces. I might be able to identify them by their voices alone. Originally, I intended to track down the culprits and bring them to justice—however long that might take—but at present, carrying out my plans would seem highly unlikely." Blackie's head hung even lower.

I let out one low whistle. "*K'yoti* Hell! Maybe I was right in the first place, Tin Man. Maybe those two bastards in the alley weren't gunning for me. Maybe they were after you, making damned sure you got dumped into the incinerator and burned along with the rest of the evidence!"

The bot gave me one sharp shake of his bald dome. "That scenario is doubtful, Rand, since the murderers were unaware I witnessed their crime. Had they so much as *suspected* the truth, they most certainly would have dismantled and destroyed me, then and there. No, I firmly believe you were the target of that attack. And judging by his response upon seeing you, I am now as firmly convinced Torrance is *not* the party responsible for the price upon your head."

"Well, *I'm* not—convinced, that is. Make no mistake: Torrance wants me *dead!* He just didn't have guts enough to go after me himself and risk getting caught. Since the jackings started so soon after his parole, he must know he's on the ISF's radar. No, Torrance put the price on my head and the *fleggin* target on my back. I'm dead sure of that."

"Then, obviously, Rand, we have a slight difference of opinion," the bot said.

"So what else in Bloody Hell's new, Tin Man?" I heaved a sigh. "Tired—gotta shut down for a bit and save my energy." I dropped my head onto my forearms, which were still folded on top of my knees, and tried my damnedest to get some sleep.

Near as I could figure, it was two days later when Torrance's goons finally came and hauled me and the bot outta the damn pit. With their blasters trained on the back of my skull, Morgan and Drake marched me back to the cavern. Two guys I'd never seen before followed, keeping their eyes and their blasters glued on the bot.

But Blackie obediently followed me, meek as hell.

The four goons forced us into a huge cavern. The jackers'd taken great pains to light it mighty damned well. Torches were burning every couple feet; the glassy walls—at least the ones not stacked with boxes and bins of stolen goods—reflected the torchlight like mirrors. We didn't get to stay in the cavern long, though. Torrance's goons forced us outside into the open air.

The bot never once made the slightest attempt to escape, damn him!

Seemed Torrance's new smuggling buddy insisted on inspecting the goods in broad daylight. That gave me a brilliant idea. I figured, if this Breego guy had enough brains not to trust Torrance completely, maybe, somehow or other, I might be able to win the *fleggin* smuggler over to my side. Maybe bribe him to let me go or agree to split Aguilar's five-mil reward with him—or some other spacey, long-shot ploy like that.

After being trapped at the bottom of the eater's pit for two long, boring days with only a tube-torch for light, my eyes weren't used to daylight. It blinded me for a bit; had to blink a helluva lot before I could make out a damn thing.

Then, I saw two ships parked on the plain far below us, right at the edge of the foothills around Mount Hope. I knew the old fast-ship belonged to Torrance. Didn't recognize the one sitting beside it.

Several figures were struggling up the mountainside, headed for the mouth of the cavern. Four brawny men bore the poles of a litter on their broad shoulders. I figured the big guy seated on it had to be Breego.

When they finally reached the cavern's mouth, the brawns carrying the litter went down on their knees. The other guys hauled Breego to his feet.

Soon as I got my first good look at him, I took a step back and cursed under my breath.

Torrance hadn't been exaggerating, not one bloody bit! Breego was fat all right, so damned fat he could barely waddle. Blubber larded his belly. Rolls of fat jiggled under his chin. Two bright, dark eyes struggled to peep out from above his bulging cheeks. Large, pointed ears flapped like pale batwings on either side of his round, bald head.

I'll be damned if Breego didn't look exactly like an over-sized, over-fed mine-rat!

The microsecond the bloody letch caught sight of me, his beady little rat-eyes lit up. His fingers flexed, as if he were having trouble controlling them. I almost gagged.

Old Rat Eyes was dressed in a full-length robe made outta bright-yellow, damned expensive Anjellian silk. A broad red sash wrapped around his middle made his belly look *twice* as big around as the planet Jupiter! Judging by his fancy getup and the general look of him, I pegged Breego for a full-blood B'treeni who at least fancied himself a *gurundi*: one of the B'treeni's mid-rulers. The *gurundi* are notorious throughout the explored galaxy for carousing. Those bastards wallow in sinful pleasures like a *kareeb* bathes in mud.

A thought hit me: Breego must finance his lush lifestyle by smuggling and reselling jacked goods, including the stuff he bought from Torrance.

The microsecond my former boss got a load of the lust plastered all over Breego's fat face, he grinned from ear to ear. I gritted my teeth. If my hands'd been free, I would've clamped them around Torrance's scrawny neck. But for their own safety, Drake and Morgan—damn the bloody cowards!—had tied my hands together behind my back. No matter how hard I tugged and twisted, my bonds were too damn tight to loosen—probably a stroke of luck for me. Still, I thought it'd be worth getting smoked, just for the pleasure of throttling Torrance.

Given my druthers, I probably would've chosen such a quick, clean end over becoming the personal property of Old Rat Eyes!

After eyeballing me up, down, and sideways, Breego had the *fleggin* gall to reach out and poke me with one fat finger.

I hissed, "Touch me again, you bloody bastard, and you'll be *missing* that finger!"

My threat only amused Breego. He chuckled, which made his whole bloated body shake like jelly. "A feisty one, this fem! She has spirit as well as beauty, Torrance, my dear friend. A prize, a genuine prize, easily worth, shall we say—three-hundred *zoltari?*"

Torrance frowned and shook his scruffy head, plainly unhappy with that offer. "Six," he said in a firm tone, crossing his arms on his chest.

Old Rat Eyes let out a gasp of phony-as-hell outrage. "Come now, Torrance! This deal is between friends! Remember who takes the ill-gotten goods off your hands in return for *zoltari,* which are perfectly safe for you to spend wherever you please!"

Torrance's scowl didn't fade one damn bit. "This isn't a simple case of unloading a few hijacked goods, now is it, Breego, old boy? This deal's strictly on the side, just between the two of us. You can take it or leave it, as you please."

If his own *fleggin* life'd been at stake, Breego couldn't have kept his beady, little rat-eyes off me. He was nearly drooling, licking his thick lips over and over again. Any microsecond, I expected he was gonna drool all down the front of his expensive Anjellian silk.

"Four-hundred *zoltari,*" Breego countered, upping my price by a hefty amount.

I caught the gleam of downright greed in Torrance's dark eyes. "*Five*-hundred!" he insisted stubbornly.

Making one helluva show of dismay, Breego waved both chubby arms in the air and cried, "*Ah, too much!* Far too much! Four-fifty."

"Four-seventy-five," Torrance said flatly. "And no damn lower!" The hard, cold look on his face told me this time he meant what he said.

"Done!" Breego agreed. His pale, round face beamed like one of Milo's moons at its fullest.

Thought I was gonna be sick all over my dust-covered boots. Damn good thing I had nothing in my stomach to heave, or I would've.

"Now, moving on to the bot here," Torrance said to remind his disgusting ally their business wasn't done yet.

Breego waddled around Blackie, making a wide circle. The fat bastard was too wary to get within the bot's reach, but wasn't satisfied 'til he'd inspected every last inch of him. Old Rat Eyes acted like a guy buying a used fast-ship. Wouldn't have surprised me one damn bit if he'd kicked the bot in the shins.

Making his suspicions plain, Breego demanded, "What manner of bot *is* this?"

Torrance shrugged. "Just an ordinary service bot, but as you can see, it's in damned-good condition. One hell of an expensive model, too—top of the line, I'd say."

Breego still eyed the bot with mistrust. "This machine appears dangerous and untrustworthy. Most certainly, it is *not* a servant model—no, no, not at all!" He shook his round head, making all his chins wobble and his bat-ears flap.

"No problem. To get the bot to cooperate, all you have to do is threaten the fem you just bought," Torrance explained, nodding in my direction. "For some reason, it's attached to her, maybe thinks of her as its master, but the bot could easily be reprogrammed to obey *you.*"

I growled, "I'm *not* his bloody master! He's a damned-obnoxious hunk of junk that won't stop following me around like a stray dog!"

Breego eyed the bot again, then casually reached out and snatched a blaster right outta the hand of Torrance's nearest goon. Old Rat Eyes swung the muzzle on me and snapped at the bot, "Kneel! *Kneel, I say!* Or I burn down the fem!"

With quite a bit of difficulty, Blackie clunked first to one silver-jointed knee, then to the other. When Old Rat Eyes saw how easy it was to bring the bot to his knees, he let out a cry of triumph. His whole bloated body shook with laughter. Suddenly, Breego found guts enough to close in on the bot. He raised one fat foot and kicked him right in the crotch. Blackie didn't react, not even to that grossest of insults. Old Rat Eyes roared even harder.

I was forced to watch as the poor bot suffered such indignities. My face burned hotter than Hellfire, but a stern, calm voice inside my head reminded me Blackie couldn't feel pain, let alone any real emotion. Still, I couldn't keep from yelling at Breego, "Stop playing games with him, you *fleggin* coward!"

I lunged for the smuggler, intending to give *him* a good, swift kick where it'd do the most damage, but Drake and Morgan grabbed my arms and held me back.

Satisfied Torrance hadn't lied to him, Breego shoved the blaster into his wide, red sash and offered, "Two-hundred *zoltari.*"

"Uh-uh! It'll take *six*-hundred for the bot," Torrance quickly countered, "*and* my blaster back, damn your greedy B'treeni hide to Hell!"

Breego reluctantly handed over the weapon. "Three-hundred, and that is far, far more than this bot is worth!"

"Five-fifty."

"Three!" Breego insisted shrilly, turning bluish-red in the face. "This bot is used, all but worn out!"

Torrance gave his smuggler-pal a hearty laugh, amused by the old ploy. "The hell it is! *Five* and that's firm! Take it or leave it, my friend. If you aren't willing to go that high, I know a hell of a lot of others who'll be more than happy to pay."

Breego flashed Torrance a sullen glare, then signaled his manservants, who were silently watching the bargaining from a respectful distance. One scurried forward and counted into Torrance's outstretched hands a pile of glowing *zoltari*: the rare gems the B'treeni use as currency.

Torrance took his time, admiring the quality of the crystals and double-checking their number. "A damn-fair price for both items," he assured Breego, giving him a grin.

"Torrance, my friend, you presume far too much upon our successful partnership," Old Rat Eyes protested. He motioned a pair of his brawniest servants forward. "Take my newly-acquired property down to my ship. Secure both in the hold, so I can conduct the remainder of my business with Mr. Torrance. And should the bot fail to cooperate fully, wound the fem—not fatally, of course, but painfully."

Giving Blackie a snooty look, Breego ordered, "On your feet, Robot!"

The bot struggled to stand upright. Once he was on his feet, the two B'treeni brawns tried to shove him forward, but they might as well've tried to move the whole damn mountain. Breego pointed one fat finger at me and babbled some alien gibberish. I didn't understand one damn word of it, but his men drew their blasters and turned them on me. Blackie instantly started down the side of Mount Hope.

As I passed Torrance, I spit right in his ugly, mocking mug; my aim was perfect. Cussing a blue streak, the bastard swiped at his face with his shirtsleeve. He turned purple with rage and made a lunge for me.

But like a giant red-and-yellow boulder, Breego's fat belly barred his way. "Ah, no, no, no! None of that, Torrance, my friend! The fem is now *my* property. Under no circumstances will I allow you to mar her beauty!"

Seething with rage, Torrance threatened, "Then you damn well better get the *fleggin* bitch the hell off this planet, or I swear I'll tear her limb from bloody limb with my bare hands!" He settled for aiming some of his more colorful cusswords in my general direction.

I cursed the rotten bastard right back and silently vowed to get even with him—that is, if I managed to escape Breego's clutches alive!

We had one hell of a struggle climbing down the side of Mount Hope and through the foothills. The whole way, Breego's brawns kept a nervous eye on the bot. Blackie trudged along behind me, meek as a *kareeb* kitten, without so much as a word of protest. It was downright amazing—and damned annoying!—to see what a blaster jammed into my ribs did to the bot.

I mumbled under my breath, cursing a steady stream, damning him and his robotic laws to Hell and right straight back again. Being a slave to laws like that was a helluva lot worse'n being the prisoner of Old Rat Eyes—or so I thought at the time.

We came to the edge of the foothills; on a flat stretch of barren, red-brown plain sat an old B'treeni trader. She was a fast-ship that'd seen much better days. Hell, she was so beat-up she made *Jammer* look like a luxury class!

When we reached the miserable excuse for a ship, the two brawns shoved me up its wide loading ramp. They forced me astern, down a long, central corridor, past empty cargo holds. A narrow ramp led deep into the belly of the ship. There, we stopped, and one of the brawns opened a hatch. The hold inside was pitch-dark. By the light from the corridor, I barely made out its interior.

I saw chains bolted all along the bulkheads, and attached to those chains were shackles for wrists and ankles!

In a flash, I realized, besides being a smuggler, Breego was a *fleggin* slaver! He bought and sold sentient beings kidnapped from their home worlds, torn from everything they'd ever known and loved! And here I'd pegged the bloated piece of space-scum as your average, run-of-the-mill smuggler.

The brawns dragged me into the slave-hold and none too gently chained me to the starboard bulkhead. They locked my wrists and ankles in restraints, then for good measure, wound another length of chain around my waist. One of the brawns held his blaster to my temple, while the other nervously chained the bot right beside me.

Once that was done, both brawns scurried outta the slave-hold in one helluva hurry; they were scared to death of the bot, even when he was in chains. They slammed the heavy hatch shut behind them, leaving me in total darkness. I heard the whir of the lock mechanism engaging, then nothing but silence.

I tugged at my chains, then desperately strained to break free. My efforts got me nothing but a helluva lot of pain. The chains were too damned strong for me to break. "Great jewelry, eh?" I said to the bot. "Bet *you* could break them, though. Right, Tin Man?"

"Most likely, but to what end? For once, will you employ your brain cells as nature intended? We find ourselves securely locked in a hold, within an alien ship that will shortly be traveling through deep-space. What is more, we are outnumbered by heavily-armed guards. Should I reveal my true strength prematurely, Breego would merely increase his security measures or perhaps deactivate or dis-assemble me. In that case, I would be of absolutely no value to you, Rand."

I grumbled, "You're not exactly doing me a whole helluva lot of good right now, Tin Man." In sheer frustration, I rattled the chains and gave my restraints another furious yank. "*Damn* bots and their idiotic laws! The bastard who invented your kind oughta be put outta his misery for the good of all mankind!"

At that insult, the bot clamped his metal mouth shut. For a long spell, he said nothing. After a while, he spoke: "Rand, since we appear to no longer be in imminent danger, might I suggest our best strategy is to play along with our captors, bide our time, and wait for an opportune moment to make our escape?"

I shot Blackie a glare, knowing he'd see it even in the darkness. "*If* we manage to stay alive that long, Tin Man! Did you get a load of Breego? Got no intention of letting that disgusting lard-bucket of a *slaver* have his way with me." I shuddered violently at the thought. "Rather be dead!"

Blackie didn't say one snarky word to that. I yanked hard on the manacles fastened around my wrists, tested the strength of the chains one last time. No luck! I rattled them helplessly and groaned,

"How in the name of Bloody Flaming Hell do I manage to get myself into these *fleggin* messes?"

That flight was long, miserable, and boring as Hell on a Monday afternoon. Locked in the dark, airless slave-hold, I had no clue where in the Cosmos the B'treeni ship was headed. Spent most of the time snoozing off and on, which wasn't too damned uncomfortable once the ship hit zero G.

During my awake-time, I tried to figure out where in bloody-blue-blazes Breego and his crew of slavers and smugglers hid out. I was damned sure of only one thing: it wasn't Esperance. Without more clues to go on, there was no way in hell for me to narrow down the location.

The old trader finally arrived—somewhere—and descended into some planet's atmosphere. Gravity kicked in with a vengeance. Both Blackie and I hit the deck in the slave-hold. Not long afterward, the B'treeni ship came in for a landing and settled down with a loud groan of protest.

I quipped, "How much ya wanna bet the bastards lost our *fleggin* luggage?"

"Rand, this is hardly an appropriate occasion for levity!" the bot scolded. "We are in an extremely serious predicament!"

"Aw, hell, Tin Man! I'm in one fix or another more often than not. No reason to take it so damned seriously."

"*Humph!* Well, *you* may refuse to take the present situation seriously, but I certainly—"

With a whir and a hiss, the lock let go. The slave-hold's hatch swung wide open. Light from the corridor outside streamed in, making me wince. Three guards came in; one kept his blaster trained on me, while the other two removed my chains. Then, eyes wide with fear, the pair removed the bot's chains. The microsecond Blackie was free, both backed off in one helluva hurry.

The brawn holding the blaster pointed toward the hatchway and muttered a string of gibberish. I wasn't stupid enough to argue with him or play dumb. I went where I was told.

At the top of the loading ramp, I stopped dead in my tracks. Sure as hell wasn't expecting to see what I saw. The scene was mighty familiar, though I'd never been here before. We'd landed at Zan Siba!

"*K'yoti* Hell!" I swore softly under my breath, awestruck. I stood and stared.

Ancient ruins stretched from the landing pad to the far horizon. Milo's Sun, huge and blood-red, was setting in a brilliant orange sky streaked with pale-purple clouds. All the vids I'd ever seen of Zan Siba had come to life!

To be honest, there wasn't a whole helluva lot left of the true-B'treeni's oldest city. The stone walls of what once must've been grand structures were crumbling badly. Centuries ago, their towers had toppled.

Jumbled piles of stone blocks lay half hidden beneath tangled blue-and-purple vines. Here and there, ruined columns stuck up, draped with vines. Reminded me of broken teeth jutting from the jawbones of long-dead corpses. What once must've been the main drag of a bustling city now lay dead-silent, littered with rubble, and covered in a thick carpet of green-gold moss.

Every school kid in the explored-galaxy knew the history of Zan Siba. Once, it'd been the capital city of the whole damn B'treeni Empire; now it was nothing but a fading memory. An alien civilization had built this city on one of the dozen planets orbiting Milo's Sun. That civilization was long gone, wiped out by plagues, wars, and other disasters. Like the city, the empire itself'd crumbled. Breego's crude mongrels—sweet people who now had the *fleggin* gall to call themselves "the B'treeni!"—had picked off most of the true-B'treeni left. Far as I knew, only a handful of them survived on distant planets.

I shot a glance over my shoulder as I whispered to the bot, "Know where we are, Tin Man?"

"Of course," he replied, "Zan Siba, the City of the Sun."

Might've known the obnoxious know-it-all wouldn't be so easily stumped. His creator, this RBS guy, had been a bloody genius; he knew damned near everything, and he'd programmed the bot.

But I was betting I knew a few things RBS *hadn't* known.

I mumbled under my breath, "Zan Siba's said to be haunted by the ghosts of the ancient B'treeni who lived and died here. Once

again, the fear factor keeps nosey tourists at bay. Makes these ruins
a damned-near-perfect spot for smugglers and the like to hide out."

The guard planted the flat of his hand between my shoulder
blades and gave me a rude shove. Fuming, I started down the ramp.
The bot followed. Gesturing with their blasters, the brawns steered
me to the right and down Zan Siba's main drag.

The bot and I picked our way through fallen stonework, 'til we
came to the remains of a huge building. Its crumbling front wall was
covered by a curtain of vines, which I pushed aside. Underneath,
I discovered an entrance. Beyond, stretched a long hallway, lit by
electric torches overhead.

The brawn shoved me again. I bared my teeth in a snarl, but went
in. At the far end of the hall stood an open doorway. When I saw
what was inside, I got another helluva shock.

Within the ancient ruins, the smugglers'd built a palace! And this
room had been decked out to be a *fleggin* throne room. *Delusions of
grandeur*, Torrance'd said about Old Rat Eyes. I'll be damned if he
wasn't dead-right. Breego'd spent a bloody fortune fixing up this
joint. His "throne room" was so damned posh it was a sin!

Under my feet, the floor was covered in brightly-colored glass and
metal mosaics. I'd never seen most of the alien patterns before. High
above my head, swanky light fixtures dangled from a gold-covered
ceiling. Full-length *Garzantine* mirrors hung on every wall, reflecting
the room's lights and colors a hundred-fold. Took one helluva lot of
credits to finance such a gaudy display.

Judging by Breego's "palace," slave-dealing and smuggling were
damned lucrative rackets. But then I figured, Old Rat Eyes probably
kept the best swag for himself and sold whatever he didn't want to
folks off-world, folks who didn't give a fast-flying damn how he'd
come by any of the shady stuff he had up for sale.

Breego'd left the slave-ship before we had and was lounging
on a massive, gold throne set atop a raised platform at the front of
the room. The throne sported a fortune in gleaming jewels; it was
ancient, probably'd once belonged to some long-dead B'treeni ruler.

The microsecond Old Rat Eyes spied me, a sickening smirk
spread across his round, fat face. His beady, little rat-eyes glittered
like twin black jewels. I shuddered in disgust.

"Ah! Here come my latest acquisitions!" Breego announced with a hearty chuckle. "See what my vast fortune has bought, my lovelies!"

He was speaking to a bevy of scantily-clad fems seated about the golden throne and fawning at his feet. As soon as they caught sight of Blackie, all the fems let out a gasp and scrambled to surround him. Reminded me of mine-rats in a feeding-frenzy, but they totally ignored me. One fem got bold enough to reach out and touch the bot's metal chest.

When he didn't pull away or offer any other sign of protest, the giggling fems crowded closer. They rubbed their hands all over his polished body, murmuring excitedly among themselves, admiring his build. But their entertainment came at the bot's expense.

Blackie turned his head and looked at me, as if he were begging for help. He seemed embarrassed as all get-out, but I could only grin at him and shrug.

"You're the star-attraction here, Tin Man. By the way, who sculpted that awesome body of yours? Michel, ah—Michael—?"

"—angelo," the bot muttered under his breath.

"Y'don't say! Could've sworn the guy's name was Michael Something-or-other. Anyway, this Angelo did one helluva job on you."

The bot let out a little sigh. He stared up at the gold-plated ceiling and, in his usual snooty tone, said, "I will so inform him the next time I see him, Rand!"

Wasn't sure whether or not he was putting me on.

"E'kali manoti! Akree! Akree!" Breego began screeching at the top of his lungs, his jealousy and his fury pretty damned obvious.

The fems instantly stopped going gaga over the bot and scurried to grovel at Old Rat Eyes's feet once again. With a wave of one pudgy hand, Breego motioned to our guards. "Take my new property down to the slave quarters and imprison them there. I shall deal with the fem later, when the mood strikes me."

Two guards came up, one on either side of me, and grabbed my upper arms. *"Something* sure as hell will strike you, you fat bastard!" I yelled across the room. "And it'll be my *fleggin* fist!"

Breego scowled. His pale jowls drooped even lower. "If that miserable shrew of a woman opens her mouth again, silence her!" he ordered. He gave me a broad smile—the most sickening smile I'd ever seen! "Until later then, dearest lady."

For a microsecond or two there, thought I was gonna be sick all over Breego's fancy mosaics, but the guards hauled me roughly toward the doorway. The third brawn trained his blaster on my head. Poor Blackie had no choice but to follow meekly.

I stumbled outta Breego's fancy throne room, pinned between the two B'treeni brawns. I was angry as hell at being held captive and treated like crap, but mighty damned glad to be going anywhere outta sight of Old Rat Eyes. By that point, I'd had as much as I could take of that *fleggin* slaver!

9 Outta the Frying Pan

Breego's *fleggin* guards dragged me through corridor after corridor, then down a long flight of rough stone steps. They led to a narrow passageway where armed guards were stationed every few yards. It was lit by smoky torches set in niches carved outta the rock walls. This place was one helluva cry from the throne room far above—no sparkly gems wasted here! No electrical power, either.

Cells lined both sides of the gloomy corridor. Had no doubt this was the slave quarters Old Rat Eyes'd mentioned. The brawns pushed me through one of the open doorways and into an empty cell. Without resisting, Blackie followed me inside. The cell door slammed shut and locked behind him.

The heavy, metal door was bolted on the outside—no way to open it from within.

As I gave the cell a quick scan, my upper lip curled in disgust. No windows; some dim light filtered down from a small metal grating set into the overhead. In one corner, a miserable excuse for a sleeping pallet lay on the filthy floor.

"Dammit all! No way outta here 'cept past those *fleggin* guards," I complained bitterly to the bot

"That would not be a wise choice," he noted matter-of-factly.

Hands on hips, I faced him. "I'd be willing to bet my last credit *you* could bust down the door and force your way past 'em, Tin Man."

Blackie gave me a long, hard look. "Not if they threaten to harm *you*, Rand."

I'd had about as much of the bot's spacey ethics as I could take. "Damn you and your *fleggin* laws! What the hell good are you? You won't *obey* me. You won't *help* me. You're bloody *useless!*" I threw myself down on the thin pallet and sulked.

The bot stood where he was, motionless as a block of spectromium. Finally, he broke his silence: "Rand, I sincerely regret not being of more assistance to you."

I heaved a sigh of disgust. "Hell, you can only do 'what you've been programmed to do', right, pal?" I knew damned good and well that mimicking him was cruel.

"That is, essentially, correct."

I sat bolt upright and shot him a suspicious look. *"Essentially?"* Didn't like the way he'd said that word. "What in bloody hell d'you mean by *that?* You're a bot; you've got a nano-computer for a brain. You can only do what it's been programmed to do. Am I right, or am I wrong?"

"You are partially correct, Rand; however, as I have told you on previous occasions, I am a prototype—one of a kind."

His answer fed my growing suspicions. I gave him the stink-eye. "So? Explain, Tin Man!"

"I am the first of my kind—that is, the first robot to be programmed with—well, I suppose you would refer to them as, ah, 'human memories.'"

"The hell you say!" Astonished, I scrambled to my feet to look the bot square in his metal face. "Let me get this straight: You're telling me Robert Benton-Smythe had the *fleggin* gall to program you with *human memories!"*

"He did indeed."

One of my notorious hunches punched me in the gut. *"Whose* memories did he program you with, Tin Man?" I demanded to know.

The bot hesitated a microsecond before he replied, "Why, his own, of course."

I couldn't have been more surprised if the bot'd dumped a whole freighter load of spectromium on me. "His *own* memories!" I gasped.

"Along with his speech patterns? His fancy-schmancy manners? His education? His beliefs? In short, his whole *fleggin* personality?"

"Once again, essentially true."

The all too obvious fact smacked me like a fist to the face. I let out another gasp. "*K'yoti* Hell! Then—for all intents and purposes, Tin Man—you *are* Robert Benton-Smythe!"

The bot said quietly, "In any case, I am all that now remains of him."

Stunned, I let out a low whistle. "*Knew* there was something mighty damned peculiar about you, Tin Man. You act way too human to be an ordinary bot, but I had no *fleggin* idea—! *K'yoti* Hell!" I repeated in a whisper.

"Although I may *seem* somewhat human to you, Rand, I am simply a machine," Blackie insisted. I caught the note of resignation plain in his voice.

My suspicions raging like wildfire, I flashed him another look. "Tell me you're not one of those newfangled *cyborgs,* Tin Man—half human, half machine?"

"No, Rand. I am merely a piece of machinery, hardware—as you seem to enjoy reminding me frequently." Now the bot sounded downright depressed.

I gave him a little shrug, but had to clear my throat. "Uh, nothing wrong with being a machine, I guess. But I still say you're a helluva lot *more'n* a machine, Tin Man!"

"Am I?" His tone held a hint of bitterness.

For some unknown reason, I broke out in a sweat. "Hell, being a machine can't be as bad as all that, can it? *Jammer*'s a machine, and I'm pretty damned fond of her."

"*Jammer* is *not* sentient," the bot pointed out glumly. "Rand, I could never expect you to fully understand my plight, unless you found yourself in a similar position, which I pray will never happen! Becoming accustomed to being a machine, rather than a living man, is indeed a difficult adjustment."

I racked my brain, searching for something positive to say, something to comfort him. "On the outside, you may *look* like a bot, but on the inside—well, I guess you're still RBS, sorta."

"My *proper* appellation is RBS02," the bot corrected in a quiet voice, turning his face away from mine. "And an entire universe of difference separates being a man from being a machine. Unfortunate, but true. I never truly appreciated what it was to be fully human until far too late.

"Finding myself trapped within this cumbersome body was a shock of incredible magnitude; it is far worse than being forced to wear a suit of armor that can never be taken off and put aside. As I am still in the process of discovering, in my present form there is an impenetrable barrier between myself and—and the rest of the Cosmos."

I'd never seen the bot so upset. It made me damned uncomfortable. My throat started to ache, then threatened to close up. A feeling crept over me, something I hadn't felt—hadn't *allowed* myself to feel!—for one helluva long time.

I didn't have a *fleggin* clue what to say or do to comfort the bot.

I tried to clear my throat. "Ah, listen—um, about the 'Tin Man' stuff, if it bothers you, I'll do my damnedest to can it. *Aww, dammit all!* Sorry, Tin Man! That just sorta slipped out. No offense intended, I swear!"

I expected the bot to get huffy on me, as usual, but to my surprise his broad metal shoulders squared. His unblinking crystal lenses looked me straight in the eyes. "I prefer you continue to be yourself, Rand. I cannot ask you to change who you are on my account. I must accept the truth, bitter though that truth may be: I *am* a tin man."

I was stunned to hear such grim words come outta the bot's mouth. I shook my head and murmured, "No, *not* tin! You've survived a helluva lot. You're made outta tougher stuff than tin."

"That remains to be seen," the bot replied stoically.

I flopped down on the filthy sleeping pallet and lay flat on my back. Laced my fingers under my head and did some real deep thinking. Hell, that was becoming a new habit for me.

But for the life of me, I couldn't figure out *why* RBS01 had pulled such a dumb-ass stunt; why had he programmed the poor bot with his own pernickety personality? What in the Cosmos made him do something so *fleggin* weird to a helpless creature? To his own creation—his Frankenstone's Monster!

The blood within my veins started to simmer.

I sat bolt upright again and demanded, "So answer this for me, Tin Man: what in bloody hell's so great about being a man? Never met a man I trusted completely, 'cept for my father. He was a good man—honest, hard-working, reliable, God-fearing. And look where *that* got him!"

"Your father?" Blackie repeated. The word seemed to perk him up.

"Yeah, I had a father—and a mother!—once upon a time, long, long ago. I'm not made outta metal like you are, pal."

The microsecond those harsh words left my mouth, I bit down hard on my tongue, but it was too damned late. "*Dammit all!* Sorry again, Tin Man! Force of habit. I honestly didn't mean to—!"

"I gather your meaning, Rand—quite vividly in fact. Thank you for being so forthright and setting me straight in regard to the matter of my existence."

I bristled. "Hey, look here, pal—!"

"The entire subject is best dropped. It was a colossal error on my part to confide anything of a personal nature to *you*!" The bot pivoted on one heel and turned his broad metal back on me. Once again, he stubbornly refused to move or speak.

Disgusted, I let out a loud groan and flopped back down on the pallet. "Okay, what the bloody hell! Go ahead! Give me the *fleggin* silent treatment, Tin Man. I deserve it."

No matter what I said or did, I just couldn't win as far as the damn bot was concerned. I decided, *To hell with Robert Benton-Smythe, man or machine!*

Determined to ignore the bot, I curled up on my left side, facing the dank wall of the cell, and tried my damnedest to get some sleep.

Evidently, Old Rat Eyes was giving me and the bot plenty of time to stew in our own juices, to let our hopeless fix sink in good and deep. I was tired, hungry, and in one helluva rotten mood.

Outta the blue, the bolt on the cell door shot free. With my senses instantly on high-alert, I jumped to my feet, ready for anything.

The cell door creaked open. Breego himself waddled in. I was surprised as hell to see him in the slave quarters.

With a lecherous gleam in his beady rat-eyes, he said, "Dear lady, I find your present garb *far* from attractive. Kindly clothe yourself in more suitable garments." He tossed me a small, tightly-wrapped bundle.

I let it drop to the floor at my feet and swore at him. "Don't dress to please anyone, least of all *you*, chum!" I drawled, glaring daggers at the rotten piece of space-scum.

Breego had guts enough to waddle a bit closer. "Perhaps you require *assistance* in dressing, my dear?"

He raised one chubby finger. Two brawns stepped through the open cell door. They came up behind him and stood glaring at me, leaving no doubt they meant business.

One good look at that pair of half-dressed, muscle-bound brutes quickly changed my mind. "Uh, thanks for the offer, chum, but I've been dressing myself for quite a few years now. Guess I can manage after all."

"Very good, very good!" Breego said, smiling that disgusting smile of his. The smirk made me feel like puking my damn guts out. "If you expect to receive food and drink, you will obey me to the letter! I assure you, my dear lady, you shall *need* every ounce of energy you possess." Giving me one last, lecherous leer, he turned and waddled outta the cell.

The microsecond Old Rat Eyes left, I breathed a huge sigh. Both guards followed him out. I made a move toward the open doorway, but before I could get near it, one of the brawns came back. He bent down and slid a battered metal tray across the cell's stone floor. He slammed the door shut. I heard the bolt slide into place.

In sheer frustration, I gave the cloth bundle at my feet a vicious kick, wishing it were Breego's fat behind. "Dammit!" I growled. "This is all I need! But to tell you the truth, I'm kinda shocked Old Rat Eyes didn't wanna stay and watch me undress! *K'yoti* Hell! How *do* I get myself into these *fleggin* messes?"

The bot agreed with me. "You do seem to possess a unique talent for enmeshing yourself in some extremely calamitous situations, Rand."

Those damned-big words were the first Blackie'd said to me in several hours.

I checked out the food on the metal tray and was damned glad I didn't have to share with the bot. But the miserable excuse for a meal wasn't one bit appetizing. They'd given me only a couple pieces of rock-hard bread and a cupful of warm water. The stuff made me gag, but after soaking the stale bread in the water, I managed to choke it down.

Breego'd been dead-right about one thing: I needed food and water to keep up my energy. If I wanted to get outta this miserable cell alive, I had to do whatever the hell it took.

After downing the lousy food, I picked up the bundle of cloth. I sat on the sleeping pallet with a resigned sigh and began to untie the bundle. I pulled out wisps of sheer fabric: shimmering golds, sparkling reds, bright purples—real tasteful colors! If these duds were any example of the fashions worn by Breego's harem, a fem's nights in Zan Siba must get mighty damned cold!

I got to my feet, heaved a heavier sigh, and started to strip.

The bot acted as if I'd zapped him with a laser-bolt! He snapped to attention and protested, "*For God's sake, Rand!* Have you absolutely no sense of decency?"

That spacey attitude took me by complete surprise. I let out a little chuckle. "Seems to me you've got more'n enough modesty for the both of us, Tin Man! Sorry I embarrassed you."

"Rand, that is not—" Blackie started to say, then evidently thought better of it, and switched gears. "You might at least give me time to turn my back before you proceed to undress."

I couldn't resist flashing him a sarcastic grin. "So your RBS was a real gentleman, eh? Hell, they're an endangered species these days! Do as you damn please, Tin Man," I said, giving him a slight shrug of my shoulders.

Without another word, the bot pivoted on one metal heel and stood back to me once again. I finished stripping as fast as humanly possible, then began to dress. But as I discovered, Old Rat Eyes hadn't given me a whole helluva lot to put on. The toughest part was trying to figure out what wisps covered what and what was left bare! I tried to recall how the fems I'd seen in Breego's throne room were dressed.

When I finished dressing, I decided to put my boots back on.

Breego hadn't given me any footgear, and the hard stone floor of the cell was as cold as Hell's Icebox in Winter.

Satisfied I was at least halfway decent, I said, "Okay, Tin Man, what d'you think?"

Blackie turned around cautiously, then froze in place. For a microsecond or two, he stared at me, as if he'd never seen me before.

"Oh—m-my—Lord! What the half-dressed slave-girl is wearing this season, I presume?"

Never'd heard the bot stutter before. My face went up in flames. "Hell, it wasn't *my* damn idea to wear this *fleggin* getup!" I snapped. "On top of all the crap I've put up with lately, pal, I don't need you insulting the way I'm dressed!"

"I assure you, Rand, I meant no insult. On the contrary, I think you look stunning—absolutely stunning!"

I growled, "Oh, yeah? I'll just *bet* I do!"

The bot tried to explain away his odd reaction. "I must confess, however, to being somewhat shocked. After all, your customary attire is rather, ah—is so, um—"

I raised one eyebrow, daring him to finish the dangerous sentence. "*What?* Masculine? Unattractive? Ugly?" I finished for him. "Hell, the outfit goes with the job, pal! I'd look real sweet kicking some guy's lights out, or diving for cover, dressed in skirts and high heels!"

"The word I was so unsuccessfully grasping for was 'concealing'. Once again, I had no intention of insulting you, Rand. Not in the least! Must you *always* take everything I say as an insult?"

"*Huh!* Saves a helluva lot of time. But enough of this damned foolishness! We need to come up with a workable plan to get ourselves outta here and do it mighty damned fast. I don't like the way Old Rat Eyes has been drooling over me. Not one damn bit!"

This time, plain as day, I heard Blackie murmur, "Nor do I!"

Now it was my turn to stare at him. "And what in hell was *that* supposed to mean?"

"I was simply pointing out that you appear to be in imminent danger, Rand."

"Brilliant deduction, Eisenstein!"

"I believe you meant to say 'Einstein', Rand. *Really!* Where in the

Cosmos did you receive your education? Your lack of even the most basic knowledge is utterly appalling!"

I shrugged off that dig. "Who the *flegg* cares? If you must know, I pretty much educated myself. Look, the faster we get our butts the hell outta here, the better. For God's-green-snake, Tin Man, use the brainpower your master gave you! You're the one who's supposed to be so *fleggin* smart, *not me!*"

The bot surprised me by obeying for once. He began to study the cell, taking in every detail. Afterward, he was forced to admit, "Short of ripping the cell door off its hinges, thus attracting a great deal of unwanted attention—and most likely getting ourselves shot in the process!—a means of escape, ah, escapes me at the moment."

"*Hah!* So much for your superior mind! Let me give it a try."

For the next couple hours or so, I searched the cell, looking for even the tiniest cranny. But the cell's walls were solid rock, too damned smooth and slippery to climb. Tried standing on the bot's shoulders again, but the grating overhead was too high for me to reach. Besides, even if I'd been able to reach it, the opening was way too small for *me* to crawl through, let alone the bot.

I racked my brains 'til I gave myself one helluva headache.

Outta sheer desperation, I started pulling every trick in my playbook, one by one, no matter how old or how feeble. I played sick. I pretended to be injured. I screamed that I saw ghosts coming through the walls. The bloody guards were stone-deaf to all my pleas for help.

Next, I tried my damnedest to seduce the brawn who was standing guard just outside the door. Promised him a whole vidcatalog of sensual delights, if he'd only open the door and come into my cell. But every damn one of Breego's brawns ignored me. I began to think *they* were the ones made outta tin!

Finally, I admitted defeat. Swearing a blue streak, I dropped down on the sleeping pallet to rest, my back pressed against the cold wall of the cell.

Sometime later that night, the bolt shot back. The cell door opened a crack. I straightened up, on high-alert. A bare, muscular arm reached in and set down a long-necked purple bottle trimmed with golden tassels. Then the door quickly slammed shut and locked again.

Giving in to curiosity, I got up and went over to give the bottle a better look. If I guessed right, it held high-grade *hahk-teem*, my favorite poison. My hackles went up; Old Rat Eyes'd waved a red flag under my nose.

Furious, I grabbed the fancy, purple bottle by its neck, whirled, and, with all my might, hurled it across the cell. The bottle exploded against the far wall, making a satisfying crash. *Hahk-teem* trickled down the wall and made little silvery puddles on the stone floor.

"That *fleggin* bastard! *Trying to get me drunk!*" I roared. "Damn him to Unholy Hell!"

The bot shot me a sideways, worried look, shocked by my reaction. "Violence is uncalled for, Rand. If we are to escape this predicament, we must maintain cool heads."

Tried my damnedest to heed his advice. I took several slow, deep breaths before I finally managed to calm down, then went over to inspect what was left of the bottle. Purple glass was scattered over the cell floor, the pieces too damned small to be of any use. But the bottle's long neck, which was made of *thicker* glass, was still in one piece, now sharp-edged and jagged—dangerous enough to be used as a weapon!

I tore a strip from the tail of the shirt I'd taken off and carefully wound it around the bottle's neck to pad the sharp end. I stuffed the whole business into the top of my right boot, so I could reach it in a hurry when the time was right. The glass shard was a far cry from my laser-handle, but having a weapon of any kind in my possession made me feel a whole helluva lot better.

I gave my boot a pat. "Now if Old Rat Eyes wants to tussle, he'll pay for it in blood, his *own* blood!"

The bot protested, "Rand, should you attack Breego, he is far more likely to kill you, or have you killed. Please consider the consequences before you act in such a rash manner!"

"Some things are worse'n dying, Tin Man. But you wouldn't know a damn thing about that, now would you?"

"I am aware that such a foolish act would be tantamount to committing suicide, Rand. I simply cannot allow you to throw your life away in such a manner, as if—"

The bolt on the outside of the cell door shot back with a crash. I jumped an Akadran mile.

The door swung open, and there, in all his magnificent fatness, stood Old Rat Eyes. He was dressed in a long, metallic-green robe, belted with the same wide, red sash he'd worn before. Once again, he had the gall to step into my cell. He noticed the smashed remains of his little "present" and waddled straight for me, an angry scowl on his fat face.

I stiffened, not liking the look in those beady little rat-eyes of his, not one damn bit! Breego looked like a starving man about to dig into a feast, and I was the main course!

I backed up. My shoulder blades met the ice-cold wall of the cell. I got ready to reach for the shard of glass in my boot.

Blackie stood like a bronze statue, not moving one metal muscle.

Breego ignored the bot. "Ah, my dear, dear lady! Do not shrink from me," he said, giving me one of those sickening smiles of his. He was trying his damnedest to be charming, with no success.

Breego went on, "May I say, you look delectable, absolutely delectable. Come, dearest one! I have arranged more suitable accommodations, so that we may spend the entire night together. And there I shall shower you with delights you have only dreamed of thus far in your life."

That flowery little speech really set my teeth on edge. I hissed at the bastard, "In my worst nightmares, chum!"

Either Old Rat Eyes had guts enough or was stupid enough to take another step toward me. I snatched the bottle-shard from my boot and ripped off its wrappings. I held the jagged piece of broken glass out in front of me.

"You so much as *touch* me, chum, and you'll end up missing a couple real important body parts!"

My bravado amused Breego. He chuckled and exclaimed, "Aha! A show of resistance! That only serves to *enhance* the sport, does it not, my lovely one?"

"*Sport?*" I snorted my opinion of his choice of words. "Never been anybody's sport, and sure as hell don't intend to start now!"

But the overstuffed dumb-ass kept coming, not taking my threat seriously. His sickening grin widened. I felt sick to my stomach again and wished to bloody hell I *hadn't* eaten the damn bread and water!

I steeled myself and got ready to make good on my threat. To defend my virtue—what little was left of it!—I might actually have to carve up the bastard. But if I so much as wounded Old Rat Eyes, I knew damned good and well what was bound to happen next.

Suddenly, it seemed to dawn on Breego that I wasn't playing games here: I was dead-serious. His smile faded. He heaved a gusty sigh.

"*E'kashini!* I truly hoped to avoid using this, my dearest one." He drew a pocket-sized stun-gun outta his red belly-sash, and aimed at me.

Every inch of my skin crawled. I had to make another helluva choice and make it damned fast!

Deep down inside, I suddenly felt dead-calm. In a quiet, steady voice I drawled, "Hell, using a gun on me would spoil your plans for a night of fun, wouldn't it, Breego, old chum?"

Old Rat Eyes shook his round, bald head. His bat-ears flapped. His chins and jowls jiggled. "Not at all, my dear," he said with an evil snicker.

"*Flegg* you! You're a disgusting bastard!"

With his free hand, he reached for my arm. My muscles tensed. I made ready for a fight I knew wasn't gonna end well for either one of us.

But Breego made a real dumb-ass mistake: he stepped in front of the bot. I didn't see Blackie move, but suddenly his metal hand was clamped like a vise around Old Rat Eyes's throat. The bot lifted the struggling tub of lard clear off the floor.

Damned impressed by the bot's superhuman strength, I let my mouth drop open and croaked, "*K'yoti* Hell, Tin Man!"

Breego blubbered like a baby, kicking and squirming for all he was worth. Reminded me of a wriggling grub about to be speared with a fish-hook and used for bait.

"*Re-release me!*" were the only words he could choke out.

One fat hand scrabbled at the metal fingers clamped about his throat. He fired the stun-gun still clutched in his other chubby fist.

A bolt of energy hit the cell's high ceiling. A shower of sparks and dust rained down. I dove for the nearest corner and covered my head with both arms.

Two guards stationed outside the open cell door stood and stared, frozen in horror. They hadn't the slightest clue how to deal with a super-strong bot on the rampage.

"Kill—*her*!" Breego managed to gurgle, flailing one thick arm in my direction. By then, his bulging face'd turned a purplish-gray.

Like robots themselves, the dumb-ass brawns stepped into the cell and obediently trained their blasters on me.

"Aww, *flegg* it!" I swore. Disgusted, I flung the neck of the bottle across the cell and heard the smash. Slowly, I got to my feet with both hands raised.

"Let's not do anything hasty here, boys. Easy does it," I pleaded.

The bot opened his hand. Breego dropped, stumbled backward, and landed on his well-padded ass. He sat there, coughing and wheezing, rubbing the blubber around his throat.

One of the beefy brawns rushed to his aid. He took Old Rat Eyes under both arms and, after a helluva struggle, managed to haul him to his feet. Once Breego caught his breath, he faced Blackie, glaring up at him with pure hatred in his beady little rat-eyes.

"You will dearly *regret* that serious error, my large metal friend! I refuse to risk being attacked and humiliated by you a *second* time! You must be dealt with—*immediately!*"

Old Rat Eyes made a sharp, angry motion to the guards and to a third brawn who'd just showed up. "Take these fools down to my laboratory and chain them there! And should this mechanical monstrosity show the slightest sign of hostility, I order you to *kill* the woman—in as sadistic a manner as possible!"

"Whatever you desire, Your Magnanimous Munificence!" the guard at his elbow gulped, bobbing and bowing like a *fleggin* idiot before his master.

The wary brawn came up and jammed the muzzle of his blaster into my ribcage. I raised my hands higher. "*Oww!* Take it easy, pal! I'm going, dammit! I'm going!"

As I passed Breego, I shot him a glare hot enough to melt spectromium. The brawns forced me outta the cell at blaster-point. I heard the bot's heavy footsteps trudging behind me.

"Why in the name of Unholy Hell did you drop that fat bastard?" I hissed under my breath, knowing damned well the bot could hear every word I said, even if our guards couldn't. "You should've throttled that *fleggin* slaver while you had the chance!"

His voice pitched as low as mine, Blackie replied, "The taking of life does not come at all easily to me, Rand, as you well know. Besides, that approach most certainly would have placed your life in even greater jeopardy."

"*Huh!* D'you really think the situation's any damned better now?" I growled.

I grumbled and cursed all the way, as two brawns dragged me none too gently down deep into the dark, dank bowels of Breego's lair. The third guy trailed behind Blackie, his blaster drawn and ready.

By that point, I was mighty damned sick and bloody-tired of popping outta the frying pan into another one that was just as bad, if not worse.

Then and there, I made myself a solemn promise: if I were lucky enough to survive this *fleggin* mess, I'd get the hell outta the recoup business—for good!

10 Lab Rats

One of Breego's brawns grabbed me by the arm and dragged me down a long, narrow flight of steps carved outta solid bedrock. The steps led into a huge, underground chamber. Taking the stairs one careful step at a time, Blackie followed. Once again, he acted meek as a tamed *kareeb* kitten, damn his metal hide to Bloody Hell!

I scowled when I got a load of the disgusting surroundings. Outdated electric lanterns dangled from a high ceiling, flickering on and off and casting eerie shadows. Old Rat Eyes'd called this his "laboratory!" I called it a dank, old dungeon packed with a hodge-podge of dusty gadgets and gizmos, probably hijacked stuff he'd had no luck unloading. The whole setup looked like a scene outta one of the ancient Frankenstone movies I'd seen as a kid.

Two brawns chained me against a cold, clammy stone wall with both arms raised above my head. Hurt like hell! The third guy kept his blaster squarely on me. Muttering a bunch of gibberish and gesturing wildly, the first two brawns forced Blackie to back against a tilted metal table, then chained him to it.

Not long afterward, Breego came waddling down the steps, taking his own sweet time. Behind him trailed a handful of B'treeni dressed in long, white lab coats. A bunch of brawns brought up the rear.

Paying no attention to me, Old Rat Eyes puffed and wheezed his way across the "laboratory" to the table where the bot was chained.

Obeying Breego's commands, the white-coats began scurrying back and forth, attaching long wires to Blackie's metal skull.

It felt as if a damned cold fist were squeezing my guts. I remembered what Torrance'd told Breego back on Esperance: something about *reprogramming* the bot.

"You bastards leave him the hell alone!" I yelled, struggling to free myself. Got nothing but more pain for all my efforts.

Breego's white-coated witch doctors took no notice. They kept fiddling with the damn wires. The wires led to a gigantic, round gizmo. It reminded me of an old-fashioned generator I'd once seen in a museum vid-tour.

"Proceed with the program erasure," Old Rat Eyes ordered the white-coats. "In his present state, this bot is far too dangerous to be trusted. Once his original programming has been erased, you will reprogram him according to my specifications. The bot will become an excellent household servant: obedient, docile, compliant—and more than eager to please me."

My face flushed hot as a solar flare. "You can't *do* that! He's not an ordinary bot, not some hunk of machinery you're free to tinker with. He's a prototype! He's part human! Wiping his nano-circuits would be like—like committing *murder!*"

For the first time, Breego turned to look at me. He raised one eyebrow and sneered, "And what in the entire Munificent Cosmos, my dear one, leads you to believe *I* would balk at murder?" He chuckled, as if I'd told him a damned good joke.

I snarled, "You *fleggin* bastard! You damage that bot, and you'll have *me* to deal with!"

My empty threat amused Breego no end. He chuckled louder, then smirked. "Your taming is the next item on the agenda, my dear, dear shrew."

"Now what in the name of Bloody Hell's *that* supposed to mean?" I demanded.

Breego ignored my question, so I started calling the bastard every last name in the book, inventing a few more in the process.

Sure enough, the name-calling got Old Rat Eyes's attention. He waddled across the lab to glare right into my face.

"Once this wretched robot is reprogrammed, he will *never* interfere in our sport again! And now, my lovely one, you yourself shall do the honors by engaging the power." With a sweep of one pudgy arm, he indicated the control panel attached to the side of the giant generator-gizmo.

"Like hell I will! You get ahold of some really bad *hahk-teem*, Breego, old chum?" I growled through clenched teeth. "Your breath sure stinks of something mighty foul!"

Quivering with anger, Breego snapped his fat fingers. Instantly, every single one of the brawns holstered his blaster and instead drew what looked to me like some kinda pistol-sized dart gun.

After getting a load of those miserable excuses for weapons, I had to let out a snort. "Darts? *K'yoti* Hell! You really expect me to *tremble* over a bunch of little pinpricks?"

Breego's rat-eyes glittered evilly. "Ah, but *these* 'pins,' as you choose to call them, have been dipped in a nerve toxin native to Zan Siba! Even a minute amount of toxin injected directly into the bloodstream will, in time, result in a slow, agonizing death. I can assure you, dearest lady, the process is most entertaining to watch—but *not* to suffer!"

I glared my worst at him. My fingers itched to clamp themselves around the evil bastard's fat neck and throttle the life outta him.

Old Rat Eyes barked something to the nearest pair of brawns—probably an order to release me from my chains. Then he added another order, one he clearly meant for me to understand: "Should the fem be so foolish as to refuse to follow my instructions, fire at her until she obeys!"

Breego stabbed a finger at the control panel on the near-side of the generator. "Engage the power—*now!*—or my men will gradually, unmercifully, turn you into a living pincushion, temporarily living, that is!"

Breego waddled away, to watch the show from a safe distance.

I turned my glare on the brawns who were unchaining me. Wondered what my chances were of getting to Old Rat Eyes before I got darted. For what seemed like an eternity, I stood there like a *fleggin-*idiot, rubbing life back into my numb wrists.

On all sides, deadly dart guns were aimed at me. Once again, I had to make helluva choice: me—or the bot?

I eyed him and bit my lower lip. A little voice inside my head whispered, *You know damned well Blackie isn't really human. Like he said himself, he's just a machine. And a machine doesn't have human feelings!*

But in my heart, I knew the truth: if I hit that switch, I'd be wiping out a helluva lot more'n a computer program; I'd be wiping out a one of a kind human personality! A damned obnoxious personality maybe, but *human* all the same—human and unique. And once the bot's personality'd been erased, nothing and nobody in the Cosmos could bring him back.

Robert Benton-Smythe was murdered once. How in the name of Unholy Hell can I kill him a second *time?*

My feet were like solid blocks of spectromium as I shuffled toward the control panel. One of Breego's witch doctors muttered something in the B'treeni tongue, pointed out the switch he wanted me to hit, then stood back. Took a couple more steps toward the panel and paused, staring at it. I reached for the *fleggin* switch. My hand trembled. I swallowed hard and breathed a silent prayer for the courage to do this.

"*Oh, God!* I'm so sorry, Tin Man. Hate like hell having to do this to you, but it's either you or me—RBS01."

In a flash, I darted forward, but instead of hitting the switch, I grabbed handfuls of wires and jerked them free of the bot's skull. Then, with both arms covering my head, I dove behind the metal table Blackie was chained to.

I heard chains snapping, men yelling, darts pinging off metal. Then Breego let out a yowl like a scalded *kareeb.* I dared to poke my head around the edge of the table to see what in bloody hell was going on.

Blackie'd broken free of his chains, just as I'd hoped he would. The air was chock-full of poisoned darts. The dumb-ass brawns were firing wildly at the bot, but their weapons were bloody useless against his armor-plating. Darts were bouncing off his metal body like hail off a miner's tin-roof. He had one hand clamped around Breego's throat again. As I watched, he pulled the fat bastard against his metal chest and pinned him there, to act as a shield.

The white-coats were shrieking, madly ducking for cover or running for their damn lives. A couple managed to scramble up the stairs on all fours.

Breego was gurgling, "Cease fire! *Cease fire!*" As a dart bounced off his fat belly, he let out a high-pitched shriek. Half expected to see him deflate like a punctured balloon.

"Rand! *This* would appear to be the opportune moment!" the bot announced in a voice loud enough to carry above the ruckus. "Get behind me! I will shield you!"

I scrambled to my feet. Keeping as low as I could, I dashed to Blackie and ducked behind him. Still using Breego as a shield, the bot began backing toward the steps. Ignoring their boss's orders, two brawns kept firing in our direction. Lucky for us, not a single damn one was willing to use his blaster and risk accidentally smoking Old Rat Eyes.

We started up the steps, moving sideways. My back pressed against the cold rock wall, I slid one arm around the bot's waist and moved up to the next step whenever he did. Blackie, in the middle of our sandwich, kept Breego firmly pinned in front of him; the fat bastard was still struggling and screaming like a bloody banshee.

I heard a booted foot scrape against one of the steps above me. My head instantly snapped in that direction. A single brawn was coming down the stairs. He reached for his blaster.

Letting go of the bot, I raced up the steps. Before the startled brawn could aim, I rammed my head right into his gut. He groaned and sagged.

My adrenaline surging, I grabbed him by his scanty duds and flung him off the stairs and out into space. He landed on top of his cronies in the lab below and flattened them.

I yelled to the bot, "Let's get the hell outta here! *Fast!*"

Just then, a blaster-shot fired from below took a big chunk outta the wall above my head! One of the brawns'd recovered whatever wits he had.

Ducking the fallout, my ears ringing like crazy, I raced up the steps. The bot followed on my heels with his squirming shield pinned in front of him. We made the top step. The corridor beyond was deserted. I ran back the way we'd come. Blackie trailed after me, half-dragging, half-carrying Old Rat Eyes, who was still shrieking at the top of his lungs like a *fleggin* madman.

A bunch of scantily-clad fems stood smack-dab in the center of the next corridor we came to. When they saw me running toward them, they froze. I bowled right through 'em with no trouble. But the microsecond those fems got a load of the bot coming, they screeched and scattered in all directions like mine-rats fleeing for their bloody lives.

The bot and I came to the foot of another long flight of stone steps; I ran up them, taking two steps at a time, and skidded around the next corner at top speed. Hoped to hell we were headed in the right direction.

But a squad of twenty or so B'treeni brawns were headed in the opposite direction, probably making for the battle zone below.

Naturally, I ran smack into them. Just my dumb-ass luck!

I spun and side-kicked the blaster outta the lead guy's hand, then shouldered him in the chest. With the wind knocked outta him, he flew backward into the brawns behind him. I head-butted another guy. Scooping up the blaster he dropped, I got ready to fight for my damn life.

Blackie caught up with me. He lifted Breego high over his head and tossed the shrieking ball of blubber on top of the brawns who'd managed to stay on their feet. They went down. The bot and I scrambled over and through the flailing arms and legs.

Blackie pivoted and grabbed the one man left standing. Swinging the guy like a scythe, by one arm and one leg, the bot mowed down every brawn who even tried to get back on his feet.

"C'mon, Tin Man! This way out—I think!" I yelled. "*Quick!* Before they call in more reinforcements!"

"I will be with you presently, Rand! Do not wait for me! *Go!*"

I dashed to the far end of the corridor. Heard more screaming behind me, then the bot's heavy footsteps dogged mine. Sure enough, at the next turn I passed Breego's gaudy throne room. The exit was just ahead.

I urged Blackie, "This way! For God's sake, hurry up, Tin Man!"

I pushed through the heavy curtain of vines and out into waning sunlight. Blinking like crazy, panting for breath, I got my bearings mighty damned fast. I turned left and raced down the moss-grown main drag of Zan Siba with the bot right on my heels.

Far down at its Eastern end, I saw two ships parked beneath the electronic scan-net designed to prevent overhead scans. Skirting chunks of the crumbling walls, I made a beeline for the nearer ship, a fast-ship that'd seen better days. But she was in a helluva lot better shape than the other ship: the old slaver the bot and I'd been chained in.

Blaster-fire came from behind us. I ran even faster, then turned and fired an energy-bolt to slow down the bloody bastards who were chasing us.

By a stroke of luck, the fast-ship's ramp was down. Without hesitating so much as a fraction of a microsecond, I darted straight up it. The brawn standing guard aboard thought he was the bloody welcoming committee and stuck his nose out to see what all the ruckus was about.

Before he had a chance to draw his blaster, I doubled him over with a fist to the gut. Groaning, he crumpled to his knees. I kicked his lights out and watched him topple from the ramp to the ground below.

A handful of Breego's brawns'd almost reached the ship. I figured if anyone could mop up any unwelcome visitors and raise the ramp, it was the bot. I wasted no time dashing into the control room. Threw myself into the pilot's seat and strapped in. At the same time, I tried to figure out how to work the alien controls. I located and engaged thrusters, then in one helluva hurry switched the ship to hover-mode.

I figured the heat from the thrusters oughta keep Breego's brawns at bay long enough for me to get the B'treeni ship airborne. Blackie joined me and quickly strapped himself into the co-pilot's seat.

But, as usual, he couldn't resist pointing out my flaws. "Rand, you do realize this constitutes vessel-stealing, which is considered an extremely serious offense throughout the explored galaxy?"

After all the *fleggin* crap we'd been through, I couldn't help chuckling at the bot's crazy logic. "Aw, hell, Tin Man! All those damn rules were made for bots and people like 'em, not for fems like me."

As soon as I shifted thruster-power to max, the B'treeni ship lifted skyward, busting through the scan-net. Any brawns below who didn't have brains enough to get their butts as far as possible from a launching fast-ship probably'd been fried to a crisp.

"That red-hot lesson oughta teach those bloody bastards not to deal in slaves!"

The B'treeni ship's main engines kicked in with a vengeance, letting out an ear-splitting roar. In no time at all, she'd left Zan Siba far behind her, then the planet's outer atmosphere and gravity itself. We headed out into the cold, dark reaches of deep-space. I felt a whole helluva lot safer there.

At the co-pilot's station, Blackie looked up from monitoring our back-trail and began calmly inspecting his metal hide.

"You okay?" I asked him.

"I appear none the worse for wear, no thanks to the B'treeni," he said, "although I could, perhaps, use a bit of polishing once again." His black dome swiveled in my direction, and twin crystal lenses fastened on me meaningfully.

I ignored his less than subtle hint.

Several microseconds later, Blackie said, "Rand, I have been wondering *why* in the Cosmos you put your own life at risk in order to save me from a simple program-erasure."

Didn't feel like giving him an answer, so I concentrated real hard on the alien ship's instruments. The readouts seemed to be getting fuzzy. I rubbed my eyes. My head started to swim, as if I'd drunk way too much *hahk-teem*. Chalked all this up to the aftereffects of going into zero G, or to the running and fighting I'd done back in Zan Siba. Maybe I was feeling so damned odd because I'd gone so long without food and water.

Anyway, I finally came up with what I thought was a logical answer to the bot's nosey question. "Hell, Tin Man, I figured, as is, you still might be worth a few credits—that is, if we ever make it back to Milo's Planet."

Blackie seemed satisfied with that answer. He contented himself with monitoring the aft viewscreen, watching our wake for pursuers.

Suddenly, I noticed he was staring into space at nothing.

In a damned-odd voice he said, "Rand!"

"*Now* what in bloody-blue-blazes is the matter?" I demanded, annoyed with him yet again.

He pointed. A bunch of tiny red beads hung in midair above my head, slowly floating upward. The bot stretched out a long, silver-jointed arm and captured one on the tip of a black-metal finger.

He drew back his arm and studied the bead, then shot me a look of alarm. "*Blood!* Rand, you must have been wounded!"

"You sure, Tin Man?" Frantic, I felt my body, searching for signs of a wound. Nothing. Then I checked my limbs. My upper left arm was wet with blood. The broken stub of a B'treeni dart stuck outta my bare flesh! I stared in shock as more tiny beads of blood formed and drifted upward.

"*K'yoti* Hell!" I swore; my voice was no more'n a hoarse whisper. In all the ruckus back in Zan Siba, with my adrenaline pumping like crazy, I hadn't felt the least bit of pain—'til now!

I grimaced at the bot. "Just my damn luck, eh, Tin Man?"

Blackie unfastened his restraining straps a damn-sight faster than I thought he could. "Where is the emergency medical kit usually stowed aboard ship?" he demanded in a no-nonsense tone.

By that point, I was feeling really woozy. I jerked my head toward the overhead. "Check the starboard compartment, right behind the—right behind—"

Without waiting for me to spit out the rest, the bot launched himself to starboard. His long legs dangled behind him. I watched him catch one of the hand-loops attached to the bulkhead. With his free hand, he slid aside the storage compartment door and grabbed the med-kit. Then, head down, he propelled himself back toward the control console.

Blackie caught the pilot's headrest and rotated his body 'til it was in an upright position. He slipped his metal feet into a pair of foot-holds on the deck, so he wouldn't float off while he tended to me. In one helluva hurry, he opened the med-kit and began laying out supplies in midair.

As he worked, I kept one eye on the ship's aft monitor. There was an off chance Old Rat Eyes was enough of a lame-brain to send the old slave-ship after us. But I was pretty damned confident I could out-fly any ship he had—as long as I stayed conscious, that is.

Blackie picked up a shiny pair of med tweezers. With it, he pulled what was left of the B'treeni dart outta my arm. The pain made my eyes water. He pressed a damp med-pad tight against the still-bleeding puncture-wound. The sharp breath I drew made a hissing sound. Had to grit my teeth.

"Watch it, will ya, Tin Man! That smarts like hell!" I complained, feeling more than a little cranky.

"I sincerely apologize for causing you more pain, Rand; however, this procedure is an absolute necessity. I must staunch the bleeding and prevent infection from setting in."

The shock of discovering I'd been wounded was wearing off. I felt intense pain slowly creeping over my body and remembered something damned important, something I'd all but forgotten.

"Tin Man, Breego said—he said the B'treeni darts are *poisoned!* They're tipped with some kinda fatal nerve-toxin!"

Startling the crap outta me, Blackie exclaimed, *"Damn it all to Bloody Hell!"* He rummaged madly through the med-kit. Stuff floated off in all directions. "I *pray* that their medical kit stocks the B'treeni version of a universal antidote! Ah, yes! Here it is, I do believe."

"Swell," I murmured. By then, I really didn't give a fast-flying damn about much of anything 'cept my pain.

"Rand, I must administer a dose of this antidote, in hopes that it will counteract the toxin. The only drawback is that, since I do not read B'treeni, I have no idea how much of the antidote to administer!"

Without saying another word, he prepared a hypo-dose and shot it into the muscle of my right arm. Once that was done, he applied a dressing of sterile micro-gauze to the wound in my left arm. Even though I was no longer bleeding, he took his sweet time fussing over the bandage.

I mumbled a groggy question: "Who in hell taught you first-aid, Tin Man?"

"Now *that* is an eminently stupid query, if ever I heard one, Rand!" the bot snapped, suddenly getting mad at me.

He wrapped the stub of the broken B'treeni dart in the used med-pad and discarded both down the ship's trash chute. Then he cleaned the med-equipment, recovered and packed up the rest of the scattered med-gear. Finally, being his usual picky-neat self, he suctioned up the stray droplets of my blood still floating about the cabin. He stowed the med-kit back in the starboard compartment where it belonged, returned to the co-pilot's station, and strapped himself in.

I barely had strength to mumble, "Thanks a helluva lot, Tin Man." Had to admit I didn't *sound* one damn bit grateful. I flexed my bandaged arm and stifled a wince of pain. "Not sure I could've done such a good job, not all by my lonesome anyway."

"You are entirely welcome, Rand," the bot replied. Oddly enough, my surly tone hadn't put him off. "I am indeed grateful you were not more seriously injured, and even more grateful that the universal antidote was so fortuitously at hand. Robert Benton-Smythe never studied *advanced* lifesaving procedures."

"Uh, so tell me, Tin Man—why in hell d'you give a mine-rat's ass what happens t'me? I'm not really your master."

His voice was a helluva lot softer'n usual as he reminded me, "Had you not intervened on my behalf in that shockingly-primitive excuse for a laboratory back in Zan Siba, I would be nothing more than a mindless metal shell by now. And had Breego succeeded in carrying out his maniacal plans, for the remainder of my miserable existence, I would have been merely his slave, his plaything—his *pet*, if you will!"

I let out a groggy chuckle. "*Huh!* Maybe I'd like you better that way, Tin Man." Definitely felt as if I'd had way more *hahk-teem* than I could handle, which would be one bloody helluva lot!

"Very well, Rand, treat the matter lightly if you must, but I remain indebted to you for your heroic, selfless actions."

"No reason t'feel that way," I scoffed. "Can't very well sell *damaged* goods, now can I? Always act in my own self-interest. Haven't you smartened up to that hard, cold fact yet, Tin Man?"

"Evidently not," he said quietly.

A sudden wave of weakness hit me pretty damned hard. I realized I was about to lose consciousness. I panicked and fought like hell to stay awake and aware.

"*Tin Man!*"

"Relax, Rand; the universal antidote is simply beginning to take full effect. The best remedy now is sleep."

I felt cold metal fingers loosening my restraining straps. Once free, my whole body drifted upward, and I seemed to be floating in some kinda dream-state. Then a pair of strong arms wrapped around me, pulling me in.

Ever so gently, the bot was guiding me toward the B'treeni sleep-cocoons, which were attached to the overhead, forward, just like the ones aboard *Jammer*.

For the first time since I'd stumbled across the damn bot, I didn't bother arguing with him. I simply let myself relax in his metal arms. With a resigned sigh, I rested my head against his all-too-solid chest. No matter what in the Cosmos happened next, somehow or other, I knew he'd take damned-good care of me.

And right about that point, my whole *fleggin* world went as dark as the far corners of Hell on a cloudy day.

I slept, but I had bad dreams again.

This time, I was standing atop my favorite perch: a huge boulder jutting outta the flank of Mount Hope. I shaded my eyes with one hand to look out over the plain of Esperance. A shadow passed overhead. I looked up to see a big ship swoop past. Then I heard loud noises, explosions! On the plain far below, fires started to spring up, first one, then another and another. From my perch, they looked like wiggly, yellow-orange dots. But the fires were spreading faster'n Esperance's hot winds could blow them.

Terrified, I jumped down and ran for home, scrabbling through the foothills, stumbling over loose rocks, sliding on my butt down dusty slopes. When I hit the plain, I ran as fast as my stubby little legs could run. But hard as I ran, I wasn't gaining an inch of ground!

Suddenly, fire was all around me: I was trapped! The solid ring of flame wasn't gonna let me go. Thick, dark smoke poured down my throat, choking me. I started to cry; hot tears ran down cheeks black with smoke. I screamed for Mum and Dad, over and over again 'til my throat was raw.

No one answered.

I woke up, soaked in sweat and trembling from head to foot. Hadn't dreamed that godawful nightmare for several years now!

Thought I'd finally beaten it, but the monster trapped inside me'd just taken a long siesta. For what seemed like hours, I tossed and turned, fighting the B'treeni sleep-cocoon. At last I fell back into another restless sleep.

God only knows how long later I woke up. Found myself tangled in a B'treeni sleep-cocoon, feeling like a Cyrelian moth struggling to break free and stretch brand-new wings. I was still pretty damned groggy. I managed to pry my eyes open, but had one helluva time trying to focus them.

Soon as I could see straight, I took a look down at the B'treeni ship's control console. Found myself gazing into a familiar pair of crystal lenses. The damn bot'd taken over the pilot's station and was staring up at me.

"Ah, Rand! You are awake," he said. No mistaking the note of relief in his voice.

I wondered how the hell long I'd been sleeping, and how long *he'd* been sitting there, keeping an eye on me.

"How do you feel?" Blackie asked.

I knuckled my eyes, stretched, and let out a little groan. *"God-awful!* My left arm's throbbing. Hurts like hell. Aw, dammit! My other arm hurts, too! What in bloody-blue-blazes did you do to me, Tin Man?"

"You were feverish, Rand, so I decided to administer a second dose of the universal antidote, just to be on the safe side, as you would say."

"Great!" I grumbled. "So you went ahead and made me into a

bloody pincushion after all. Old Rat Eyes'd be happy as hell to hear that. Disappointed I didn't *die* on you, Tin Man?"

Too damn quietly for my liking, the bot said, "You know better than that, Galaxy."

I squirmed and shot him one of my darkest scowls. The *fleggin* nerve of the bot! Using my *given* name! Ah, well, actually, the name I'd given myself. "For God's-green-snake!" I snapped. "Don't you dare get all sloppy on me, Tin Man. Can't stand it. Not my style."

The bot swung the pilot's chair into its correct position. "I shall continue to pilot the ship, Rand, until you have recuperated sufficiently to resume its controls."

"I'm perfectly capable of that right—uhh!" The microsecond I moved, my damn head buzzed and threatened to rocket into orbit.

"Nonsense, Rand!" the bot scolded. "Use your head for something beyond mere decoration, will you? Take my advice and attempt to go back to sleep. Undoubtedly, sleep will speed your recovery, and as long as you remain disabled, I am permitted to pilot this vessel— *legally*."

Much as I wanted to argue with the stubborn bastard, I decided to take his advice. I closed my eyes and let out a groan. "Thanks, Sir Lance—ah, Lance something or other—?"

"—elot," the bot said, giving a little sigh.

"Yeah, thanks a lot, Tin Man. But what in bloody hell was that knight-guy's name? Can't remember at the moment. Don't go hitting any asteroids, y'hear me?"

I could feel myself already drifting back to sleep and didn't bother fighting it. Heard myself murmur some real dumb-ass thing like: "This ship's in damned good hands—even if they aren't human."

The next time I woke up, I felt a whole helluva lot more like my old self. The bot was still seated at the ship's controls and hadn't yet noticed I was awake, so I decided to stay put and turn the tables. For a while, I'd spy on *him*.

Blackie was running through the B'treeni ship's data banks, intent on the readout screen.

"Snooping *again*, Tin Man?" I asked, giving him a soft chuckle.

"Ah! You are awake once again, Rand. If you feel up to it—?" He swept one black metal arm toward the control console.

Took that as an invitation and disentangled myself, slowly and awkwardly, from the B'treeni sleep-cocoon. Once free, I launched myself toward the pilot's station. But the bot reached out, snagged me in midair, and gently guided me down into the co-pilot's station instead.

"Let us not rush your recovery, shall we, Rand? While you were sleeping, I came across some pertinent information I think may prove of considerable interest to you. In Galaxy-parlance, I believe you would term this particular data 'damned-odd.'"

"*Huh!* So what the hell'd you find out, Tin Man?"

"I discovered an inventory of the latest contents of this ship's hold."

"Must be all the stuff Breego just bought off Torrance."

"Acting upon what you most likely would term 'a hunch,' I ran that list against the data from Roman Aguilar's plastidisc. The list matches, almost gram for gram, the goods stolen during the most recent Remoxa hijacking. Only several of the more unique items are missing and are, no doubt, now in Breego's possession."

I double-checked the bot's findings, comparing the two lists of data side by side on the readout screen.

"*K'yoti* Hell! I'll be damned if you're not right, Tin Man! This cinches it beyond the shadow of a doubt. Torrance and his gang've been jacking Remoxa's shipments and selling the stuff to Old Rat Eyes!"

"Indeed, Rand. Breego, in turn, takes his personal pick of each shipment, then smuggles the remainder back to Milo's Planet, as well as to other colonies in this solar system. There, it is resold at a huge profit. A rather lucrative arrangement, I must say!"

"You can say that again, Tin Man!"

The bot cocked his shiny black dome to one side and gave me an odd look. "Rand, I fail to see the necessity of repeating myself, unless the B'treeni toxin has effected your hearing?"

Couldn't help rolling my eyes and giving him a lopsided grin. "Aw, forget it, Tin Man! That's just a damned old-fashioned figure of speech. It's—hang on a microsecond! *Where* in bloody hell did you get that data—I mean the info on the Remoxa jackings? The plasti-disc I got from Aguilar is still aboard *Jammer*!"

The bot looked mighty damned pleased with himself. "I committed the information to memory, 'just in case', as you would say. While you were sleeping, I downloaded the relevant data into this ship's data banks. Something else of great importance occurred to me, Rand: If *you* were able to deduce the whereabouts of Torrance and his gang, the ISF most assuredly *could* have done so—and *ought* to have done so long before this."

I shrugged off his theory. "*Huh!* Warned you the ISF was nothing but a pack of *fleggin* morons, didn't I?"

"Some of them, perhaps, but hardly all of them, Rand," the bot contradicted. "I am led to an inescapable conclusion: The highest authorities in the ISF have been paid quite handsomely to search for Torrance, but *not* to find him!"

"If you expect me to swallow that bucket of bilge, hook, line, and stinker, Tin Man, you gotta be *fleggin* crazy! A two-bit piece of space-scum like Torrance sure as hell doesn't have enough credits to pay off the ISF's higher-ups. That'd take millions! Breego's witch doctors must've fried your nano-circuits!"

"*Humph!* My brain is sufficiently intact to realize the word you mistakenly used should be 'sinker,' not 'stinker'!" the bot said with an uppity sigh; then insisted, "I am dead-serious, Rand. I suspect some unknown individual, quite powerful and extremely wealthy, is determined that Torrance remain free to continue his hijacking spree, unhindered."

"And why in the name of Unholy Hell would anybody in their right mind go that far to keep *Torrance* in business? He's just one lousy jacker! The galaxy's chock-fulla guys like him."

"You yourself said it, Rand: Hijacking is a lucrative profession."

Still not convinced Blackie's weird ideas were right, I shook my head. "Can't see one damn reason why the ISF would risk its *fleggin* reputation just to protect an operation like Torrance's."

"Unless his operation is considerably more profitable than it would at first appear," Blackie suggested slyly.

"I dunno how. That's one helluva load of speculation there, Tin Man."

"Speculation is the father of ideas, Rand," the bot said. "However, I possess further evidence, which perhaps might serve to convince you." He called up another list on the readout screen and pointed it out with one silver-jointed forefinger.

"This is a record of ISF activities for the past several planet-months. As you can clearly see, Rand, routine patrols were frequently diverted from their regular routes, often mere hours prior to hijackings. The ISF authorities offered multiple lame explanations for their unwise and unfortunate actions, excuses which ran the gamut from malfunctioning equipment to unproductive tips."

I stared at the screen, trying to take in the data. Couldn't believe my own damn eyes. Instantly suspicious, I demanded, "Tin Man, where in bloody-blue-blazes did you get this? *I* sure as hell never saw any of it before!"

"My master uncovered this incriminating information, shortly before his murder."

Shocked, I let out a gasp. "*K'yoti* Hell! You mean RBS managed to hack into the ISF's top-secret files? Stumbling across *this*—and having the gall to record it—must be what got him killed!"

"Most assuredly so."

"Then how in bloody hell did you get ahold of this info, Tin Man?"

"Robert Benton-Smythe programmed me with all the information he had accessed—data he thought necessary to implicate the ISF in the hijackings. In the event he were to be captured and imprisoned—or murdered—I was to avenge him and try to bring the culprits to justice. You might say I became his 'backup plan.'"

"Tin Man, this data *proves* the ISF's corrupt as hell! Every last bastard in the outfit must be in on this little scheme!"

"Not necessarily," the bot objected. "Rand, the ISF is an extremely close-knit organization and practices a strict no-questions-asked policy. Their agents are trained to do exactly as they are told. Mere loyalty, or simple obedience to the orders of superiors, may account for their actions, or lack thereof. But it is perfectly clear to me that whoever is responsible for corrupting the ISF has no fear whatsoever of being blackmailed."

"In other words, if I follow you, Tin Man, the payoffs were meant to be long-term arrangements. So long as the ISF's higher-ups play ball, they're set for bloody life," I grumbled, growing more and more indignant by the microsecond.

"True enough, *unless* someone in the organization should become greedy or suspicious or have a sudden attack of conscience. In that case, I am certain the individual in question would meet with an 'accident' of some sort. One must, therefore, question the deaths of the six ISF agents who were killed on duty within the past planet-year," the bot pointed out soberly.

I was outraged. "This whole *fleggin* mess makes me sick to my stomach! People in trouble are forced to rely on the ISF! Damn the bloody bastards to Hell and back!"

"Surprisingly, in this particular instance, Rand, one of your notorious hunches did indeed prove correct: The ISF is *not* to be trusted and, in all likelihood, has not been completely trustworthy for a good many years past."

I wondered out loud, "Twenty-two years past?" Couldn't keep bitterness from creeping into my voice. "The ISF never managed to pin the Esperance Massacre on anyone, did they? At least, not on one damn soul who was still alive!"

The bot went on, "Another burning question must then be asked: Was the ISF legitimately *unable* to establish guilt, or were they *unwilling* to do so?"

That question made me even more thoughtful. "You mean the ISF might've known damned good and well who was behind the Massacre? Tin Man, I spent ten miserable years of my life at my uncle's place—*ten years!*—with the ISF knowing exactly where I was! *K'yoti* Hell! Those *fleggin* bastards could've taken me out anytime they wanted to. So why in bloody hell didn't they?"

The bot seemed stumped. He shook his metal head in an all too human way—the way I supposed Robert Benton-Smythe once had. "After your rescue from Esperance, ISF investigators must have grilled you at some length. Were you able to provide them with any useful information?"

"Not one damn thing! During the Massacre, I was off playing all by myself up in the foothills. I was too damned far away to see much of anything. All I saw was a ship overhead and the fires the murdering bastards set!"

"Rand, undoubtedly, the sole reason you are still alive is the fact that you *did* see nothing. But as I can well imagine, since your disappearance, the mastermind behind the Massacre has been searching diligently for you. He—or she—must be absolutely petrified. Suppose the lone survivor of the Esperance Massacre should suddenly recall a vital piece of information, even at this late date!"

I snorted and muttered in a sullen tone, "A helluva lot more'n my name's changed since the Massacre, Tin Man."

"However, your DNA has not, Rand, nor have your fingerprints," the bot pointed out sternly. "Should a concerted effort be made to locate you—!"

That all too grim thought rocked me back on my heels. "What can I do about it? Sure as hell can't go to the ISF for protection, and what law there is hereabouts is bloody well useless. So's Surety Galactic, for that matter." I heaved a disgusted sigh.

After he'd thought over the situation for a few microseconds, the bot said, "I perceive one definitive method of delving further into this case, in hopes of finally solving it and bringing the guilty party, or parties, to justice."

"And that is—?"

"I must break into ISF Headquarters, access their covert data files, and, ah—snoop."

I nearly choked, unable to believe the dumb-ass idea Blackie'd come up with. "Are you outta your tin-plated skull, Tin Man? ISF Headquarters has state-of-the-art protection: round-the-clock surveillance, internal and external barriers, hacker-screens, passwords, codes, encryptions, armed-guards—you name it, pal, they've got it!"

"Rand, you seem to be forgetting one thing: Until his recent murder, Robert Benton-Smythe was *employed* by the ISF. He was engaged in biomechanical-design and robotics-engineering; these projects were conducted in top-secret laboratories at ISF Headquarters. Therefore, he held the highest security clearance possible. In the aftermath of his untimely death, the ISF may very well have neglected to invalidate that clearance. Under the usual circumstances, a dead man poses no security risk whatsoever. Am I not correct?"

"Aren't you forgetting something, Tin Man? You're *not* RBS! You're a *bot*!" I reminded him sharply. "And a bot can't just stroll into ISF HQ without creating one helluva ruckus! You'd be caught for damn sure. And the microsecond those *fleggin* bastards connect you with RBS, they won't hesitate to take you out—for good!"

"Perhaps, if I were to conceal myself in some type of disguise, I might be able to gain entrance to the robotics laboratory without being detected. Once inside, with RBS's clearance, I could safely access their computers. And it so happens, Rand, in the course of exploring the B'treeni ship, I discovered some items of clothing in the crew's quarters."

That bit of news brightened my mood a helluva lot. "You don't say? Stay here at the controls, then, Tin Man, and keep a sharp eye on things. I'm going amidships. I'm dying to get outta these duds; they're bloody uncomfortable. Besides, I can't set foot outta the ship dressed in this damn-skimpy outfit. I'd attract way too much unwanted attention. And *you* sure as hell aren't going anywhere, especially without me, y'hear that, pal!"

"But, Rand—!" the bot started to protest.

Not about to stop long enough to listen to any more of his bilge, I released my restraining straps and launched myself toward the cabin's hatchway. I floated out into the main corridor and headed amidships.

In the crew's quarters, I found the clothes the bot'd told me about. Picked out a halfway-clean outfit closest to my size and changed in a hurry.

Didn't care for the *fleggin* crazy plan the bot'd come up with, not one damned bit! I knew better'n to mess around with the ISF, especially not on their own turf! That was begging for trouble, a whole freighter-load of trouble! Too bloody much could go wrong, and I was already smack on the top of the ISF's least popular list.

Dressed in a guy's long-sleeved red tunic and a pair of black pants that were a wee bit too short for my long legs, I launched myself back toward the cabin. Now that I felt more comfortable, I couldn't wait to resume the controls.

The microsecond the bot got a look at me, his head snapped up.

"*Now what?*" I growled. Felt my face flushing to match the color of my shirt. "You got some snarky comment about these duds?"

The bot slowly shook his metal dome. "No, not at all, Rand—that is, if I am correctly interpreting the word 'snarky.'"

We swapped places, and this time he didn't object. I strapped myself into the pilot's seat, then adjusted our course. Wasn't exactly easy; the *fleggin* B'treeni navcomp was badly outdated.

Making his suspicions all too plain, Blackie asked, "And what, may I ask, is our present heading?"

I snapped, "If you must know, Tin Man, we're headed back to Esperance. Got a problem with that?"

To my surprise, Blackie protested indignantly, "Good Lord, Rand! Have you learned no lesson whatsoever from our recent misadventures?"

I gave him the slightest shrug of one shoulder. "Have t'get *Jammer* back before I do another damn thing. She's my ship. I'm not about to abandon her to the likes of Torrance and his *fleggin* gang!"

"Galaxy, for God's sake stop and think this over! Is any vessel in the entire universe worth the risk of your life?"

"Yes, dammit!" I roared. "We've been through a helluva lot together, *Jammer* and me. I depend on her!"

"*Humph!* I must say your priorities leave much to be desired!"

"Wouldn't expect a damn bot to understand how I feel about *Jammer!* She's all I've got, Tin Man. Hell, she's not just transport—she's *home!*"

"I do understand your feelings of attachment, Rand; however, *you* are of infinitely more importance than any ship!" Blackie said stoutly.

I flashed him an annoyed glare, hoping he'd get my less than subtle hint and be smart enough to shut the hell up. "Thought I told you not to go getting all sloppy on me, Tin Man. Got no damn use for sentiment. Space that bilge, y'hear me!"

The bot made that sighing sound again, pushed the co-pilot's chair back as far as it'd go, and stared up at the overhead. "Very well, then—suit yourself, Rand. First, we will attempt to recover *Jammer.* Second, with a great deal of regret and genuine sorrow, I will bury your dead body somewhere on the barren plains of Esperance. Then will you be satisfied?"

I glared daggers at him. "Nobody said *you* had go with me, pal! I'll swing by Milo's and drop you off. I'm a big girl now. I can handle this whole *fleggin* mess all by my lonesome. Sure as hell don't need *you*!"

The bot sat bolt-upright and turned to look me square in the face. "Rand, I am *begging* you to reconsider this course of action, before you get yourself killed! By now, Torrance may very well have hidden, disabled, destroyed, or even sold *Jammer*. Doubtless, he has discovered the fissure we used to gain entrance to Mount Hope and has either sealed it off or placed it under guard.

"In addition, our friend Breego most likely has informed Torrance of our escape. Consequently, the latter may very well be expecting us to return to Esperance. Have you forgotten the dire fate Torrance originally had in mind for you?"

"*Huh!* How could I forget? But I sure as hell don't need you to nursemaid me, pal. I can manage on my own. I'll be fine," I declared stubbornly.

"If you insist upon pursuing this reckless course, I intend to insure that you are fine and *remain* so!" the bot said, being his usual damned stubborn self.

I rubbed my aching forehead. "*K'yoti* Hell! You're enough to make a plaster saint swear and take up drinking!"

After that snarky remark, the bot kept his mouth shut. Should've known he was thinking up something I wouldn't like.

"Very well, then," he said at long last, "Apparently, you remain adamant and determined to pursue this extremely foolish and dangerous course of action. My presence will undoubtedly increase the odds in your favor; however, if we are to have the slightest hope of successfully carrying out this impossible mission, we will require *outside* assistance. And that fact is not open to debate!"

I rolled my eyes and swore a colorful stream under my breath. But much as I hated to admit the bloody bot was right, he *was*! I wasn't in topnotch condition, not with a wounded arm. Even with the bot's help, I might not be able to handle whatever came up. And getting *Jammer* back was way too damned important to risk failing.

Knowing I was beaten, I sighed. "Okay, you win this round, Tin Man. We'll go back to Milo's and see if we can rustle up some help. Then we'll head straight back to Esperance, recover *Jammer*, and nab Torrance—if that plan suits you?"

This time the bot didn't object, so once again I corrected our course on the B'treeni navcomp. Still wasn't one hundred percent sure I was making the right decision, but I sat back and started brainstorming.

Who in the name of Unholy Hell'd be stupid enough, greedy enough, or *fleggin*-crazy enough to be talked into helping me out? I had damned few credits left, nowhere near enough to pay for the kinda help I needed. The job ahead was beginning to look bloody hopeless!

The microsecond the B'treeni ship I'd, ah, "borrowed" drew within comm range of Milo's Planet, I sent out a direct call to Surety Galactic Insurance. Asked to speak with Krol Kramer. When his stiff-as-a-board image appeared on the commscreen, I wasn't exactly filled with a shipload of confidence.

"Kramer."

"If I may ask, Rand, where the ruddy hell have you been?" he demanded. "Larking about, carefree, through the entire solar system, or did you simply decide to remain incommunicado?" His fancy feathers were all in a huff before I had a chance to explain myself.

"Er, well, it's a damned long story, Kramer. The upshot is, I managed to locate Torrance and his gang."

"Did you indeed?" Kramer said with a sniff.

"Yeah, but in the process I sorta lost my ship. Need a little help getting her back and rounding up the jackers."

Kramer raised one elegant eyebrow. "I certainly hope you don't expect *my* assistance in accomplishing either of those risky endeavors."

"Ah, well, yeah. Not you personally, of course. Just thought maybe Surety'd—"

Kramer let out a delicate snort. "Rand, when it comes to getting into untenable predicaments, you're positively expert. It's your own responsibility to extricate yourself, not mine and not Surety's."

"But, Kramer, I've got proof-positive Torrance's behind the Remoxa jackings. Isn't *that* worth something to Surety? And to Mr. High-and-mighty Roman Aguilar?"

"Only if you succeed in capturing Torrance and his entire gang, thus bringing about a halt, once and for all, to their hijacking spree. Then I'm sure Mr. Aguilar would show his appreciation, at least in a monetary fashion."

"But you won't lift so much as a *fleggin* finger to help me out, eh, Kramer? Hoping I'll get myself *killed*, so you can mop up after me and claim the five-mil for yourself?"

Kramer gave an extra loud sniff. "Claiming rewards is not my business, Rand; however, recouping is *yours*! I'm certain you can manage on your own. You pride yourself on that, don't you?"

I protested, "But this time, it's gonna be a whole helluva lot harder, Kramer. Thought you might be just a tad more helpful— and more grateful!"

"Apparently, Rand, your thought process is radically flawed," Kramer said. The edge to his voice told me he was done talking.

I glared my worst at the prissy image on the screen and swore under my breath. At that point, I didn't give a fast-flying damn whether or not Krol Kramer heard me. He was in luck; from this distance, all I could do was swear at the ungrateful son-of-a-bitch!

"Thanks a helluva lot! Your concern's touching. See you in Hell, Kramer!"

I blanked out the viewscreen before I put my *fleggin* fist through it. "Damn his hide!"

"Well! I must say your friend Kramer was no help whatsoever," the bot observed. "What is our next step, Rand?"

Still fuming, I leaned back in the pilot's chair and brooded in silence, doing my damnedest to cool down my jets so I could think straight. Outta the blue, a good-looking face on a holo-badge flashed to mind.

I repeated the name on the badge aloud: "*Jeffries!*"

Startled, the bot said, "I beg your pardon, Rand?"

"Just thinking out loud, Tin Man. But I think I might have our guy!"

Using the B'treeni version of a comm-link again, I composed a secure vid-message and addressed it to Armando Jeffries, Inspector Second Class. Sent it to ISF HQ.

Located subject in question. Willing to split Aguilar's reward fifty-fifty in exchange for your help. Still want in? Meet me tonight at The Black Hole, Habeeb's Outpost, twenty-three hundred hours. Come alone or the damn deal's off.

I sent out the message and sat back to wait for a reply.

If I'd read the guy right, Jeffries couldn't resist that offer. I was betting the greedy bastard would swallow the bait whole! And if he wanted his cut of the five-mil as bad as I thought he did, he wouldn't want to share it with any of his ISF buddies.

"That oughta interest him," I told the bot, chuckling smugly at my own savvy.

"Do you think we can really trust this Jeffries person?" Blackie asked. "After all, he is an ISF agent."

I shook my head. "We need Jeffries, but *trust* him? Hell, no! Just using him. He's stupid enough and greedy enough for me to control, even over the orders of his *fleggin* superiors."

We headed back to Milo's Planet. Blackie sat as lifeless as a lump of spectromium, staring straight ahead without saying one damn word to me, like he does when he's worried about something. Wished to bloody hell I knew what he was thinking, but it's a whole helluva lot harder to read a bot than a human and that's for damned sure.

When the ship reached Milo's Planet, just to play it safe, I decided to berth her at one of the space stations. I figured the bastards who were hunting for me weren't likely to connect me with the B'treeni ship. Plenty of "B'treeni" passed through Kaswali City, but it was pretty damned odd to see any in the outposts. Might raise suspicions if I were to land the ship on-planet.

Once the ship was safely docked and within the station's artificial-gravity field, I left the bot in the cabin to keep an eye on things. Going to the crew's quarters, amidships, I flopped down on one of the bunks to grab a quick nap before my late-night meeting with Jeffries.

When I woke up from my catnap, the damn bot was missing. He wasn't in the cabin; he wasn't in the crew's quarters. He sure didn't need to use the head, so where in bloody hell had he gone?

The answer suddenly dawned on me, as bright as a bolt of desert lightning in a sandstorm! He'd gone to break into ISF Headquarters!

Why the flegg *didn't the damn idiot at least* wait *for me?* I wondered. Grimly, I shoved the blaster I'd come by in Zan Siba into my waist-band and pulled the red shirt down to hide the weapon. Deep in my gut, I knew the answer to my own question, but didn't want to stop and think about it.

If Blackie were caught breaking into ISF Headquarters or tampering with their computer system—!

A cold shiver of dread ran through my whole body. The bastards'd probably lock him up, interrogate him, then deactivate him. And sure as Hell's hot, whoever'd ordered RBS's murder wouldn't so much as flinch at demolishing a bot!

If the ISF caught *me* breaking in—hell, that'd be a completely different story, but I knew damned good and-well I wouldn't like *that* ending one bit better. My chances of seeing free space again would be next-to-nothing. Probably'd find myself locked in stasis for the next three or four hundred years, either that or left to rot on some godawful penal planet out in the hind-end of space.

The ISF didn't exactly like me to begin with. Recoups competed with their 'gents, did some jobs they couldn't, or wouldn't, do. Recoups often made them look bad; truth be told, that really didn't take a whole helluva lot of doing.

I kicked myself mentally for going to sleep without taking better security measures. I cursed myself as I headed for the B'treeni ship's ramp. Why hadn't I kept a closer eye on the damn bot, especially after he'd come up with that hare-brained scheme to break into ISF HQ? Should've realized the tin-plated know-it-all would pull a dumb-ass stunt like this.

Outta the blue, it hit me like a brick smack in the face: I was *worried* about the bot, damn his metal hide to Hell and straight back again! Me! Worried about *him*! I let out a snort of disgust.

Still, we'd come this far by sticking together. Both of us were searching for answers, maybe not the same answers, but massacre and murder were in the same general sector.

No telling how long ago the bloody bot'd left the ship. In one helluva hurry, I lowered the ramp and ran full tilt down it and into the station. I raced across the berthing foyer of that level. Ignoring the move-walk as too damned slow, I charged through one of the transparent tubes leading into the station's central shaft.

At the tube's far end, I ran smack-dab into the bot.

In surprise, he demanded, "Rand! Where are you going in such a hurry?"

Panting for breath, I managed to gasp, "*K'yoti* Hell! I was looking—for *you*! Where in bloody-blue-blazes—have you been, Tin Man?"

He showed me the foil-wrapped package in his silver-jointed hand. "I went into the station proper in order to purchase food for you. If you expect to recuperate fully, Rand, you must eat something much more nutritious than space-rations."

I gave him a blank stare. "You went—to buy *me*—food?"

"Indeed I did. Why in the Cosmos do you appear to be so upset?"

"Upset? *Huh!* I was worried outta my damn mind! I looked for you everywhere, Tin Man. What's the big idea of leaving the *fleggin* ship without telling me where the hell you were going?" I demanded, my voice and my temper both rising.

The bot deflated. "I apologize for neglecting to do so, Rand. But why on Earth are you—? Oh! Am I mistaken, or were you under the impression I was on my way to ISF Headquarters, as I previously suggested? Is that the true reason you are upset with me?"

Damned furious, I whirled and stalked back to the B'treeni ship in sheer disgust, fuming all the way. I heard the bot's heavy footsteps behind me.

"The next time you decide to jump ship, pal, at least have the *fleggin* decency *to tell me first!*" I roared, without turning around to face him.

"But, Rand, I assure you, I had no intention whatsoever of 'jumping ship,' as you say. I was returning, was I not? I simply thought—"

Seething, I spun on my heel to confront him. "You *thought*? No, you sure as bloody hell didn't think! Look, pal, from here on out let *me* do the thinking. Of all the dumb-ass stunts you could've pulled—!"

I stomped up the ship's ramp and forward into the cabin. I threw myself into the pilot's seat, crossed my arms on my chest, and fumed in silence.

A few microseconds later, the bot came in and apologized again. "I *am* sorry, Rand. I failed to realize how much my temporary absence would upset you. Had I realized, I would have waited until you awoke before setting out upon my errand."

He gently placed the food packet on the console in front of me. Had to admit the packet smelled pretty damned good. I was starving, but I just sat there, glaring and stubbornly ignoring it.

"You should eat," the bot said, nudging me gently, "while your food is still warm."

"Not hungry!"

"I rather doubt that to be true." Blackie took his usual seat at the co-pilot's station. For a bit, he had enough smarts to keep his damn mouth shut, then he said, "While you were napping, Rand, I experienced a strange phenomenon. I believe you might term it 'a hunch.'"

I snapped, "Oh, really? Thought you didn't trust hunches, or is it only *my* hunches you don't trust, pal?"

He ignored my snit. "You once mentioned the Mines Bureau, in reference to Esperance. After repeated attempts, I succeeded in accessing the restricted data in their archives."

"You *hacked* their files?"

"Basically—yes, I did."

Damned and determined not to give in to my curiosity for once, I tried to ignore the bloody bot. Several microseconds passed, but I finally couldn't resist the urge to ask, "So what'd you find out? Anything interesting?"

"Indeed! I began my search with the original holder of the mining rights to Esperance, then attempted to trace that ownership to the present holder: a company calling itself Omega Mining

Enterprises. Following the twenty-two-year-long trail proved to be an extremely difficult task, almost impossible, in fact. Apparently, every subsequent owner of those rights did everything within its power to falsify or obscure the title data. Over the ensuing years, the rights were sold, resold, assigned, or transferred an astonishing number of times. That, as you can imagine, created quite an intricate puzzle. I rather enjoyed the challenge."

I was immediately hooked. "That's mighty damned odd, Tin Man! What in bloody hell were all those companies trying to hide? Or were they simply afraid of being linked to the Esperance Massacre? If I remember right, an outfit called Alpha Mines, Incorporated, wangled the mining rights outta the heirs of the murdered colonists. Including my *fleggin* Uncle Clive!"

"Your memory is indeed accurate, Rand," the bot said. "During the course of my investigation, I came across a record dated two years *prior* to the Massacre. Said record named the registered owner of the newly-incorporated Alpha Mines as one A. Aguilar."

My ears perked up. "Aguilar? As in *Roman* Aguilar?"

"Not quite, Rand. After doing more research and enlisting other sources, I discovered a reference to Roman Aguilar's grandfather, whose name happened to be Agamemnon Aguilar."

"*K'yoti* Hell! Aguilar's *grandfather* owned Alpha Mines? Was he the *fleggin* bastard who bought up the mining rights to Esperance after the Massacre?"

"It would appear so, Rand. And since then, every entity involved has taken extraordinary pains to keep that fact out of the records— as well as from the general public."

"*Hmmm!* Aguilar claims his parents were lowly asteroid miners. Never said one damn word about his family owning a mining company!"

Absently, I reached for the food packet; it was still warm. I picked it up, unwrapped it, and took a bite of the sandwich inside.

I chewed thoughtfully, swallowed, and said, "*K'yoti* Hell! This's a damned peculiar development, Tin Man—one I sure as hell never suspected. So Roman Aguilar's family scooped up the first mining rights to Esperance. Mighty suspicious!"

12 Jeffries

At twenty-three hundred hours on the dot, I stepped inside The Black Hole. Right off the bat, my "uh-oh" sense kicked in. At that hour the bar was usually standing room only. Tonight, it was only half-full, if that.

Spotted Jeffries seated at a table tucked into the darkest corner. As I made my way over to join him, I gave the bar a quick scan, hoping to hell I'd see J'neen.

But there was no sight or sound of her. I felt sick to my damn stomach.

Figured I wouldn't find her here, but you know that old saying about hoping for Spring eternal, or something like that. If J'neen *had* sold me out to Torrance, sure as hell she'd already got what she deserved. And if J'neen *hadn't* sold me out—aw, dammit!—I didn't even want to think about what that *fleggin* piece of rotten space-scum had done to her!

I'd left the bot outside to watch my back. Figured I wouldn't be in too much danger inside; I could handle Jeffries. Casually, I lowered myself into an empty chair at his table. Sat side-to him with my back to the wall, so I could keep one eye on the door and one eye on him.

"Jeffries," I said. Slowly, carefully, I spread both hands out on the none too clean tabletop to show him they were empty.

I saw him relax his guard. He flashed me a grin and raised a half-empty glass of booze in a snarky salute. "Rand. *Hahk-teem*'s your usual poison, right? On me."

I eyed him suspiciously, but gave him a quick nod. He tapped out the order on the serving disk set into the center of the grungy table. When the disk rose, Jeffries dropped a cred chip into the payment slot and grabbed the drink sitting underneath. Holding the glass between two fingers, he passed it to me, then took a slug from his own glass and eyeballed me over its rim.

I raised the glass to my lips and pretended to take a sip of *hahk-teem*. Wasn't stupid enough to actually swallow any of the powerful stuff, even if Jeffries hadn't drugged it. Something warned me to keep my *fleggin* wits about me 'cause I was gonna need every last one of 'em.

Jeffries set down his glass, folded his arms on the tabletop, and leaned toward me. "So where's Torrance hiding out?" he asked, keeping his voice low so it wouldn't carry to the bar's sleazy patrons. Without giving me a chance to answer, he said, "Let me take a good guess: Esperance?"

That caught me off guard. I leaned back in my chair and stared at him with a shocked look on my face. *I'll be damned! The bot was right: The ISF knows exactly where Torrance's holed up.*

"How in bloody hell'd you figure *that*?" I demanded, more suspicious of Jeffries now than ever.

He shrugged, but his blue eyes twinkled. The bloody bastard enjoyed being one jump ahead of me!

"Esperance is a pretty good-sized planet," I pointed out. "Has one helluva lot of great places to hide out, y'know?"

"But you managed to find Torrance?"

"I did."

"Where exactly?"

I shook my head and gave Jeffries a mighty cold smile. "I'll *take* you to him, pal, but I won't *tell* you where t'find him. Hell, no! I'm not that much of a dumb-ass to risk losing my half of the reward. Besides, it's a damned sight easier to show you where he is than tell you."

"Not really." Jeffries' own smile turned bitter; he looked as if he'd just swallowed a mouthful of some really bad *hahk-teem* and was trying his damnedest to pretend he could handle it. "Still don't trust me, eh, Rand?"

"Should I?"

As if I'd waved a wand in his face, his phony smile disappeared. His eyes got colder'n space on a Winter's day. He sat back in his chair, puffed out his chest, and flexed his muscles. Knew he wanted nothing more'n to challenge me to a fist-fight then and there.

"I'm an ISF agent. Remember, sister?"

"My point exactly! Ego as damned big as the planets Jupiter and Euphrates put together, not to mention all the morals of a *kareeb* in heat. Hell, I wouldn't put it past you to ditch me out in the boon-docks of Esperance and take all the credit for capturing Torrance."

Jeffries made a lousy attempt to look innocent. "Not me, Rand!" he protested. "I wouldn't stab you in the back like that. This deal's strictly on the up and up!"

I pretended to believe him. "Okay, pal, I'm willing to take my chances and split the five-mil with you—but nobody else, y'hear? We leave right this microsecond, just you and me. I'm not stupid enough to give you a chance to share this info."

Jeffries didn't look one damned bit pleased.

"So? Are you in or out?" I demanded, in no mood to waste time trading barbs with an egotistical idiot like him. *Wow! A good five-syllable word!* I thought. Wished I could brag to the damn bot about that one.

Jeffries gritted his teeth and gave me a sullen stare across the table. "All right, have it your own way, Rand. I'm in. Let's go get this the hell over with." He downed the last of his booze in one gulp and got to his feet. The dark scowl pasted on his pretty-boy face left no doubt about his opinion of me.

I got to my own feet and looked him square in the baby-blues. "You bet we do this my way, pal, or we don't do it at all. Got that?"

"I don't appreciate your brand of sass, sister, but under the cir-cumstances, I don't have a hell of a lot of choice, do I? We'll do things your way—unless you *flegg* up. Then I'll take over. Agreed?"

I glared at Jeffries. My fists clenched all on their own. "I won't *flegg* up! See to it that you don't," I warned him. Pretended to take one last swig of my *hahk-teem* without downing a single drop, then licked my lips with longing and followed him outta the bar. That's my standard practice; I never let anyone carrying a blaster walk *behind* me, doesn't matter if it's friend or foe!

Once we hit the street outside The Black Hole, I told Jeffries, "We use my ship, make no stops along the way and no calls. There's, ah, only one slight problem, pal—something I need to warn you about."

"What's that?" he asked, giving me a thunder-cloud scowl.

"Some *fleggin* bastard put a price on my head. On our way up to the space station where my ship's parked, both of us could get smoked."

Jeffries gave me a damned-nasty grin. "Peachy! So I'm not the only one in this solar system who hates your *fleggin* guts, eh, Rand?"

"Yeah, I'm real popular."

I whistled to signal the bot. The microsecond Blackie stepped outta the shadows and into the light of the gas orbs, Jeffries jumped an Akadran mile. His right hand flew to the butt of his blaster.

Before he could draw on the bot, I said, "Relax, pal! He's with me." Couldn't help chuckling at the stunned expression that'd come over the ISF 'gent's face.

In a hoarse voice, Jeffries demanded, "Where in hell did you get *that bot?*" In the orb-light his face was dead-white. He stared at Blackie, as if he'd come face to face with a ghost.

To needle Jeffries, I played dumb. "That bot?" I asked, innocent as all get-out.

Jeffries growled, "Yeah, *that* bot! You see another bot anywhere around here? It looks a hell of a lot like one of our prototypes, a robotic agent we're working on."

"*Robotic agent?*" I repeated, shocked to hear that coming outta Jeffries's mouth. Then I tried to shrug away my reaction. "*Huh!* That so? This bot's only salvage I managed to repair."

"If you ask me, it looks in damn good shape for junk," Jeffries drawled. He eyed the bot, making his suspicions all too obvious.

"Well, uh, he was a little the worse for wear, but I polished him up a bit."

Jeffries sneered, "You, Rand? Can't picture *you* polishing a damn bot." He gave me a real snarky laugh.

"Yeah, *me*! Always have had a way with mechanicals, y'know?"

"Ships maybe," Jeffries allowed, raising one blond eyebrow.

"Bots? Didn't think robots were your area of expertise, Rand. Sure you didn't *hijack* this one somewhere?"

"He's mine by right of salvage, pal, fair and square!"

"After we wrap up this operation, the ISF might be interested in finding out *exactly* how you came by him—it."

"Haven't got one damn thing to hide, Jeffries, but I don't appreciate a jackass like you accusing me of doing something wrong when I didn't."

"Nobody's accusing you of anything, sister. I'm just curious, that's all. One damn-fine piece of workmanship, that bot."

Jeffries was acting nervous as hell. He kept a real close eye on Blackie. As for the bot, he stood stock-still, not saying a word. Wasn't like him to be shy or quiet.

"Whereabouts did you say you picked up this bot?" Jeffries asked, getting a tad too nosey for my liking. "Was it here on Milo's?"

"Didn't say. None of your damn business where I came across him!"

Jeffries snarled, "It's the ISF's business!"

I took that as a threat. "Look here, pal, like I told you, I stumbled across the bot during my travels. Figured he might be worth a few lousy credits. That's my *only* interest in him."

My "uh-oh" sense started to tingle again. I took a quick look around us. "Uh, Jeffries, we make great targets standing out here in the open, jabbering away like a pair of *fleggin* idiots. We need to get our butts up to the station—the sooner, the better!—before we end up getting smoked."

Without so much as a shred of protest, he heeded my warning. We started toward the local transport station. Broke out in a grin when I saw how careful he was to keep a good distance from both me and the bot. Jeffries might be a dumb-ass, but he was smart enough to realize being anywhere near me could be damned dangerous—maybe even fatal.

The walk back was a long one. The whole way I kept my eye peeled for signs of trouble and was surprised as hell when we didn't run into any. The three of us took the next scheduled shuttle up to the space station.

The shuttle docked on the outermost ring of the station. We disembarked and took a lift down to the sixth level, where I'd berthed the old B'treeni trader. She was parked in her slip, right where I'd left her. The bot climbed aboard first to make damned-sure no one had come visiting while we were gone. Once Blackie cleared the ship, Jeffries and I started up her loading ramp. As long as we stayed docked, attached to the berth by a flexible umbilical-tube, the ship would be within the station's artificial-gravity field.

When Jeffries got a load of the old ship's battered side, all that was visible of her while she was in dock, he made no effort to hide his disgust. "This beaten up excuse for a ship's yours, Rand? *Hah!*"

"Right at the moment, she happens to be all the transport I got, pal," I growled.

I raised the ramp and pushed my way past Jeffries. Stalked straight into the control cabin and strapped myself into the pilot's seat. The bot was already seated at the co-pilot's station.

Soon as Jeffries saw that arrangement, he bristled. "*What the hell's this?* Don't tell me the damn bot's your partner, Rand? Hell, a bot can't fly a ship! It's illegal. He's a *fleggin* machine!"

"So? What of it? But get the dumb-ass notion he's my partner right outta your head, pal. I don't need a partner, never have, never will!"

Jeffries shook his head, shooting dark looks at me and coming to a slow boil. "After this action's over, sister, you'll have to answer one hell of a list of questions at ISF HQ."

"Great! Nothing in the galaxy I like better'n a little chit-chat with my friendly, neighborhood ISF 'gents. Now, if you don't mind, pal, I have to get off this bloody station before some *other* dumb-ass up here starts getting too nosey for his own damn good."

I jerked a thumb aft, toward the main corridor right behind him. "It's getting late, and we've got a damned long way to go. Might as well grab a bunk back in the crew's quarters, strap yourself in, and try to get some sleep. You can come forward again when you wake up, if you really want to."

Jeffries snorted. "Wouldn't want me to get exhausted, huh? That'd just about break your heart, eh, Rand?" Swearing and grumbling under his breath, he headed aft, madder'n hell. Heard one of the hatches amidships slam shut.

Now that Jeffries was outta earshot, I hissed to the bot through clenched teeth, *"Did you hear what he said?"*

"Of course! I heard every word, Rand. My hearing is extremely acute."

"Then, for once in your sorry so-called-life, Tin Man, tell me the God's honest truth. Are you a robotic ISF agent?"

Blackie looked me straight in the eye. The focus of his twin crystal lenses didn't waver a fraction of a centimeter. "I suppose that, technically speaking, I could be regarded as such."

My scalp crinkled. Every hair on my damn head stood at attention. I gasped, *"K'yoti* Hell! Why didn't you tell me the truth *sooner?"*

"I assumed you realized the purpose for which I was originally designed and constructed."

I clapped one hand to my throbbing forehead and let out a string of the most colorful cusswords I could come up with. Furious as hell, I spluttered, "Do you want the *fleggin* ISF to pick me up on charges of stealing their property?"

"Of course not, Rand. I simply failed to realize my origins might present a problem for you."

I let out a loud groan. "Let me tell you something, pal, we're *both* gonna have one helluva problem if the ISF investigates your 'origins!' They might very well claim you as their rightful property!"

"Strictly speaking, Rand, I do not, legally, belong to the ISF," Blackie protested. "RBS01, as you refer to my late master, developed, designed, and constructed me entirely on his own time, employing his own resources. Consequently, I am—or at least I *was*—the sole property of Robert Benton-Smythe. And unlike the prototypes he was developing for the ISF, I am unique."

I demanded, "Could the ISF connect you with their robotics program?"

"I most certainly hope not, but that might prove possible."

"Wish to bloody hell you'd told me there might be a problem with the ISF *before* I involved Jeffries in this little outing! The guy's rumored to be damned-good at sniffing out mine-rats, even though he is an ISF 'gent. And he'd gladly sell his grandmother for spare parts just to get something on me."

I let out an exasperated sigh. "Something tells me, supposing I actually live through this *fleggin* disaster, I'm gonna have a helluva lot of nosey questions to answer."

No help for it now! I told myself grimly. Aloud, I said, "Okay, Tin Man, let's get our butts off the station and clear of this damn-blasted planet before anything *else* can go wrong."

I contacted station-control, requested and received clearance to depart. The B'treeni ship left berth. She wasn't anywhere near as responsive, or as fast, as *Jammer*, but she'd have to do. I programmed the navcomp with our new heading and set course back to Esperance.

The damned-annoying, pain-in-the-ass bot sat totally silent. I figured he was mad at me for some reason or other and giving me the silent treatment, as usual. Then, outta the clear-blue, he asked, "Rand, do you consider him good-looking?"

"Who?"

"This ISF agent—this Jeffries."

I shrugged. "Suppose so. Hadn't really given it much thought. Why?"

"I am simply curious. If my understanding is correct, human females place a high priority upon a male's outward appearance, do they not?"

"Yeah, some do, I guess."

"Do you, Rand?"

I chuckled at the question. Pretty damned odd coming from a bot! "Ever hear the ancient saying 'never judge a book by its cover'? Well, I happen to believe that's also true of men."

"Then you do not judge a human male by physical appearance alone?"

"Try not to. After all, Tin Man, looks aren't everything. A guy can be handsome as hell and turn out to be a royal snake."

"From what you have said since our first meeting, Rand, I gather you do not hold a high opinion of the male of your species."

I gave him another shrug. "Not most of 'em, no. To tell you the God's honest truth, I haven't had all that many good experiences with men. But y'know, while we're talking about looks, you're not half bad yourself, Tin Man—for a bot, that is."

Blackie's metal head bobbed silently. I had no idea in hell whether he were agreeing with me or not. But thank God, he went back to his monitoring duties and let the whole awkward subject drop.

The B'treeni ship I'd borrowed—okay, stolen!—entered the outer atmosphere of Esperance. I checked the monitors and was relieved as hell to see *Jammer* sitting right where I'd left her. Far as I could tell, she was still in one piece. Torrance hadn't bothered to hide her from view; he must be pretty damned confident nobody in their right mind'd come out this far.

I spotted two vessels parked on the surface below; one was Torrance's ship; the other was a newer model I'd never seen before. Both sat close to the foothills, right below the mouth of the cavern. Looked like Torrance had company: more smugglers maybe? Or had he invested in a new ship?

To make damned-sure we weren't seen, I brought the old B'treeni trader in on the far side of Mount Hope. Set her down a good distance from *Jammer*, figuring Torrance might've posted a goon or two to guard my ship. I didn't want to oblige the bastard by springing any traps set for me.

I released my restraining straps, got my legs under me, and tried to get used to gravity after the long flight. A microsecond later, Jeffries hurried forward, acting for all the Cosmos as if *he* were in charge of this operation—the arrogant bastard!

"I'm surprised as hell you managed to land this outdated piece of crap without crashing, Rand," he said, leaning over the console to scan the images on the monitors. "Now what?"

"We walk."

Jeffries straightened up fast and snarled, "*Walk?* What the hell! We're *miles* from anywhere that Torrance could possibly be! Why didn't you park the damn ship closer to our objective?"

"And risk being spotted? Not on your *fleggin* life, pal! It's safer for us to hike from here. Torrance'll have a tougher time spotting *us* coming than the B'treeni ship landing."

Jeffries swore under his breath.

The bot came up behind me and tried to get my attention. In a low, urgent tone, he said, "Rand, I must speak with you—in private. It is imperative!"

But I waved him off impatiently. "I know damned well and good what you're gonna say, Tin Man, and you can stow it! That rotten hunk of space-scum's gonna pay for the hell he's put me through," I vowed.

"Rand, that was not—," Blackie started to say, then stopped. He gave Jeffries an odd look before continuing. "For God's sake, Rand, think before you act! In the first place, how in the Cosmos do you intend to enter Mount Hope this time? You most certainly cannot mean to take the cavern entrance by storm. That would be sheer insanity, as well as amounting to suicide!"

"Cavern entrance?" Jeffries echoed, giving me a questioning look.

I ignored him. "Use your damn nano-circuits, Tin Man. The answer's obvious, isn't it?" I swept one hand toward the monitors still busily scanning every square inch of the surface of Esperance. "Over twenty years of mining operations left this planet one giant hunk of Terran Swish-cheese! It's nothing but a huge network of mine shafts and underground tunnels. And I'm willing to bet my life at least *one* of those tunnels links up with the asteroid eater's handiwork—or gut-work."

The bot contradicted in a grim tone, "Not necessarily, Rand."

"Hell, there's only one sure way to find out, isn't there?"

Jeffries gasped, "*Asteroid eater!*" The scowl on his face instantly darkened. "Rand, you never said one damn word about a *fleggin* eater! Hell, I'm not crazy enough to go prowling through any tunnels where an asteroid eater might be lurking! Not for any amount of credits!"

"Sorry about that, pal. Guess it slipped my mind to mention the eater," I excused myself, giving Jeffries a little shrug.

I checked the B'treeni blaster I'd stolen, made sure it had a full charge, then tucked it into my waistband. Opening the port storage compartment, I pulled out the B'treeni emergency kit and slung the strap over my left shoulder.

"You in or out, Jeffries? Decide, and make it snappy!"

He seemed to be having trouble making up his mind. He licked his lips, acting real nervous. "Uh, tell you what, Rand—why don't I go around to the other side of the mountain and scope out this cavern entrance you're talking about? If Torrance is holed up inside, I'll make damn-sure he and his mine-rats don't escape our net. Just give me a signal when you're ready to close in. A whistle will do, okay?"

I had to chuckle. "Aww! You'll miss out on the fun part! But have it your own way, pal." I turned to the bot, who was still hovering at my elbow. "Coming or not, Tin Man? Your choice."

"Have I a choice?" he replied. "Rand, you possess an absolutely remarkable talent for getting yourself into predicaments from which someone must extricate you."

His lack of enthusiasm all too obvious, Jeffries followed me aft. Blackie brought up the rear. When we reached the exit, I lowered the B'treeni ship's ramp. For several microseconds, we stood looking out over the bleak landscape.

The barren plain stretched from the rugged foothills rising on our left all the way to the far horizon. I was barely able to make out a distant line of mountains on our right. As far as the eye could see, the plain was littered with rubble, scarred by mining operations that'd run rampant for the past twenty-odd years. The sight was just as damned-depressing as it'd been the last time.

The three of us trudged down the ramp, single file, and headed for Mount Hope. The farther we walked, the more Jeffries grumbled. He stumbled often on the rocky ground. After every stumble, he swore colorfully. Even put *me* to shame; almost singed my ears!

As for Blackie, for a nice change, he was glued to Jeffries' heels, not mine. Had to wonder if the bot were developing a man-crush on the tall, good-looking ISF 'gent.

Blackie kept his mouth shut tight. He wasn't talking, didn't say one damn word. That made me wonder even more what the bloody hell was going on inside that thick metal skull of his.

To be on the safe side, we gave *Jammer* a wide berth. Not rushing to board her went against every damn instinct of my mind and body. I was itching to take back my ship, even if it meant blasting to Unholy Hell any lowlife who was waiting inside to smoke me.

First things first, I told myself sternly, trying my damnedest to be patient and cool-headed for once in my life. I *had* to capture Torrance! After that, I'd get *Jammer* back. Both my job and my rep would be safe, and I'd be two-and-a-half-million credits richer!

At the edge of the foothills, we came to a section heavily-pockmarked with abandoned mineshafts. I decided this was as good a place as any to part ways with Jeffries, so I could get down to serious business. To be honest, I wasn't real keen about shepherding *him* through the tunnels deep beneath the surface of Esperance. The bot and I'd be much better off navigating the maze alone. Jeffries would be nothing but a bloody nuisance, tagging along and getting under our feet.

Couldn't see the cavern's mouth from this side of Mount Hope, so I gave Jeffries directions. He started off without so much as pausing to rethink his decision or giving us a backward glance—the lousy coward! Blackie and I stood and stared at his back 'til Jeffries was only a black spot in the distance.

"Good riddance!" I said, heaving a sigh of relief.

The bot finally spoke. "Rand, now that he is gone, there is something I *must* tell you, something of great importance concerning this Jeffries—"

I cut him off with a snarled, "Not now, *flegg* it, Tin Man! Tell me later. We need to find a way down into these tunnels *pronto!*"

I went to the edge of the shaft nearest the foothills. Bracing my hands on my knees, I leaned over and peered down. The shaft was as deep and dark as the bowels of Hell Itself, and then some!

Just below the rim of the hole hung an old tailings bucket. It dangled from a chain hitched to a scaffold high above. The chain was wrapped around a sprocket wheel with a winch that was meant for raising and lowering the huge bucket. The whole damn setup was thick with years of rust.

I reached out and gave the chain a tug to test its strength. "Any hope of getting this to work?"

The bot inspected the winch mechanism. "Primitive indeed! Besides being barbarically outdated, the equipment is unfortunately, rusted solid."

"*Dammit!*"

"I believe there is, however, another possibility."

"And what the hell's that, Tin Man?"

"Step down into the bucket, Rand, and I will show you," he said. "Trust me!"

Without giving the bot so much as the whiff of an argument, I perched my butt on the edge of the shaft and slid feet-first over the rim and into the bucket. The old chain let out a groan as it took my weight. The whole setup creaked a protest.

Once I was safely inside the bucket, I rummaged through the emergency kit hanging from my shoulder 'til I found a couple of tube-torches. I took one and held out the other to the bot.

"Rand, you know perfectly well I do not require a light," he reminded me.

I shoved the tube-torch toward him anyway. "Take it, damn you, and don't give me any back talk! Never know when we might need a spare. I don't fancy mucking around in the pitch-dark again. Besides, Torrance's stooge, Drake, said the eater doesn't like light, remember? Torch-light might keep it at bay, maybe save your sorry metal ass."

"Very well, Rand, if you insist."

Bending at his silver-jointed waist, Blackie reached for the torch. His cold metal fingers closed about the clear tube, barely touching mine. He held his hand there and avoided meeting my eyes. "Rand, this escapade is extremely foolhardy and dangerous. I venture to predict that neither one of us will survive."

An all too familiar ache suddenly rose into my throat. I tried to ignore it and shrug off the bot's gloom and doom attitude. "Damn you, Tin Man!" I croaked. "I *have* to give this a try. Whatever the hell happens—happens!"

Blackie made that odd, sigh-like sound and let go of the torch. "Hold onto this for me, then, Rand. I will need both hands in order to lower the bucket."

Again, I wasn't about to argue with him. I watched as he freed the rusty chain from the sprocket wheel. Gripping the chain with both metal hands, he swung himself into the bucket with ease.

Hand over hand, he began to release the chain. Slowly, in irregular jerks, the bucket dropped, sending us deeper and deeper into the gloom of the mineshaft. I imagined this was what it felt like to gradually go blind.

Ever since the Massacre, I'd hated being underground, hated that trapped-like-a-mine-rat feeling. My recent run in with the asteroid eater sure as hell hadn't helped matters! But I was desperate to capture Torrance and his goons, and this was the only way to get the job done.

Darkness closed in around us, growing thicker and thicker. I activated the tube-torches. They blossomed into brilliant blue-white light. Once I could see again, I felt a whole helluva lot better—'til I noticed the shaft getting narrower. The rocky walls were closing in on us. Still, we hadn't hit bottom. My grip on the rusty edge of the bucket tightened. With the other hand, I clung for dear life to both tube-torches.

"Dammit, Tin Man! Can't you lower us any *faster?*" I whispered.

My voice sounded damned-odd, even to my own ears, kinda raspy and strained. The bottom rim of the bucket scraped the shaft walls. The sound it made gave me cold shivers. I could feel the vibes through the soles of my boots.

"I dare lower us no faster, Rand," the bot replied. "This chain has definitely seen its day and could very well snap at any moment. Are you, ah, 'getting cold feet,' I believe, is the customary expression?"

"Hell no! I'm dying to get my hands on Torrance. Don't want that bloody bastard to escape."

Foot by foot, the bucket bumped and grated downward. I was forced to grit my teeth. Without warning, the bucket hit bottom! I felt a tooth-rattling jolt. If my jaws hadn't been clenched together so tightly, I might've bitten my own damn tongue.

"Thanks for the smooth landing, Tin Man!" I said, giving the bot a glare.

"Any time," he replied, as he swung one metal leg at a time over the rim of the bucket.

A helluva lot more awkwardly, I crawled over the side and stood staring at my surroundings. In the bluish light from the torches, a damned-spooky scene spread out before me; tunnels branched off in every direction, all leading into the same pitch-blackness. But the main tunnel, the widest of the bunch, seemed headed straight for Mount Hope. Holding both tube-torches high, I started off in that direction. Without protesting, the bot followed.

The sound of our footsteps echoed eerily through the long-abandoned tunnel. Couldn't help wondering, *How the hell many years has it been since any living human set foot down here?*

The bot spoke, so suddenly that I jumped. "Rand, according to my sensors, several meters ahead on our right, a side tunnel branches off. It appears to lead in the exact direction we wish to travel."

Even with two tube-torches to light the way, the tunnel was too dark for me to see far ahead. I decided the bot's infrared sensors were gonna come in damned handy.

As usual, Blackie's sensors were dead-on. We took the next right and walked for one helluva long way before the tunnel came to a sudden fork; we were forced to stop and chose our path.

"Well, brainiac, which way from here?" I demanded, getting impatient and snarky for no particular reason.

"Regrettably, Rand, the closer we get to Mount Hope, the more difficulty my long-range sensors are experiencing. The residual metal ore within the tunnel walls, as well as in the foothills above us, must be impeding my scans."

"Okay then, we'll take a damned good guess—I guess." Turning right, I plunged ahead. Again, Blackie didn't argue, but followed obediently.

The tunnels turned and twisted, crisscrossed and merged. We walked for what seemed like hours. With the bot's sensors down, we ran a terrible risk of getting hopelessly lost in this bloody maze! I remembered Blackie's grim prediction that neither of us would survive this. My gut twisted into a knot.

There was one hopeful sign, though; so far, the walls of all the tunnels we'd traveled were rough, human-made, not the work of the asteroid eater. Getting lost down here—where I could slowly starve to death!—would be bad enough without having to worry about getting *eaten alive*!

A short distance farther on, the tunnel took a sharp left turn. I stopped dead in my tracks and stared in horror. Every surface of the tunnel ahead was smooth as polished glass, reflecting the bluish glow of the tube-torches. Reminded me of the hall of mirrors in Breego's throne room!

"Aww, *flegg* it!" I swore. "The damn eater's been at work here, Tin Man!"

Standing right beside me, Blackie stared at the reflections. He didn't say one damn word, but this time I had no problem imagining what was going through his mind. It was almost as if I were developing some kinda link with his half-human nano-computer-for-a-brain.

Trapped in the acids from the eater's gut, a big hunk of metal like him would dissolve a whole helluva lot *slower* than soft human flesh. If the eater got the bot—hell, it might take *days* for the monster to dissolve and digest him! And the worst part was that the bot would be *conscious* the whole *fleggin* time!

That godawful thought made me shudder from the top of my head to the tips of my toes. If *I* dreaded meeting up with the asteroid eater, how must Blackie feel about running such a terrible risk?

I turned to look the bot square in the face. "Uh, Tin Man, I really don't need any help carrying out the rest of this operation. I can take it from here. The eater's been through this tunnel so, sooner or later, it *must* join up with the ones in Mount Hope. And Jeffries'll be waiting for me outside the jacker's cavern. Go back the way we came. See if you can recover *Jammer*, and wait for me aboard her."

But the damned-stubborn bot stood his ground and insisted, "I prefer to remain with you, Rand, no matter the personal consequences."

"I'm your *fleggin* boss, pal, and I'm giving you a direct order! *Go back to my ship!*"

Those unblinking crystal lenses stared straight into my eyes. "I think not."

That made me spitting-mad. "You disobedient, tin-plated bucket of bolts! *Do as you're told, damn you!*"

"You are in grave danger, Rand; therefore, I refuse to abandon you. My duty is to protect you at all costs," Blackie declared.

"*Costs?* Have you stopped for even one microsecond to think about the costs, Tin Man?"

"Of course I have! I am not a fool, Rand."

"Look here, pal, you don't owe me one damn thing, least of all loyalty! Hell, you're just a fancy piece of junk I salvaged in hopes of making some quick credits. Now obey me. Get the hell outta here!" I roared.

Still, the bloody bot refused to retreat.

I crossed both forearms on the bot's broad metal chest and shoved with all my might, straining to force him to back up. Might as well've tried to move a ton of spectromium by myself. I couldn't budge him so much as a fraction of an inch.

Suddenly, my eyes stung. In a raspy whisper I croaked, "*Damn your metal hide to Bloody Hell!*" I spun and raced down the tunnel as fast as my legs could go.

From the darkness behind me, the bot was shouting, "Galaxy, *no!* I failed to tell you something that may prove vital! *Galaxy, come back!*"

I shut my ears and ran like hell. Figured the only way to get ridda the damn bot was by outdistancing him. For a while, I could hear the clumping of heavy metal feet. Then the bot's footsteps faded in the distance, 'til all I could hear was my own ragged breathing, my own running footsteps. At the snail's pace that was his top speed, Blackie'd never catch up with me, and with his sensors on the fritz he'd never be able to track me down.

I darted through tunnel after tunnel, always choosing the ones with the shiny walls. As soon as I was damned-sure the bot was far behind me, I paused to catch my breath. Told myself I really didn't give a fast-flying damn what happened to Blackie. That was *his* lookout. Just didn't wanna feel responsible, in case something godawful happened to him. Already had a helluva load of guilt on my shoulders—almost more'n I could bear!—and enough damn nightmares haunting my sleep. Sure as hell didn't need to add to my burdens.

Grudgingly, I had to admit I owed the bot. He'd saved my *fleggin* life on more'n one occasion. I wondered if he'd saved me because his robotic laws *required* him to, or was it because—?

I shook off that thought mighty damned fast. If the bloody bot'd saved my life only so I could meet my doom down in these gloomy tunnels, then maybe he hadn't done me much of a favor after all.

Maybe the bot'd been right; maybe this *was* my final scrape: the one I wouldn't walk away from.

But if I didn't survive this—what the hell! At least *Blackie* knew the truth about Torrance and his rotten conspiracy. The bot had the data to prove the ISF was corrupt—*and* he'd uncovered Roman Aguilar's family-connection to the Esperance Massacre. Maybe, just maybe, justice would finally be served, even if I didn't make it outta here alive.

But a snarky little voice inside my own head snickered, *And who in their right mind—who in all the* fleggin *universe?—would take the word of a damn bot over any human's?*

For the first time, that cold, hard fact struck home like a fist to my gut. Neither of us had any *solid* proof to back up our story. It was still only a theory—even though that theory was based on damned-good, circumstantial evidence. *Huh!* A good four-syllable word, that one.

If both Jeffries and I got ourselves killed out here in the boondocks of Esperance, who in bloody hell would ever find out—or bother to avenge us? And even if Blackie managed to get off Esperance in one piece, who the hell would believe his story?

And here I was, like a *fleggin* dumb-ass, risking my sweet neck all for a hopeless cause!

Did my damnedest to keep track of every change of direction I made, hoping I was still going toward Torrance's lair. A time or two, I wished to bloody hell I hadn't been in such a damn hurry to ditch the bot. But when the eater's tunnels began to slope steeply upward, I had a hunch I was getting closer to the cavern.

Just thinking about the eater made the hair on the back of my neck stand at attention. Bad as it'd be to meet up with Torrance or one of his goons, running into the asteroid eater'd be a whole helluva lot worse. The *fleggin* monster was lurking somewhere in the maze, always moving, always hungry. Damned gruesome thought!

I took a better grip on the tube-torches clutched in my left hand. I was counting on their light to protect me from the beast. The first time I'd met up with the *fleggin* thing, my blaster sure hadn't had much effect.

But I knew damned good and well the light could also give me away to Torrance. And this time, he wouldn't settle for selling me to Breego, not on my life! The bloody bastard would finish me off, make sure I was done for. And the way he'd end me sure as hell wouldn't be pleasant—or quick!

I was still weighing my choices—to douse the light or not to douse the light—when I was forced to stop short. I found myself at the rim of a dark, deep pit smack in the middle of the tunnel floor.

Swearing under my breath, I broke out in a sweat as I backed off real fast.

"*K'yoti* Hell! That was one *damned*-close call!"

I figured the pit had to be the one Torrance's goons'd tossed me and Tin Man into. That meant Torrance was somewhere in the neighborhood.

Keeping one eye peeled, I bent down and lay one of the lit tube-torches on the lip of the pit. In case I was forced to beat a retreat back this way, I didn't wanna risk falling into that *fleggin* pit. Alone, down in the pitch-blackness—with a possible broken bone or two!—I wouldn't stand a snowball's chance in Hell's Furnace against the eater, blaster or no blaster. And Torrance'd be more'n happy to leave me trapped so he could watch me slowly starve to death or be eaten alive. Either way, he'd love to see me suffer.

I gave the pit a wide berth and walked on, clutching the last tube-torch. Wished I had the bot's sensors.

Not far ahead, I saw the first faint light. Figuring any light besides mine must be coming from Torrance's cavern, I flattened my back against the glassy wall and shoved the torch back into the emergency kit on my shoulder. With both hands now free, I drew the B'treeni blaster from my waistband. Silent as a mine-rat, I slid along the smooth-as-glass wall, inching my way toward the source of the light.

I heard voices coming from that direction; two men were talking in low tones. Right off the bat, I recognized one voice as Torrance's. The other sounded damned-familiar, but I couldn't quite place it.

I reached the side tunnel's entrance and took a quick peek. The tunnel beyond was deserted. Bright light came from the end where it entered the cavern. The voices were louder here.

I slid the emergency kit off my shoulder and let it drop silently to the tunnel floor. Clutching my blaster in both hands, I held it at arm's length. Ready for damn near anything, I crept toward the voices, taking one small step at a time, so I'd make no noise to warn them I was coming.

Knew I had to get the drop on Torrance—and every single one of his goons—or I'd be good as dead! Next, I'd signal Jeffries, and together we'd round up the whole gang.

I stopped at the cavern entrance, pulled the blaster in close to my chest, and flattened my back against the wall. Then I risked poking my head around the corner. What I saw inside the cavern hit me harder than a fist straight to the gut!

Torrance was there all right, and just as I'd suspected, he had company—the second man was *Roman Aguilar!*

Quickly gathering my wits about me, I extended my blaster again, and stepped out into their full view. Torrance was the first to see me. The blaster in his hand was trained on me, as if he were expecting me! He flashed an evil grin.

Kept my weapon squarely on him, at the same time wondering, *What in the name of Unholy Hell is going on here? What have I stumbled onto? And what the* flegg *is Roman Aguilar doing* here, *of all places?*

Aguilar turned sideways and caught sight of me. "Ah, Ms. Rand!" he said, coming forward. "We were expecting you to arrive at any moment. How kind of you to join us, and I must say, how convenient!" He flashed a pleasant enough smile, baring his perfect, whiter-than-white teeth.

I scowled at him and demanded, "What the hell are you doing on Esperance, Mr. Aguilar?"

The great man pursed his lips. "I believe you recoup agents would refer to my current mission as conducting 'mop up operations.' I intend to eliminate a few loose ends."

"Mop up operations? Now what the bloody hell is *that* supposed to mean?" I growled. The situation was getting more and more spacey by the microsecond.

Had Roman Aguilar grown so impatient he'd come out here, in person, to find and capture Torrance? If so, how the hell had *Aguilar* figured out, all on his own, exactly where the jackers were hiding out? I was pretty damned sure he *hadn't!*

Down in the deepest pit of my stomach, I got a real sick feeling; my "uh-oh" sense maxed out. Torrance *and* Aguilar. Had the two of them been working together all along? It just couldn't be!

But I'll be damned if the whole stinking-to-high-heaven mess suddenly didn't make perfect sense!

Roman Aguilar paid the ISF bigwigs a small fortune to look the other way, while Torrance ripped off Aguilar's company. And Remoxa, in turn, ripped off Surety for the insurance reimbursements. Then, Torrance sold the hijacked goods, and the two bloody bastards split the profits! An "extremely lucrative" arrangement, as Tin Man would put it! The only loser was Surety Galactic—and me!

Now I got a sinking feeling in my gut. So far, the biggest loser in this whole *fleggin* conspiracy was Robert Benton-Smythe: he'd lost his life—and I might be about to join him shortly!

Aguilar watched the expressions flitting across my face as I figured out what in bloody-blue-blazes was going on. He said, "Two birds, one stone, you might say, to use your crude parlance, Ms. Rand."

My eyes darted about the cavern, looking for Torrance's goons. The place was too damned silent. The flaming torches spaced along the rocky walls cast their flickering light over a grisly scene. Bodies were strewn here and there about the cavern floor—dead bodies! I recognized Drake, Morgan—even Blondie. She was still wearing J'neen's dazzling *star-shi* earrings. Wisps of smoke were rising from some of the corpses.

This massacre was mighty recent!

I looked from the blaster in Torrance's hand to his ugly mug and hissed, "*You* did this?" All I could get out was a hoarse whisper.

He answered with a sharp snort. "Thought I was rid of *you* once and for all, Rand. Now I've got the chance to even the score between us—*personally!*"

"Helluva partner you picked to do business with, Mr. Aguilar," I said. "Torrance here is a real sweetheart of a guy. Neat financial arrangement, too, got to give you that. I have one question I want answered: Which one of you *fleggin* bastards put the bounty on my head?"

Torrance smirked. I'll be damned if it wasn't one of the nastiest smiles I'd ever seen in my life! "Which of us do you think?"

I did some fast figuring. Torrance probably had a better *reason* to put a price on my head, but Roman Aguilar had a helluva lot more *credits* to back him up—and a helluva lot more to lose in case I stumbled across their sleazy deal.

Taking my best guess, I replied, "Aguilar."

Aguilar gave me a little bow. "How astute of you, Ms. Rand! Quite astonishing for a simple, brainless recoup agent." He smiled at that compliment-slash-insult. "I was going to reward your old compa-

triot, Mr. Torrance here, for accomplishing said task—that is, before
a third party informed me you were still very much alive."

In a surly growl, Torrance said, "So you owe me even more now,
Rand!"

"Aww, you're breaking my damn heart, Torrance, old pal." I let
out a long, shrill whistle to signal Jeffries. "Now, if you know what's
good for you, you'll drop your blaster. I brought company with me,
and I'm a helluva lot better shot than you are. That's a damned fact."

A third, all too familiar male voice came from over my shoulder.
"That might be true, sister, but right now I happen to have the drop
on you!"

Jeffries! He'd come up behind me without making a sound.

I groaned. "You *fleggin* bastard! Might've known you'd sell me out
first chance you got!"

"Drop the blaster, Rand, or I swear you'll die in your tracks!"

Jeffries' voice was cold. I realized he'd love an excuse to smoke
me. Slowly, he moved to face me, never taking his blaster off me
for a microsecond. The dead-serious look in Jeffries' baby-blues told
me this was no practical joke he was pulling, no ploy. I dropped the
B'treeni blaster and raised my hands.

"Take it easy, Jeffries, old chum." My frustration level growing,
I took a hard look at the three men in front of me and demanded,
"What in bloody-*fleggin*-hell's going on here?"

"And you think you're so damn *smart*, Rand," Jeffries growled,
giving me a curl of his lip. "I was praying I'd get a chance to smoke
you myself and collect Aguilar's bounty. If that damn bot didn't
follow you around like a *fleggin* watchdog, I would've!"

Jeffries gave the cavern a quick scan. "Speaking of the bot, where
is he?"

I shrugged. "How the hell would I know? His sensors are on the
fritz. Got himself lost in the maze, I suppose. He's probably wandering around, searching for a way out. Told you he was a worthless
hunk of junk!"

"*Ahem!* If we could get back to the business at hand? Ms. Rand,
would you be so kind as to kick your weapon over to me?" Aguilar
said in a no-nonsense tone.

I did as I was told. Wasn't about to argue with *two* blasters held at such damned-close range; wasn't anxious to get myself smoked, not even once. Aguilar picked up my blaster with two fingers, as if it were filthy-dirty.

"Your opinion to the contrary, Ms. Rand," he said, "according to Inspector Second Class Jeffries here, your robotic friend is an extremely valuable piece of property. Apparently, it is an unauthorized prototype, a prototype the ISF erroneously thought had been destroyed."

I scowled at Aguilar. "How in the name of Unholy Hell do you know so much about *the bot?*" I demanded, dead-determined to be curious to the bitter end. The gears inside my own head were whirring and meshing on hyper-drive. Desperately, I tried to put together every last piece of the puzzle before I got smoked.

Aguilar gave me one of his phony smiles. "My dear young woman, I know everything there is to know about every single person involved in this matter, including the late Robert Benton-Smythe. A most unwise young man! Highly-intelligent, extraordinarily ambitious, but overly inquisitive. He had the misfortune to stumble across my arrangement with the head of the ISF, thus endangering my grand political plans. In order to protect myself, I was forced to eliminate him."

"How in bloody-blue-blazes could a harmless guy like RBS hurt a man like you: the great and powerful Roman Aguilar?" I wanted to know.

Aguilar replied, "He couldn't be bought. As far as I am concerned, such integrity is a fatal flaw. Can *you* be bought, Ms. Rand?"

My upper lip curled in a snarl of disgust. "*Hell, no!* For all your floating towers and vast wealth, you're no better breed of scum than Torrance here. You might even be *worse!*"

"*Tsk, tsk!* Let us remain civil until the denouement, shall we, Ms. Rand?"

"Whatever the hell *that* means!" I flashed Aguilar my darkest scowl to let him know I held a low opinion of him. "Next, I suppose you're gonna promise to let me live if I make nice!"

Aguilar raised one eyebrow at that snarky remark, as if my cocky attitude amused him. "You are everything I have been told about you,

Ms. Rand: attractive, feisty, crude, ill-educated, undisciplined, impulsive, and extremely foolhardy."

"So y'don't care for my table manners. Big *fleggin* deal! Don't tell me *that's* the reason you put the price on my head?"

Roman Aguilar pursed his lips again. He seemed to be debating with himself or having trouble making a last minute decision. "I assure you, my dear, whatever I do, I have extremely good reasons for every single one of my actions."

"But you're not gonna spill 'em to me, even now, when I'm good as dead?"

Aguilar shook his head. His dark eyes were hard and cold, reminding me of the shards of flint I used to collect up in the foothills when I was a kid. "Revealing my secrets to you would be *most* unwise of me, especially since I am forced to take present company into consideration."

Both Torrance's and Jeffries' heads swiveled in Aguilar's direction, as if they'd become robots themselves.

I snorted. "So I get to die without even knowing the real reason why?"

"Precisely. I am sorry about that, Ms. Rand, truly I am. In fiction, does not the villain *always* reveal his motives to his intended victim? But this is real life, my dear, and I am far from a villain." Aguilar laughed, as if he'd told a good joke.

Damned and determined to poke around 'til I found a tiny chink in the great man's armor, I taunted, "You're one helluva sport, eh, Aguilar? Never figured a bigwig like you'd be afraid of a backwater nobody like me."

"He who fears *nothing* is a complete and utter fool," was his reply—but I'd expected Aguilar to *deny* he was afraid of anything!

A sudden hunch hit me with one helluva wallop. I had a gut-feeling Roman Aguilar *was* afraid of me! *But why?*

What in the name of Unholy Hell could a lowly recoup agent like me do to someone as rich and powerful as he was? What was it Blackie'd once told me? Seemed like *fleggin* ages ago now. Someone wanted me dead because he either *hated* me or *feared* me.

Aguilar heaved a sigh of phony regret. "Now, Mr. Torrance, if you would be so kind as to rid me of this thorn in my proverbial side—permanently!"

Torrance's finger hovered over the firing-button. Then, he paused and grinned. Holstering his blaster, he reached for the other side of his belt and drew a laser-handle, the laser-handle he'd taken from me before he'd tossed me and the bot into the pit. He thumbed the switch to activate the blade. A three-inch laser beam tipped the handle—a deadly three-inches!

My whole body tensed. The *fleggin* bastard wasn't gonna make this easy on me! He was gonna carve me up, slowly, painfully, with little or no blood loss.

My mind racing at maximum speed, I made a last-ditch effort to get outta this fix. I swallowed hard, then croaked as loud as I could croak, *"The Esperance Massacre!"*

Those three little words had one helluvan effect.

Torrance and Jeffries frowned and looked puzzled. Roman Aguilar's hawk-nosed face paled, as if I were draining his blood. He looked stunned, but not one damned bit puzzled.

"That's what all this crap's really about, isn't it? Not teaming up with Torrance to hijack Remoxa's shipments, not scamming Surety, not bribing ISF bigwigs to look the other way! It all boils down to Esperance and the *fleggin* Massacre!"

Torrance'd obviously taken note of Aguilar's sudden change of color. He demanded, "Mr. Aguilar, what the hell is she talking about?"

Aguilar silenced him with a curt hand gesture. "She is simply babbling in a feeble attempt to stall for time. Her pitiful ploy will not succeed. Finish her off and make it quick! We have no time to play your crude games, Mr. Torrance!"

But I babbled on, as fast as I could babble. "Both of my parents were massacred here—remember, Torrance? Aguilar had all the colonists *butchered* because every last one of 'em refused to sell the mining rights to their land—to Alpha Mines, Incorporated, *his grandfather's company!* I'm willing to bet my last damn credit that it was Aguilar himself who hired the mercenaries to do the deed. And after the Massacre, he rigged their ship to blow up in mid-space, making damned sure none of 'em would ever talk or blackmail him.

"I was only a snot-nosed six-year-old, but by some miracle I managed to survive. You and me, Aguilar—we're *the only survivors* of that Massacre. And no one alive suspected you were behind it—not even me!—up until this very microsecond."

Aguilar looked even more stunned. The expression on his face told me the whole bloody truth. He was afraid of me all right: afraid I might be able to ID him, afraid I knew what he'd done, afraid I was only biding my time before blackmailing him or muscling in on his action!

Torrance made a fatal mistake.

He eyed Aguilar with more than a little interest, made it all too plain he recognized a business opportunity when he saw one. "So the great Roman Aguilar got his start by murdering a bunch of helpless colonists and a handful of hapless mercenaries?" He let out a harsh bark of a laugh. "Damned good thing we're friends, eh, Mr. Aguilar?"

Aguilar lost his focus on me and shifted it to the jacker. "No, Mr. Torrance, I am afraid you are very much mistaken. We are *not* friends—not in the least!" He smiled one of his phony-as-hell smiles, a smile as deathly-cold as space itself. "No matter how much I pay them to do my biding, there is no man—nor woman—in the entire universe whom I would trust with such potentially damaging information."

Torrance's face slowly turned dead-white. "But—but I've always done exactly as you said, Mr. Aguilar. I never told one *fleggin* soul about our arrangement, not even any of my late colleagues here. You know damned good and well you can trust me!"

Roman Aguilar's lousy excuse for a smile vanished. "Inspector Jeffries, would you kindly disarm the gentleman?"

None too gently, Jeffries jammed the muzzle of his blaster into Torrance's ribs. The bloody turncoat snatched the laser-handle outta Torrance's hand, switched off the beam, then had the gall to slip *my weapon* into his shirt pocket! He yanked the blaster outta Torrance's holster and tucked it into his own belt. Once Jeffries had obeyed orders, he backed off to a safe distance.

His trigger finger hovered over the firing button. He gave Aguilar a quick sideways glance and got a curt nod.

Torrance had time enough to scream, *"No!"* before a single blaster-bolt cut him down. I watched, frozen with horror, as his body sagged, then crumpled to the cavern floor. He lay still; a thin plume of grayish smoke drifted upward from the hole burned into his chest.

I gulped and started praying harder'n I'd prayed in many years. I was next!

"Now, Mr. Torrance, *now*, at last, I can fully trust you," Aguilar said in a real quiet voice.

"*K'yoti* Hell!" I croaked, staring at Jeffries. "Was *that* really necessary?" He didn't bother answering me.

Aguilar strolled toward me; his flinty eyes narrowed. "Unfortunately for you, my dear Ms. Rand, you have made rather a nuisance of yourself. And as you well know, I refuse to tolerate any interference with my plans."

I forced out a chuckle. "You by any chance referring to your plans to be elected president of the Consortium? You wanna run the whole damn galaxy, don't you? Maybe even get yourself crowned Emperor someday? What danger could *I* be to your grand plans? Like you said, I'm nothing but a lowly, dumb-ass recoup agent with nowhere near your power or influence. Who in their right mind would even listen to me?"

Aguilar shook his head. "What you possess presents an unacceptable danger: information—along with a rather tedious tendency to pry into affairs you ought to leave well enough alone. If you were to be perfectly honest, I am certain you would agree with me. I simply cannot allow the current untenable state of affairs to continue.

"I sincerely regret having to kill you, Ms. Rand. I truly do. However, that course of action appears to be necessary. You have a great deal of spunk and have provided a bit of diversion, a dash of much-needed spice, to my often-dull life. You have kept my edge keen, shall we say? I shall miss that, at least somewhat."

Aguilar heaved a heavy sigh. He seemed to find me too damned stupid to enjoy dealing with any further, now that I didn't offer him any challenge. "Twenty-two years ago, when two of my agents discovered a filthy child wandering amid the ashes in the aftermath of the Esperance Massacre, they made the grievous error of failing to kill and dispose of her, then and there."

"*Your* agents?" I gulped. The fact hit me as hard as a fist to the gut.

"Of course, my dear Ms. Rand! Who else do you think I would

trust to 'investigate' the crime? As you may very well know by now, I own the ISF; I started small, but I have owned the entire organization for a good many years now. Obviously, you succeeded in linking me with that obscure mining company my family began all those years ago. *Brava!* Quite possibly, you possess a touch more intelligence than I have given you credit for thus far."

My anger was about to boil over; it was growing hotter by the microsecond. My jaw muscles tightened. "Bet you'll shed real tears when I'm dead and gone, eh, Aguilar? You're a helluva lot more concerned about your own *fleggin* welfare than you've ever been for human life!"

Aguilar's hawk-nosed-face hardened. "In this instance, Ms. Rand, your customary sarcasm is not going to save you."

"Well, I'm sure as bloody hell not gonna beg *you* for my life, Aguilar, if that's what you're waiting around for. I don't expect one-damn drop of mercy from you: the lowlife bastard responsible for murdering my parents, along with thousands of other innocent colonists!"

The corners of Aguilar's mouth twitched. "Rightly so, Ms. Rand, rightly so! Believe me, I did not get where I am today by being merciful."

Fists clenched by my sides, I took one foolish step toward him.

Instantly, Aguilar aimed the B'treeni blaster straight at my heart. "No farther! I am well aware of your formidable reputation, including your talent for hand-to-hand combat. Oh, yes! Once your name popped up on my radar screen, Ms. Rand, I researched you quite thoroughly. I know everything there is to know about you."

"Flattering, I'm sure!" I snapped. "Didn't realize I was so bloody interesting."

Aguilar gave me the faintest shadow of a smile. "Now I must bid you *adieu*. Shortly, you shall be joining your late parents in death, as well as your old friend, Torrance, here. Should anyone discover your bodies, it will appear that the two of you killed each other during a massive shootout, which resulted in multiple casualties." He turned toward Jeffries. "Inspector."

More'n eager for the kill, that bastard actually grinned as he took aim. His finger hovered over the firing button.

"Warned you you'd need saving, didn't I, sister? Say goodbye, Rand."

A black blur shot past me.

Blackie knocked Roman Aguilar galley-west and charged at Jeffries, ignoring the weapon in his hand. The blaster-bolt meant for me hit the bot square in the chest, at point-blank range. He staggered backward. Blue-white bolts of energy crackled and arced about his armored body.

I nearly choked on the stench of scorched metal that filled the cavern. The bot teetered, then fell over backward. He crashed to floor and lay still.

"*Tin Man!*"

Jeffries recovered his balance. He closed in on the helpless bot and took dead-aim at his head, intending to finish him off.

Heard myself scream, "*No!*" as I launched myself at Jeffries.

I caught him off-guard, bowled him over. He went down with me on top of him. I pounded his face with both fists. He punched at me with one of his, pelting me with body blows and trying his damnedest to bring his blaster to bear. I got in a jab to his jaw, letting him have it with every ounce of strength I had left. Jeffries went limp as a rag-doll. I rolled off him and snatched the blaster from his hand.

Roman Aguilar was back on his feet. I looked up at him just in time to see him raise his blaster. Flat on my belly on the dusty cavern floor, I swung my weapon in his general direction and got off a shot. I was relieved as hell to see the bastard drop.

Ignoring the pain shooting through my ribcage, I scrambled to the bot's side. A lazy thread of gray smoke rose from the scorch-mark in the center of his chest.

"*Tin Man!* Speak to me!" I pleaded. "Say something, damn you!"

The bot didn't reply, didn't so much as twitch. *How in bloody hell do I check a bot's vitals?* I thought wildly, fighting the wave of panic rising from deep down in my gut.

"C'mon, Tin Man—please don't do this to me! We make a damned good team, you and me." I shoved Jeffries' blaster into my waistband, leaned over, and put one ear to the bot's metal chest, listening—*for what* I couldn't tell you.

"Tin Man, can you hear me?"

A familiar voice, right in my ear, made me jump.

"Of course I can hear you, Rand. My auditory circuits are still functioning normally, although I rather doubt you actually *wanted* me to hear your last remarks."

I sat upright and scowled down at him. "Damn you, Tin Man! You scared the *fleggin* crap outta me. What's the big idea of playing superhero? You aren't indestructible, y'know!"

I struggled to pull Blackie into a sitting position, then tugged frantically at one of his metal arms, trying my damnedest to get him up and onto his feet.

"We gotta get the hell outta here!" I hissed. "Before Aguilar's whole *fleggin* crew comes looking for him! Hurry, dammit!"

But the bot protested, "Rand, my legs are non-functional. You must leave me behind and flee!"

"The hell I will!"

"I am *not* a living creature. What happens to me is of no consequence. Listen to reason and save yourself!"

Shutting my ears, I bent over, got one shoulder into his hard-as-a-rock chest, and heaved him to his feet. I pulled one long, black-and-silver arm across my shoulders, taking most of his weight on myself.

God, he was heavy! Groaning like a weight-lifter going for the galactic record, I dragged the bot outta the cavern and into the side tunnel. Didn't dare go out the front entrance and risk running smack into Roman Aguilar's men.

I staggered under Blackie's weight as I made my way down the side tunnel. Where it joined the main tunnel, I turned left. Tried to remember how far ahead the damn pit was and whether or not another tunnel branched off before we'd reach it.

My back'd never be the same. My ribs ached. My wounded arm throbbed like hell. Knew I wouldn't be able to drag the bot much farther. I had to stop and rest pretty damned soon! Tried not to let myself think about what would happen if Aguilar's guys caught us.

"Galaxy, at the appallingly-slow rate of speed we are able to travel, Aguilar's men will overtake us in a matter of microseconds," the bot pointed out matter-of-factly. "Cease this insanity and save your own life!"

I was barely able to grunt, "Shut—the hell—up!"

He ignored me. "I am *not* human! Should Aguilar's men destroy me, I will experience no physical pain. I must insist you leave me here this instant and *run!*"

I clenched my teeth, battling my pain, and kept dragging the bot forward, inch by inch. "You can go—straight to—Bloody Hell!"

My gut was about to burst. A sharper stab of pain shot through my ribcage. Both arms were numb; still I kept going.

I saw a faint light up ahead—the light from the tube-torch I'd left on the rim of the pit!

We finally reached the deep, dark hole in the tunnel floor. I paused long enough to give the tube-torch one helluva kick. Watched it bounce and skitter down the long tunnel, lighting up the gloom ahead. Darkness closed in around us. I dragged the bot around the pit and kept going.

The tunnel was so damned dark I missed the opening in the glassy wall to my left. Luckily, I lost my balance and flung out my left arm to catch myself. Instead, I stumbled into a side tunnel and dropped the bot with a thud that sounded like half-a-ton of spectromium hitting the ground.

I flopped down on the tunnel floor, rolled flat on my back, and gasped for breath. My back ached like bloody hell. I suspected I had a cracked rib or two. I winced as I drew Jeffries' blaster outta my waistband and faced the tunnel opening, ready to meet whatever trouble showed itself.

Using his strong arms alone, the bot managed to pull himself into a sitting position with his back propped against the tunnel's wall.

I heard him whisper, "Rand, of all the absolutely *brainless*, foolhardy, irresponsible stunts you could have pulled—!"

I snorted. "Insults, Tin Man? And after I just saved your metal ass?"

"You should *not* be risking your own life to save me," he insisted hotly. "Mighty damned foolish of you!"

I let out a soft chuckle at that remark. "*Huh!* You think I'm such a bloody coward I'd run off and leave you lying there, wounded and helpless, after all you and I've—that is, after all we've—?"

I cleared my throat and started over again. "*K'yoti* Hell! If I'd done such a *fleggin* cowardly thing as *that*, Tin Man, I couldn't live with my damn self—uh, that is, in the off chance we actually survive this fix!"

"Aha! Since you are now employing the guilt excuse, Rand, you appear to have suddenly developed a conscience."

"Excuse? *Excuse!*" I echoed.

Not quite able to stifle a groan, I got on my hands and knees and crawled across the tunnel to look him right in the face, a face I couldn't see. "You obnoxious pile of nuts and bolts!" I hissed. "I broke my damn back rescuing you, and *this* is the thanks I get?"

"Were you expecting to be thanked, Rand?"

I snarled, "*Hell, no!*"

"Then you should not be disappointed, should you?" he said in a quiet voice.

I gave him a put out sniff and sat back on my haunches. "So tell me, Tin Man, how in bloody-blue-blazes did you manage to *find* me in this *fleggin* maze? With your sensors down, I thought for damned sure I'd lost you."

"Fortunately, my *heat* sensors were functioning normally. I detected the faint, residual heat left by your footsteps and simply followed your trail."

"Figures! You're chock-full of surprises, Tin Man."

"As are you, Rand."

"Me? Hell, I'm just a simple recoup agent."

The bot said, "On the contrary, Rand, there is *nothing* simple about you, far from it. You are a much more complex entity than I at first assumed. Shall we say, you are a great deal more than meets the eye—or the ear?"

My face was burning like hellfire. I was glad the tunnel was so damned dark. Once again, I began to feel a little giddy, as if I'd drunk a bit more than my limit of *hahk-teem.* "Don't go making me out to be more'n I am, Tin Man. That road'll lead to nothing but disappointment."

"I do not believe your statement to be true, Rand."

Suddenly, the bot said, "*Hush!*" as if he'd heard something I hadn't. "*Someone is coming this way!*" he warned in a whisper. "And unfortunately for us, the asteroid eater never completed this tunnel; it is a dead-end. There is no escape!"

"*K'yoti* Hell! Trapped like a pair of bloody mine-rats. *Great!*"

I plastered my aching back against the tunnel wall, right beside the bot, and listened with all my might. Sure enough, off in the distance I heard running footsteps coming toward us. Sounded to me like only one guy, maybe one of Aguilar's crew. Or had that *fleggin* son-of-a-bitch Jeffries come to and started searching for us?

I took a tighter grip on the blaster in my hand, in case the bastard discovered our little hole-in-the-wall.

The footsteps came closer. My muscles tensed. I got ready to fight for my life. But a strangled cry of alarm came from outside, followed by the dull thud of a body hitting solid ground—and the sharp crack of bone snapping! A scream of agony echoed through the tunnel system, raising goose bumps on my arms.

"*Oh, my God!*" I gasped to Blackie. "Whoever the hell that is fell into the *fleggin* pit!"

"Judging from the sound of his voice, I believe it is Roman Aguilar."

"*Huh!* You don't say? Thought I'd smoked the bloody bastard! Must've only grazed him. He recovered mighty damned fast. Either that, or he was playing possum to save his own skin."

"In either case, Rand, it would appear Roman Aguilar no longer presents a danger to us."

By that time, I was shaking all over. I crawled to the entrance and stuck my head into the main tunnel to check out the situation. Low moans of agony were coming from the pit.

I heard Aguilar shout, "I am down here! Damn you all to Hell! *I am here!*"

It *was* Roman Aguilar in the pit, no doubt about that, and he clearly expected his men to come to his rescue any microsecond.

To my left, I could see the faint light of the tube-torch. I shot a look to my right, back toward Torrance's cavern, and my whole body went stiff as a dead mine-rat.

Something moved, blocking out what light was coming from the cavern—a monstrous shape quivered and glistened! A ripple of sheer terror shivered down my aching backbone.

I ducked back into what I hoped and prayed would be the safety of the side tunnel and scrambled to the bot's side.

"The damn eater's coming this way—*fast!*" I whispered as quietly as humanly possible. I knew the bot would hear me.

"Rand, I recommend we stay absolutely motionless without making a sound!" Blackie advised. "Perhaps the beast will not sense us and pass by."

"But *Aguilar*—he's trapped down in that pit!—and from the sounds of it, he's hurt pretty damned bad!"

The bot's metal fingers clamped around my wrist like a vise, gripping me tightly, so I wouldn't be tempted to do anything stupid— or heroic. "Rand, it is far too late to save Roman Aguilar from his fate. We can do nothing whatsoever without endangering our own lives!"

"Maybe I could reach that tube-torch—get it back here in time!"

Outside, a long, drawn-out scream echoed through the maze of tunnels. I swear I'll hear that scream in my worst nightmares for the rest of my damn life!

I held my breath, my whole body frozen like a block of solid ice. I heard nothing but thick silence.

Then I turned my head toward the tunnel opening, just in time to see a large shadow. Our hiding place suddenly went pitch-black. The eater slithered past, so damned-close I could've stuck out my foot and kicked it in the ass—if a monster like that *had* an ass!

I kept holding my breath 'til I was dead-sure the beast'd gone by. Thank God, it paid no attention whatsoever to me and the bot!

In sheer relief I blew out a breath and exclaimed, "*K'yoti* Hell! That was one damned-close call, Tin Man! We need to get outta here fast. Should we go out the way we came in and risk catching up with the *fleggin* eater—or should we go out through the cavern and risk running into Aguilar's men?"

The bot released his grip on my wrist. "If you do not mind, Rand, I prefer to face *men* rather than the asteroid eater."

I shrugged. "Suit yourself, Tin Man, but if we run into those *fleggin* bastards, don't say I didn't warn you." I pushed myself away from Blackie and, with a groan, got back on my feet. "Your legs working yet? I sure hope so! We gotta get a move on, as fast as, uh, humanly possible."

After a bit of a struggle, the bot managed to stand on his own two feet, propped against the wall. "My legs appear to be recovering from the blaster-bolt. However, I am afraid I still require some assistance, Rand." He sagged against me. I steadied him with both arms, trying to keep him upright.

Taking great pains to avoid the now-empty pit, we made our slow, painful way back down the tunnel toward the cavern.

"Rand?"

"Yeah? What is it now, Tin Man?"

"Thank you."

Hoped to bloody hell the bot's infrared vision wasn't picking up the heat coming from my face. "S'nothing," I muttered.

After what seemed like one helluva long time, we made it back to the cavern. It was quiet as a tomb—which wasn't surprising since it *was* a *fleggin* tomb! Torrance's body lay right where it'd fallen. The bodies of the rest of his gang of space-scum were still sprawled about the cavern floor.

But *Jeffries* was gone!

My hackles instantly rose to high-alert. Between clenched teeth, I growled, "*K'yoti* Hell! Should've known the bloody traitor'd wriggle outta this somehow! I should've *smoked* the jackass when I had the chance—at least wounded him, so he could answer a few of my questions!"

I helped the bot reach the mouth of the cavern and left him propped against the rocks outside to act as a lookout. I went back into the cavern, in hopes of reclaiming some of my property. I came out with my own blaster back in its holster where it belonged and the tool-pack Torrance'd stolen from me fastened to my belt.

And in the palm of my left hand, I clutched a pair of *star-shi* earrings: all I had to remember J'neen by.

Ducking behind a good-sized boulder, I searched the plain below us. To my surprise, Aguilar's fast-ship was gone. Torrance's ship was there all right, but it was ablaze. I suspected Aguilar's men'd fired a parting shot with their laser-cannon and sent her up in smoke. The ship was long past salvaging.

I scanned both the plain and the skies above. No sign of Jeffries, and Aguilar's fast-ship was nowhere in sight. His crew—the *fleggin* cowards!—must've retreated, abandoning their boss to his fate. But not before making damned-sure no one could follow them or leave the planet.

An outcropping of grayish rock sheltered the mouth of the cavern from the blazing heat of Milo's Sun. The bot and I settled down in a cool patch of shade. I rested, while he tried to regain full use of his legs. Gingerly, I checked myself out, wincing at the sharp stabs of pain in my back and ribs. Knew I was gonna have some real beauts of bruises to boot!

Outta the blue, I found myself shivering.

Blackie looked at me quickly and asked, "Are you quite all right, Rand? You haven't been wounded again, have you?" He sounded real funny.

I shook my head. "No, I'm fine, Tin Man. Really. Just feeling kinda—*hollow* inside, y'know? Empty. All these long years, I've hated whoever was behind the Esperance Massacre—without knowing it was Roman Aguilar. The *fleggin* bastard finally got what was coming to him and in spades! Karma's one helluva bitch, eh? But now I wonder if that *hate* was the only thing keeping me going."

"Nonsense, Rand! You're much better than that, even if *you* refuse to acknowledge the fact. And you'll become accustomed to living without the hatred—eventually. Perhaps you might even learn to *enjoy* its absence."

"*Huh!* Maybe, for once, you should take some of your own damn advice, Tin Man!" I told him.

I got to my feet, letting a weary sigh escape me. "Enough rest for the time being, my friend. Let's drag our sorry asses back to *Jammer*. I won't really feel comfortable until we're safely back aboard her!"

15 Teamwork

The trek to *Jammer* was long, slow, hot, and damned-tiring, but the bot and I finally made it. I was relieved as hell that my ship was still there and still in one piece. So was the old B'treeni trader, sitting on the pock-marked plain right where I'd left her, a good distance from *Jammer*.

I took out my blaster, in case a welcoming committee was waiting to greet us or that *fleggin* turncoat Jeffries'd crawled back here, hoping to get his ass off Esperance.

As we drew closer, I whispered to the bot, "Read any heat signatures aboard *Jammer?*"

Blackie gave me a confident shake of his metal dome. "No, Rand, I read nothing out of the ordinary. However, my sensors may yet be malfunctioning."

Jammer's ramp was down, and the wind'd blown sand over it. No footprints in the sand; that was a damned-good sign. I eased up the ramp, nervous as hell, but dead-determined to take back my ship, no matter what. Blackie stayed right on my heels. Once aboard, I sneaked down the main corridor without a sound, then peered through the open hatch into my control cabin. Just as the bot'd said, my ship was deserted.

Blowing out a relieved breath, I quickly slid into the familiar pilot's seat and began checking out every single one of *Jammer*'s systems, looking for sabotage. Without waiting for instructions, the bot pivoted on one heel and went back to raise the ramp. When he came forward again, he sat down at the co-pilot's station and strapped himself in, as usual.

As I was running through standard lift-off procedures, the bot asked in a solemn voice, "Rand, what do you intend to do about Jeffries?"

That was one helluva thorny question. Had to think it over for several microseconds.

I gave the bot a resigned shrug. "The bastard might've escaped on Aguilar's ship, I suppose, but if he's unlucky enough to still be on-planet—and if he can't figure out how to fly the old B'treeni trader outta here—he'll eventually starve to death, I guess. And if he develops the guts to try hiding out in Torrance's cavern—well, once the torches run outta fuel, the damn eater'll probably get him. If you're asking my opinion in the matter, Tin Man, the bloody traitor deserves to get eaten!"

"Perhaps he does at that." The bot made a soft sighing sound before going on. "Rand, although I can prove absolutely nothing, Jeffries may well be one of the two individuals who murdered Robert Benton-Smythe. At least, I found his voice familiar. And he acted rather oddly around me, as if he suspected my connection to RBS."

That confession astonished me. I flashed the bot a look. *"K'yoti* Hell! You don't say? And exactly *why* in bloody hell didn't you tell me this *sooner*, Tin Man?"

"Earlier, I did consider confiding my suspicions to you, Rand, but decided against it—until it was far too late. You are *not* a proficient actress. Your change of attitude toward Jeffries might very well have aroused his suspicions. But I did try to warn you about him—as you were attempting to, ah, 'ditch' me in the subterranean maze of tunnels."

I came to a decision so damned grim it made me grit my teeth. "Tin Man, if you're right about Jeffries—hell, in my book that gives us more'n enough reason to make damned-sure he *never* gets off Esper-ance!"

I turned my attention back to *Jammer*'s instrument readings. "There've now been *two* massacres on this *fleggin* planet. The place is cursed! I swear I'm never coming back as long as I live! Let's get the bloody hell outta here!"

I engaged *Jammer*'s lift-thrusters. My sweet ship rose skyward with all her usual eagerness. Far above the ruined plain, her main engines kicked in. Seemed as if *Jammer* were as eager as I was to leave Esperance behind —and for good this time.

But before I could leave the planet with a clear conscience, I had one last job to do. I swung *Jammer* hard about, then activated the gunner's screen and targeted the old B'treeni trader's engines.

I fired my last laser-cannon charge. It was more'n enough to blow the damn ship to Unholy Hell, right where she belonged. The bot kept his crystal lenses glued to our aft monitor, watching the destruction without saying a word.

Then *Jammer* turned, left the planet's atmosphere, and reached zero G.

The bot'd been doing some real hard thinking. "Rand, it occurs to me that, most regrettably, neither of us has a single shred of solid evidence to link Roman Aguilar, personally, with the recent hijackings—let alone with the Esperance Massacre. Who will believe the word of a robot like myself and a recoup agent like you, versus the great and powerful Roman Aguilar with his vaulted reputation?"

Much as I hated agreeing with the bot, I was forced to admit, "I've been thinking the same damn thing. Hell, Tin Man, maybe the eater was the only *real* justice Roman Aguilar was ever likely to get— at least in this universe."

"Indeed. In his desperate attempt to 'mop up' those so-called loose ends of his—in order to protect himself from future consequences of his past actions—Roman Aguilar ended up destroying *himself.*"

I let out a low whistle. "That's pretty damned poetic, Tin Man!"

"Poetic indeed, Rand," the bot agreed in a solemn tone. "However—"

Suddenly, he stopped talking—never a good sign!—and drew my attention to our aft monitor. *"Rand!* Once again, we are being pursued!"

At that instant, *Jammer*'s siren began to shriek. I had only enough time to take one quick look at the monitor.

"Incoming!" I yelled, swinging *Jammer* hard to starboard. An energy-torp exploded off her port bow, too damned close for comfort!

"*K'yoti* Hell!" I swore, swerving *Jammer* even more sharply to starboard to avoid another torp hot on her tail. "Oh, crap! Who the *flegg* is it this time?"

Blackie magnified the image of our pursuers. "Rand, if I am not mistaken, that is Roman Aguilar's ship!" he noted in a grim tone. "Evidently, he must have given his crew orders to allow no one to leave Esperance alive, even should he not return."

"And here I thought the cowardly bastards'd been in one helluva hurry to leave the neighborhood! My mistake, eh, Tin Man?"

The bot was studying the data scrolling across our scan-screen. "Rand, Aguilar's vessel is state-of-the-art, heavily armored, fully out-fitted for both defense and offense," he reported. "I fear that *Jammer* is no match for her."

"And I had t'go and *waste* a laser-cannon blast on the old B'treeni ship. *Flegg* it! My damn cannon's outta power! Best I can do now is try to keep Esperance between *Jammer* and Aguilar's ship."

"So, yet again, Rand, we find ourselves in an extremely perilous predicament."

For some reason that snooty conclusion amused me. I let out a snort and chuckled, "Or as I'd put it, Tin Man, we're in one helluva heap of trouble again!"

"That, too!"

Outta the blue, an audio-visual transmission came in over *Jammer*'s comm system. I hit receive. A familiar voice said coldly, "Do yourself a favor, sister? Surrender immediately, Rand, and we *might* just let you live, damn you!"

The fuzzy image on the comm screen came into sharper focus. I couldn't help letting out a groan. "*Jeffries*, you lying, murdering bastard! I hoped to bloody hell the eater'd get you, like it got Aguilar."

"That so?" Jeffries raised one eyebrow and gave me a real nasty laugh. "His rotten luck! To tell you the truth, Rand, I hoped the same about *you*! But if you don't surrender right this microsecond, we'll be more than happy to blast your ship the hell out of space. It's up to you, sister."

"Then you might as well have a go, Jeffries, old chum. I can out-fly *you* any day, no matter what ship you're flying!"

In spite of my show of bravado, I knew damned good and well

Aguilar's fancy fast-ship had *Jammer* badly outclassed. My ship had only the basic features needed for recouping.

I quickly cut off the transmission, so Jeffries couldn't hear the colorful string of cusswords I rattled off. "This may bloody well be it for me, Tin Man, but given my choice, I prefer go down fighting. Too damn bad these bastards'll take you out with me."

But the bot was staring at our forward monitor, not paying the least bit of attention to me. "Rand, ahead of us—look!"

As *Jammer* continued to circle Esperance, a large object had come into view on our screen. "What the hell's that—another *fleggin* ship?"

The bot studied the data rapidly filling his screen. "Rand, it's the derelict we encountered on our first approach to Esperance!"

"You mean the abandoned ore-freighter?"

The old ship was headed right for us again. The spark of an idea lit up in my brain. I quickly fanned the spark into a flame. "Hang on, Tin Man! This's one damned-old trick recoups sometimes use—but there's a slight chance it might work!"

"*What* might work?" the bot asked, apparently stumped.

But getting myself outta tight scrapes like this one was *my* field of expertise, not his, as the bot would've put it. Being able to use my wits under fire was the main reason I'd managed to survive this long.

Hadn't used *Jammer*'s tractor-arm for one helluva long time, so I was terrified the whole damn contraption might be frozen. During successful recoup operations, the arm was used to capture vessels abandoned by their crews and to recover cargo that'd been ditched in mid-space.

Lucky for me, it took only a bit of struggle to deploy the long, thin tractor-arm. When fully extended, it jutted out from beneath *Jammer*'s belly to well past her bow. I fired retros, slowing *Jammer* to match the speed of the orbiting derelict. I opened the twin claws attached to the business end of the tractor-arm, then carefully maneuvered *Jammer* into position. With a shred of luck, the claws should be able to latch onto my target.

"Exercise extreme caution, Rand!" Blackie warned. "Should we collide with the freighter while traveling at this rate of speed—!"

"*Quiet, dammit!* I'm praying—and kinda outta practice!"

The bot obeyed. He shut his mouth, but kept his eyes glued on

Jammer's forward monitor, watching my first attempt to capture the derelict.

Closing like a pair of giant pincers, the tractor-claws clamped onto one of the metal fins that projected from the starboard hull of the old derelict. After making damned-sure I had one helluva good grip on her, I turned my own ship to starboard. *Jammer* came about, dragging the freighter with her, 'til she faced her pursuers. Now I was ready for the final showdown.

The gunner aboard Aguilar's ship fired another torp; luckily, it missed us and exploded just off the port bow of the freighter.

Jacking *Jammer*'s speed back up to maximum and using the freighter as a shield, I headed straight for the bow of the fast-ship. That bold move took Jeffries and the crew of Aguilar's ship by surprise. None of the *fleggin* idiots had any clue what I was about to pull next.

Dead-ahead of the rapidly-oncoming fast-ship, I opened the tractor-claws and released the derelict. The huge freighter drifted free, maintaining her speed. I quickly rolled *Jammer* to starboard and dove. Still running on max, she got the hell outta the danger zone. Tin Man and I watched on our screen as the derelict sailed smack into the path of the smaller ship. Her crew of dumb-asses tried to execute a last minute collision-avoidance maneuver, but it was way too damned late for that.

Aguilar's fancy fast-ship rammed bow-on into the huge derelict!

The head-on collision, and the explosion that followed, sure as hell killed everyone up forward instantly. With no attitude-control, the fast-ship started to tumble end over end. Her stern section smashed against the derelict's hull, causing the engines in the fast-ship's stern to explode. Aguilar's whole ship went up like a damn supernova!

The light from our forward monitor lit up *Jammer*'s cabin. I raised my right forearm to shield my eyes from the screen's glare. Of course, Blackie's sight wasn't effected one damn bit. He stared at the screen as if he were hypnotized. The freighter was still in one piece, more or less, but her hull was ruined; a gaping hole now exposed her innards to space.

As the screen dimmed, the bot said quietly, "Tragic, but quite impressive!"

"Yeah, well—serves 'em right, eh, Tin Man?"

"They left you no choice, Rand."

I shrugged off the bot's remark, even though I knew damned well he meant it to comfort me. "Hell, this time *they* made the choice for me. Those bloody bastards had no intention of letting either one of us live."

I pulled *Jammer*'s tractor-arm back into position and secured it. Then, heaving a sigh, I turned to *Jammer*'s navcomp and began plotting a course for Milo's Planet.

"Experiencing regrets, Rand?" the bot asked quietly.

"Naw! I was just mentally kissing Aguilar's five-million credits goodbye."

"You do realize that every last soul in the explored-galaxy, except for the two of us, will assume Roman Aguilar was aboard his ship when it exploded. His death will undoubtedly be attributed to a tragic accident."

I scratched my head. "Undoubtedly, Tin Man, but in the meantime, I have t'figure out how in bloody hell I'm gonna explain the deaths of Torrance and his whole *fleggin* gang to Krol Kramer and Surety Galactic Insurance!"

I needed to say something else to the bot, but wasn't quite sure how to put it. "Uh, Tin Man—"

"Uttering another word is quite unnecessary, Rand. I already know what you mean to say."

I heaved a huge sigh. "Well, that's one helluva relief! I'm no damn good with words."

All too quickly, the bot agreed with me. "How very well I am aware of that fact!"

"Look, I owe you big time, Tin Man—a helluva lot more'n I can ever repay. You're not my property, and you sure as hell aren't my slave. Soon as *Jammer* lands on Milo's, you're free to go wherever you damn please, to do whatever the hell you want to do."

Strangely enough, Blackie was silent. I figured he'd jump at the chance to be free, to be rid of a dumb pain-in-the-ass like me, to be his own man, so to speak.

"Galaxy—ah, that is, Rand—I sincerely appreciate how much it took for you to make such a magnanimous offer—"

"*Oh, for God's-green-snake, Tin Man!* There you go again with those damned-fancy big words of yours! For once in your so-called life, can't you just spit out what you wanna say, plain and simple?"

"If that's what you wish, I shall indeed attempt to do so," the bot said. He squared his broad shoulders. His head swiveled, so he could look me straight in the face; his twin crystal lenses fastened on my eyes.

"Rand, you seem to have forgotten entirely that I am *a machine,* not a human being! As such, I require direction—purpose. I was designed and constructed specifically to serve a *human* master. And since you are offering me my free choice, I prefer to serve you."

I was so stunned by the bot's decision that, for several microseconds, I blinked stupidly at him.

When I finally got my wits about me, I tripped over my own tongue. "I, um, I—oh, Bloody Hell! You mean to say that—after all the crap I've put you through—after all my snarky remarks!—you actually *want* to stay with me, Tin Man? Of your own free will?"

"I do indeed, Rand, that is, if you'll have me?" The bot's crystal lenses bored into my eyes. He waited patiently for my answer.

Under my breath, I murmured, "*K'yoti* Hell!" Doing my damnedest to shake off the shock I'd suffered, I tried to imagine what my future was gonna be like now.

"Uh, Tin Man—RBS, I mean—never in a hundred-trillion years did I think I would live to see this day! Never in my wildest dreams thought I'd team up with anyone! And now—I'll be damned!—I've got myself a *fleggin* bot for a partner!"

For no particular reason, just for the sheer hell of it, I guess, I sent *Jammer* into a joy-filled spiral before I pointed her bow back in the direction of Milo's Planet.

The End

The End